George Edward Fenety

Life and Times of the Hon. Joseph Howe

The great Nova Scotian and ex-Lieut. Governor. With brief references to some of

his prominent contemporaries

George Edward Fenety

Life and Times of the Hon. Joseph Howe
The great Nova Scotian and ex-Lieut. Governor. With brief references to some of his prominent contemporaries

ISBN/EAN: 9783337424022

Printed in Europe, USA, Canada, Australia, Japan

Cover: Foto ©Raphael Reischuk / pixelio.de

More available books at **www.hansebooks.com**

HONORABLE JOSEPH HOWE.

Hon. Joseph Howe,

(The Great Nova Scotian and Ex-Lieut. Governor.)

With brief references to some of his prominent contemporaries.

By G. E. FENETY,

*Author of New Brunswick " Political Notes," 500 pages, Royal
Octavo, (the 2nd vol. of 500 pages is half printed,) both vols.
extending over a period of 20 years—from 1840 to 1860;
also a Halifax Story, 200 pages,—"The Dress
Maker:" also " Imperial Federation—its
Impracticability:" " Early Recollections of Halifax." Also several
Pamphlets, dealing with
Fredericton Corpo-
ration matters,
etc., etc.*

ST. JOHN, N. B.

PRINTED AND PUBLISHED BY E. S. CARTER. "PROGRESS" OFFICE.

1896.

DEDICATION.

———

To E. G. W. GREENWOOD, Esquire.

Sir:—I have great pleasure
in dedicating this Book to you

AS AN OLD AND HONOURED CITIZEN

OF HALIFAX;

and in recognition of the very valuable
services which you and your fellow Jurors*
rendered (you being the last survivor) in the

CELEBRATED LIBEL CASE

brought on by the Magistrates of Halifax, in 1835,
against Joseph Howe, then Editor of the "*Novascotian*,"

WHEREBY THE LIBERTY OF THE PRESS

of your native Province was for the first time fully vindicated and established, and as a result of which

THE PEOPLE OF NOVA SCOTIA AND OF THE

SISTER PROVINCES

are under a deep debt of gratitude for
the numerous political and social
reforms which have since
been brought about.

THE AUTHOR.

———

*NAMES OF THE JURORS:—Chas. J. Hill—Robert Story—
Edward Pryor, Jr.—James W. Reynolds—David Hall—E. G. W.
Greenwood—John Wellner—Robert Lawson—Arch. McDonald
—Samuel Mitchell—Thomas A. Bauer—Duncan McQueen.

INDEX.

CHAPTER I.

CHAPTER II.

CHAPTER III.

CHAPTER IV.

APPENDIX.

ILLUSTRATIONS.

INTRODUCTION.

Biography, like History, is seldom if ever written from information based upon personal knowledge of the subject, but rather from the gleanings of others gone before, whose opportunities had been contemporaneous or in touch with the times, the persons and the things described ; and therefore such writings may be called in a great measure borrowed information, though well sifted and applied.

In offering this book to the Public—however imperfect it may appear—the circumstances are altogether different ; for the facts herein set forth, are derived, by the writer, in most instances, from personal observation and close intimacy with his subject, extending over the greater portion of Mr. Howe's private and public life ; and therefore no writer past or present has had better opportunities of dealing with the work he has undertaken in connection with this wonderful man.

At the age of sixteen I entered the office of the *"Novascotian"* (newspaper) then owned by Mr.

Howe, and in less than two years afterwards I found myself so much in that gentleman's confidence and favour that I was placed in charge of his accounts as collector, (a position which I suppose at the present day might more fashionably be called " Private Secretary,") and in the summer time I travelled through the Maritime Provinces, (stage coaching, no railroads) visiting most of the chief towns, in the capacity of collector of subscriptions to the *Novascotian.* At times I had hundreds of pounds in my hands (the subscription price was one pound or four dollars) as there were no such facilities as there are at the present day for making remittances to headquarters; and although I withdrew from Mr. Howe's employment many years before his death to go into business for myself, I always flattered myself with the belief that I enjoyed his respect up to the last hour, instances in support of this will appear hereafter in this volume. More than this with regard to my early connection with Mr. Howe need not be said. Less, I could not have very well avoided and furnished reasons why I felt myself competent, even called upon, to undertake this duty.

In 1858 the Hon. Wm. Annand published two large octavo volumes containing the " Speeches and Public Letters of the Hon. Joseph Howe," but very little (a few pages) of his biography. Several of those speeches I have borrowed, and they will be found incorporated in this book. Four years ago I published in the St. John *Progress* a series of " Random Recollections of the Hon. Joseph Howe." Beyond this I did not intend to pursue the subject ; but since then (last year) I noticed that a public meeting had been called in Halifax for the purpose of taking steps for the erection of a monument to the memory of Mr. Howe, and so I thought I might now venture, at this opportune time, upon a more pretentious field, even the reproduction of those articles, and enlarge upon them considerably, and publish them in book form—for it is likely the present generation have very little conception of the great man of whom doubtless they have heard so much, while Mr. Howe's contemporaries, fast dying out, may by this means have their recollections awakened to the trying scenes of their earlier days.

For all of the above reasons I now launch my skiff upon the waters to bring up where it may.

THE AUTHOR.

CHAPTER I.

Early Recollections of Mr. Howe.—Old Party Lines Obliterated.—The Author's First Recollection of Joseph Howe. — The Father and Brothers of Joseph Howe—William Howe, the Great Racquet Player and the Earl of Dalhousie.—Joseph Howe's Birth Place. — Halifax Society. — St. Paul's Church Dignitaries

Without attempting to more than outline the subject of these " Recollections," it has more than once of late years occurred to the writer, that the publication in an ephemeral form, of some of the incidents in connection with the career of Mr. Howe, a gentleman who for fifty years filled perhaps the most conspicuous place in the public eye in all British America, would not prove uninteresting to his old friends and admirers. Mr. Froude in a recent work entitled " Peculiarities of Great Men," in referring to Disræli (Lord Beaconsfield) remarks, as below, and the character drawn seems so apropos to our subject that I cannot refrain from quoting : " As a Statesman there was none like him before and will be none hereafter. His career was the result of a combination of a peculiar character with peculiar circumstances, which is not likely to recur. The aim with which he started in life was to distinguish himself above all his contemporaries, and, wild as such an ambition must have appeared, he at last won the stake for which he played so brevely."

The contents of this work will be given mostly from memory, as " Random Recollections," without regard to the strict accuracy of dates, or the order of the dates themselves — but near enough to answer the purpose, even if a year or two out of the way in relating some of the incidents. Literary style is not attempted in these sketches ; they are undertaken and given in an off-hand, free and easy way, as a tribute of regard and to recall many matters that have come under the personal observation of the writer. With regard to the political aspect of the subject, the writer does not deal nor entertain any feelings of his own in giving expression to Mr. Howe's views. However, the politics of his day are not those of the present. The old actors and political prejudices and animosities which then divided parties, have long since passed away. The great dividing line forty years ago was on the Responsible Government question, now settled with Constitutional solidity, so that no one today denies its importance any more, it might be said, than the people of England deny their Magna Charta privileges wrung by the Barons from King John.

The remnants of the old parties in Mr. Howe's day have become so fused of late years, or since "confederation" that the rule of discrimination is inapplicable altogether when we attempt to place politicians under their respective shibboleths. At the same time it is admitted that there are serious local and federal questions which divide parties now as of yore ; but nothing to be compared to the great issues of former years when Mr. Howe was at the front and confronted adversaries far more formidable than any that have been encountered since *he* gained for the Maritime Provinces, and it may be said all British America, a measure of freedom and independence far more precious than any statesman has been called upon to accomplish since.

My first recollection of Joseph Howe dates when he was about the age of 26. At that time he acted as Clerk in the Halifax Post Office, then kept on the lower side of the Grand Parade, towards the new City Hall. The building still stands. John Howe & Son were the Post Masters—the father and brother of Joseph. They were also King's Printers. In those days the Post Office jurisdiction embraced Nova Scotia, New Brunswick and P. E. Island. In 1837 (as far as my memory serves) Mr. Drury, the Post Master of St. John died, and Mr. John Howe, the Postmaster at Halifax, appointed his son John (still living in St. John) to the vacant post, which office he continued to fill down to a comparatively recent period, when he was superannuated by the Dominion Government. Some years before "confederation," the Post Office system was changed, whereby each of the Provinces controlled its own Department. The first Mr. John Howe was one of the Boston Loyalists, and has been dead about 60 years, passing away full of years and full of honours—a venerable patriarch in appearance ; no man was ever more thought of for his charitable deeds and kindness of heart than the father of Joseph Howe.

The sons were John, (father of our ex-Postmaster.) David, William, and the subject of this sketch by a second marriage. William and John died about the same time, and were buried on the same day, two most splendid specimens of men, tall, of great physique, altogether fine looking, as were David and Joseph. William belonged to the Commissariat Department, and was at that time the most famous racquet player in Canada, a game then very fashionable among the gentry, as base ball is at the present day among the " Boys." The Earl of Dalhousie, when Governor (about 1820) was also a good player, and could beat the best in the Garrison ; but when he invited Howe to an encounter, His Excellency invariably came off second best. He (Howe) would take up an ordinary walking stick, and play a good game with a good player, a substitute for a racquet never used by any other person. David (whose son William died a few years since in Halifax, as Deputy Registrar of Wills and Deeds) was a man of fine intellect, but not of any fixed employment, or in any way conspicuous to render his fine talents available.

So much, then, for the male members of the

JOHN HOWE, Father of Joseph Howe.

Howe family ; and now for the chief member, the late Hon. Joseph Howe.

Mr. Howe was born in December 1804 in a one and half story house occupied by his parents, situated on the Eastern bank of the North West Arm, about two hundred yards, as near as I can judge, South of the present Presbyterian Theological College. The house has long since disappeared. While yet in his teens young Howe gave promise of a brilliant future. His first effort was a Poem, his theme being " Melville Island," and the old French Prison, after the measure and metre of Goldsmith's Deserted Village. This Poem displayed so much originality of thought and talent and descriptive power in one so young and unknown, that the Lieut. Governor, the Earl of Dalhousie, invited the author to visit him at Government House where His Excellency bestowed upon him no meagre praise for his first literary flight in the realms of poesy, and he had the name of Howe registered for future invitations to Government House—to State balls and dinners. &c.; in short, to be recognized thenceforward as on a footing with the quality, as then called, of the land. Of course the official position of Howe's father and brothers gave them that right.

Now, in those days—sixty or seventy years ago —it was considered as great an honor and difficulty to pass muster and find *entr'* into Government House and become an associate with the Halifax *beau monde*, as it is at the present day to obtain admission to the Queen's drawing room receptions. No one not recognized within the magic circle had the least chance. So that young Howe in his first Parnassian flight, soared high over the heads of others of equal social calibre, but as yet unable to raise their pinions in the direction of the great society domicile of exclusives. And here is a fitting opportunity to give the state of Halifax, socially and politically, when Howe commenced his career, in order that the reader may understand at the beginning the great difficulties that stood in the young man's path, and the mountains of prejudice to be overcome, ere the silken cords of Society and the adamant political chains of official life, were forced to give way before the march of reform, led by this same Joseph Howe.

But what gave hue to Society in Halifax sixty years ago, was that reflected through its political atmosphere; the system was a monopoly of offices and exclusiveness among families dependent upon the State for their living and their grandeur, while industry and abilities formed no part of the oligarchical conception. St. Paul's Church upon the Sabbath was the grand pivotal centre next to Government House, where the great people congregated. Looking down from a front pew in the gallery, my boyish eyes were regaled by all the splendor that fashion and quality could impart, while the fancy in its incipient weakness magnified all those shreds of humanity, as worshippers some-

thing more than human. Very few persons not
"to the manor born," occupied pews below the
galleries. The Governor's pew was on one side of
the reading desk and pulpit, and the Bishop's on
the other. At that time the arrangement for
conducting the services stood in the middle of the
centre aisle, in front of the Communion table,
made in three tiers, the uppermost of which was
occupied by the Rector, Dr. Inglis, when preaching,—the second by the Curate, the Rev. Mr.
Twining—and the lower one by the Clerk (Mr.
Collupy) who made the responses and gave out the
hymns in a fine sonorous voice. The congregation
were not yet evangelized in the way of performing
this duty, but left that part of the service with
the Clerk. At both ends of the Communion table
the officers' pews were situated. There was then
no Garrison Chapel as now. The soldiers occupied
places in the gallery flanking the rear pews, where
long benches were provided. But the array of
scarlet below, the Governor and his suite, the
Bishop, and all the Judges, and all the great heads
of departments, the great merchants, for the
merchants (those especially connected by marriage
with the officials) held place among the dignitaries
—all presented a *coup d'œil,* which to me was awe-
inspiring, far more impressive than that in my
manhood days, many years afterwards, when I
occupied a seat in St. George's Chapel, Windsor,
where the Queen, Prince Albert and some of Eng-

OLD ST. PAUL'S CHURCH.

land's most illustrious Nobility worshipped beneath the same roof

And then when death overtook those of more than ordinary mark, their dust was not allowed to mingle with common clay in the old burial ground, but must needs find place beneath the floors of old St. Paul, where, as in Westminster Abbey, (the Pantheon of England's illustrious dead,) the bodies were interred. Some years ago the floors of St. Paul's, being much decayed, they were renewed, when many mounds and sarcophagi were exposed to view. The last person interred here I think, was Richard John Uniacke, Attorney General, in 1830. To-day this is all changed. Even the old burial ground is a sealed sanctuary. There is one common Cemetery now for all alike, while equality among the living appears to be more evenly balanced and recognized. In the month of August last I attended divine service in old St. Paul's ; everything looked to me as it did sixty years before, except the makeup of the congregation, which I thought had undergone a wonderful transformation. The doors of the old stately pews, which formerly shut out, as it were, all intruders, were removed and the interiors considered free to all-comers. I no longer beheld the old officials and their families, wrapped in their own exclusiveness and finery ; but a staid, respectable looking body of people of all professions, trades and occupations, resembling other ordinary mortals of other persuasions, who at the present day feel that they are dependent upon one another for the riches they possess and are working for, and not upon the Crown as of yore among the privileged classes.

CHAPTER II.

Human Nature always the Same.—The Family Compact.—And the Political System of the Times. —The Condition of the Press.—Mr. Howe's Journalistic Commencement.—Attacks upon the Public Abuses of the day—Colonel Cathcart and the Garrison Fire.

People are of course the same in all ages ; human nature is unchangeable. It is the circumstances and accidents by which we are surrounded at different epochs which account for the changed manifestations. The man of affluence and importance today, is another man tomorrow, when overtaken by adversity—he then becomes as changed in himself as if two distinct entities were bound up in the one corporeal essence. The actors under the old system which reflected a lustre on Government House and old St. Paul's, were no longer the shining stars which dazzled all beholders, after the doors of those establishments were made to turn on new hinges. Now the occupants of the old pews seem to feel as if they believed they were saying their prayers under more democratic surroundings, and that they are so many units in the great aggregation, depending upon *vox populi* for their living, and not upon a meritricious system which proscribed all who were not in some way connected with the "governing classes." And yet according to this same human nature doctrine, so peculiar and perhaps selfish, it is questionable whether if the old system could be rehabilitated, might it not reproduce the same outward and visible signs as of old, notwithstanding our advanced civilization and more apparent fraternal tendencies?

To retrace our steps. At the time to which reference has just been made the Government of the country was under the absolute control of what was called "the family compact." The Governor was sent from England, or from "home," as our Halifax friends continue to call it for some occult reason best known to themselves—clothed with plenary powers, although he had an advisroy board, consisting of twelve members, who exercised legislative as well as executive functions, in giving advice to His Excellency, whether he chose to accept and act upon it or not. Such a thing as a member of the Government holding a seat upon the floors of the House was unknown. They were all "Honorables," and would have no intercourse with the peoples' representatives, unless to cross them and clog the Royal assent to any measure that did not harmonize with their prejudices. If one of them died, another was put in his place having the most influence. If the head of a department passed away, his office was quickly filled by one of his own kith and kin; and so on in every case. The continuity or tenure was indisputable. Those officials were only amenable to themselves and the Governor ; and if the latter proved to be a simple or weak man, as some of them were, he was easily brought over to their own way of thinking. Thus all the offices in the country were in the hands of those twelve irresponsible men, whose individual salaries or appurtenances arising from their positions, were large enough to maintain their families in regal splendor, of course at the expense of " the people" who were as much under their sway as the people of Russia now are under their Czar. The subordinate Clerkships in the various departments were dealt with in the same manner—that is, all the employees were appointed by the irresponsible heads, whether good, bad or indifferent, and nobody outside the circle could utter a word of protest. Then the Press was shackled or held under the same restraining bondage—not but that there was freedom for the expression of independent thought, even to make war upon " the compact ; " but the publishers knew too well that it was at the risk of losing prestige and patronage, or incurring the displeasure or withdrawal of countenance of those who were linked in some way with the parties assailed. Indeed the political atmosphere some sixty years ago was so impregnated with the Tory prejudices and acquiescent feelings of the people themselves, (taking it for granted that all was right, no matter how wrong,) that it required a journalist of most undaunted courage and ability to dare the lions in their dens, mostly from this want of public sympathy and encouragement. It was not only the best blood in the land (as it was considered,) but the highest scholarship and talents that had to be encountered in an onslaught upon this condition of things. But the deliverer was at hand, and he came forth in due season panoplied in full consciousness of his own strength, and possessing talents of the highest order—sound judgment—rectitude of purpose—persistency of will—and a courage equal to the emergency—all of which qualifications from the right time forward were brought into activity, and with such results as will appear further on in these Memoirs.

Having then premised this much, in order to show what Mr. Howe, single handed, had to encounter at the beginning in his efforts as a reformer, we may now proceed to sketch in a fragmentary way, some of the steps taken by him as time went on to bring about a change, and thus pave the way for the entrance into office and society of a class of men hitherto unknown and uncared for.

In 1824 the *Novascotian* newspaper was started by Mr. George R. Young, brother of the late Sir Wm. Young. The office was at the foot of " Jacob's Hill," so called at the time. It was printed in quarto form. I have seen nothing of it in late years, but presume it still exists, if not sunk altogether or merged in the *Morning Chronicle*, which was an offshoot. After being in existence about two years, Mr. Howe purchased the *Novascotian* plant and copyright, and continued its publication in a wooden building situated directly at the head of Bedford Row, and nearly opposite what was then known as Reynolds' Auction Rooms. The purchase of this paper was the dawning of a new era in what may be called Independent Provincial Journalism—for its new proprietor immediately commenced his attacks upon the abuses of the day, more especially in reference to the political disabilities to which the people, the ordinary people, had to submit. The temerity displayed in his editorials was so marked that Howe was threatened by those in high places, not only with the law's vengeance, but with personal chastisement. The latter course was seldom or never put into practice—for our hero was an athlete of the most pronounced type, physically strong and powerful, standing about five feet ten in height, and could handle any two ordinary men with ease, as I have seen. But no— he was reserved for battles of another and more intellectual kind, and even in the field itself, as will be seen hereafter. But it must be observed here that Mr. Howe was not a writer who dipped his pen in gall, or in any way exhibited in his writings a rabid disposition. His attacks were always directed against existing and long standing abuses, and he would have preferred knocking these down with nobody standing behind them ; but this could not be done, for every abuse then as now, had its self-interested defender—no one hitherto having dared even to point them out, much less try to overthrow them.

About 1827 there was a fire at the Garrison Library, a building which stood in the vicinity of the Officers' Quarters, North Barrack, butting on to Cogswell street, as then called. There was no water works system—no steam engines—no such appliances as at the present day for putting out fires. Lines of troops and citizens were formed on two sides—leather buckets filled with water were conveyed up one side, while on the opposite the empty buckets passed—all conducted very slowly but systematically. The supply was generally obtained from neighboring wells, which soon became exhausted—and in most cases the fire burnt itself out, after consuming all within its reach ; the water supply at best was scant in any part of the city, unless the fire was in the vicinity of the harbor. The Fire Wardens were the great men on these occasions, running up and down the lines, compelling skulkers to fall in, even handling them roughly. There was one gentleman belonging to the Ordnance Department, named Rigby, who had been working steadily all the evening passing buckets, and at last became somewhat exhausted and was compelled to back out of the line, when immediately an officer, in the person of Colonel Cathcart, of the 8th or King's Own, (who fell as General Cathcart in the Crimea in 1855, on what is now known as " Cathcart's Hill,") seized Rigby to drive him back, and so rudely that he fell from sheer exhaustion, and might have been trodden to death had he not been raised to his feet by persons near by. But Cathcart was a martinet among his soldiers, and no civilian must disobey his orders. Mr. Howe learned of the outrage, and so did Mr. Ince, Head Ordnance Officer, and they both sympathised with the unfortunate young man. Rigby addressed a communication "to the Editor of the *Novascotian*," detailing the circumstances. [If Mr. Rigby is still alive and he reads this, I hope he will excuse me for giving away the author, no doubt for the first time after sixty years and upwards—*sub-rosa*.] The idea of attacking a Colonel, and he an "honorable" by birth, of one of His Majesty's regiments, and in a common newspaper, was enough to turn out all the troops in the garrison and make for poor Howe, not to ask but compel him to give up the writer. The Editor well knew that if he disclosed the name, poor Rigby would have gone to bed that night without his official head—for the Ordnance Department would summarily have been closed against him. The Governor and the Military and the great Heads of Departments at that time were all supreme. The day after the paper was issued the office was besieged by the great guns. The Governor's son, Captain Maitland, was one of the first callers ; and every time there was a new-comer for the author, Howe appeared at the front for interrogation, but a polite refusal was always returned, and each in turn went away disappointed and disdainful. Then His Excellency Sir Peregrine Maitland sent a peremptory demand for the author, but with the same success. Howe was inflexible, and at last began to get annoyed. The ghost, however, " evanished amidst the storm " after a nine days' chase, and so Rigby held his place unharmed. This incident will appear as of minor importance until we come to explain presently what may be called the real commencement of the Editor's career as an independent man and politician.

CHAPTER III.

*The Publishers in Halifax Seventy Years Ago.—
Editor of the Acadian Recorder, Mr. John S.
Thompson, Father of the late Minister of Justice,
—Afterwards Queen's Printer.—The Coalition
Government.—New Queen's Printer Appointed.—
The subsequent owners of the Recorder.—Halifax
Mechanics' Institute.—The Acadian School and
Dalhousie College Buildings.*

Dropping our thread for a little time, it may not
be out of place here to make some reference to the
status of the Newspaper Press of seventy years ago.
Besides the *Novascotian* there were published the
Acadian Recorder, by Anthony and Philip Holland,
started in 1812—the *Journal*, by John Munro—the
Philanthropist, by E. A. Moody—the *Free Press*,
by Edmund Ward—the *Weekly Chronicle*, by Wm.
Minns, succeeded by the *Acadian*, James Spike
publisher. These are about all I can call to mind.
There were no religious papers, so called. The
Recorder was like the *Courier* in St. John, published
on Saturday, and brought up all the news and
advertisements to date. News from England came
to hand after being on the water two or three
months, and then simmered mostly through the
United States Press, the arrivals there being much

more frequent. News from Boston or New York was generally a week or ten days old by the time it reached Halifax.

The Press in those days, it may be said was self-sustaining. The proprietor conducted every department of his paper—with one or two exceptions he was Editor, Reporter, News-gatherer, and almost "devil." Editorial paragraphs were mostly furnished from outside. There were no steel pens in those days—blood letting was done by the old style goose quill, just as effective. The proceedings of public meetings even of the Legislature were unreported, unless on very rare occasions. Trials, whether in Court House or Police Office, went on from week to week without the least notice being taken of them. Indeed the public felt little concern about public matters in which they were not individually interested, but " minded their own business." How changed all this now ! There is no scarcity of Editors, or Reporters, or Interviewers. There is nothing that escapes the lynx eye of the newsgatherer. Everything that happens is reported, and frequently things that don't happen. The Reporter goes into the Courts and brings to light all the rascality committed outside—even tries a prisoner, convicts him, and all but hangs him. We aim to get on the right side of public opinion, failing in that we force public opinion over to our side and think we succeed. If a man falls down on a slippery sidewalk it is almost published before he has time to get up again. Our age is one of steam, electricity, loud talk, tall gossip and—we had almost said, political depravity.

Before the *Novascotian* the *Recorder* was probably the most independent paper published, as the word independent was understood at the time —that is, only to tell the truth with bated breath and avoid the penalty due to boldness of speech, or the too copious use of printer's ink, and never stretch your tongue beyond the margin of a safe and wholesome intrenchment, lest dire consequences befall, which was not unfrequently the case. For example, some remarks appeared in the *Recorder* reflecting upon the management of the Commissariat Department, in which the public interests were somewhat identified, and only the rectification of which was sought. Immediately Holland's name was booked, and the advertising patronage which the paper always enjoyed, amounting to a large annual sum, was cut off as a penalty for his transgression.

Mr. John S. Thompson, father of the late Minister of Justice, was the Editor, which post he filled for many years. He was an easy-going, pleasant gentleman, good writer, but lacked the essential elements of fire and aggressiveness for those days of close sailing—hence he was more safe than successful as an Editor. Mr. Howe in after life (when Richard Nugent. a very peppery writer, had charge of the *Novascotian* in succession to Howe,) used to say that if Thompson and Nugent could be rolled into one, we should have the perfection of a genuine Editor. When the Liberal party came into power, Thompson was appointed Queen's printer, as a reward for his liberal editorial tendencies, which office he held for a year or two, until Howe's party fell through a sort of *coup-d'-etat* on the part of the Johnstone party. Responsible Government was then in its incipient stage—every concession from its enemies was gained by hard fighting and exaction, until finally the old Government condescended to take into their embrace three Liberals (Howe, Uniacke and M'Nab,) a sort of tripartite treaty, or one-sided coalition, six to three. It was considered, however, to be a point gained ; it was the insertion of the Liberal wedge, but it turned out a blunt one. The majority continued to govern as before, without consulting their Liberal colleagues. At length they over-stepped the mark, for without saying a word to the minority, they appointed a gentleman to a seat in the Legislative Council—Mr. Mather B. Almon— when Howe & Co., (who by the way, had been appointed head of the Excise Department) *struck* —(in the parlance of the day)—threw up their offices and came out of the Government. [Although breaking into our Biographical connection, the above incident is brought in for the purpose of disposing of Mr. Thompson, while we have him in hand.] When the Liberal party was re-formed outside and the old one closed up its ranks, the leader of the latter (Johnstone) requested the Queen's Printer to espouse its cause, and wage war upon the

Opposition. Thompson said " No—I was placed
in office by the Liberals, and for the sake of office
I shall never desert them." This was about 1845.
And so Thompson relinquished an office worth
probably $8,000 a year. Mr. John M. Croskill,
who owned and edited the *Daily Post*, received the
appointment—for it was all one to John what side
he espoused, for the shekels were of far more
importance to him than political principles.

When the Government Departments erased from
their books the name of the *Acadian Recorder* as
an advertising medium, the Editor addressed a long
Memorial to the Home Government, explaining
matters, and asking for a restoration of the patronage withdrawn. The only answer vouchsafed
was a reference for redress to the parties over
whose heads the shots had been fired. Of course
there could be no appeal to those functionaries in
Halifax, who dealt out the vengeful blow, unless
at the risk of receiving a humiliating refusal.
The *Recorder* did not recover the ground lost, an
extensive patronage, for many years, for its quasi-
independent manifestation on that occasion. So
much then for the independence of the Press at
that day.

Messrs. English & Blackadar succeeded the Hol-
lands in the ownership of the *Recorder*—since
converted into a Daily, and still existing in the
hands of the sons of Hugh Blackadar—fighting
the Liberal battles of the day under new auspices,
and with a freedom which its founders could

DR. GREGOR.

never have contemplated, even by Mr. Thompson himself, whose son in the Commons was the recipient of all the left handed political compliments which the present Editor of the *Recorder* appeared to pay him up to his last day.

In 1827, Mr. Howe, Dr. Gregor, Mr. Dawson (whose sons are now in business in Montreal) and a few other gentlemen, met and organized a Mechanics' Institute, at that day very popular, in Scotland particularly. Dr. Gregor, a Scotch gentleman, was elected first President, and the meetings were held for a time in the Acadian School Building. Afterwards the Society removed to one of the many vacant rooms in Dalhousie College. Lectures were given once a week, followed on each occasion by quite a lively and interesting discussion upon the subject matter of the lecture. It might have been called a veritable debating society, which brought out a display of talent highly creditable to the participants. Among the most prominent of the speakers were Mr. Thompson, before referred to, Dr. Matthew Ritchie the great Methodist Preacher, Mr. Howe, Dr. Gregor, Wm. Ward, occasionally Rev. Mr. Twining, (of St. Paul's, and a very clever schoolmaster, whose name I have forgotten. Those debates generally occupied more time than the lecture itself, but they served to bring out many pertinent matters in connection with the subject, which otherwise would have been lost upon most of the audience. In these discussions, among men of the highest learning, Howe exhibited a latent talent which in the future, promised to develop into large proportions. The shrewdness and good common sense of his observations, even upon scientific and highly literary subjects, raised him in the estimation of his confreres, as a young man who in time would be sure to make his mark upon his country's scroll.

The lectures were tolerably well attended, but never like those in St. John—the presence of the ladies in sufficient numbers was wanting, as one of the attractions—at all events for this and other reasons, the Institute languished and finally ceased to exist, after doing good work for probably ten years. The St. John Institute lasted fifty years, when it too succumbed to the inevitable—want of funds.

CHAPTER IV.

*Dalhousie College.— Kings College Founded upon
Church Principles.—The Small Pox and Cholera
Epidemics.—Sir Colin Campbell's Noble Con-
duct.—The Grand Parade.—The Able Men once
Graduates of King's College.—Generals Williams
and Inglis.*

Again. referring to Dalhousie College, it seems to
have been an unfortunate enterprise from the day
the Earl of Dalhousie laid the corner stone in 1820.
It originated as an offset to Windsor College, which
was a strictly denominational institution, under
control of the Church of England. and it so remains
to this day, but with considerable modification in
its government and management. and is now more
in harmony with the times. As everything was
" church " in the latter part of the century when
the Charter was obtained, it can very easily be
understood why King's College should have been
conducted on strictly church lines, with all its Governors and Senators and Professors belonging to
the one persuasion. The effect of this beginning
was detrimental to the College's advancement, as
it was to be sustained out of the people's money,
to which all denominations alike contributed, so that
there were heart burnings and jealousies all along

OLD DALHOUSIE COLLEGE.

from the start.   Only the sons of Churchmen felt that they could breathe freely the atmosphere of King's College, while those of other churches stood aloof and waited for the time to come when they could have institutions for the higher education, which all alike might approve and feel at home in, as their own and only Alma Mater.   Hence the Pictou Academy, under Dr. M'Cullough—hence Dalhousie College—Wolfville Academy—Sackville Academy—all now grown into the dimensions of Colleges—and all have greatly advanced. pecuniarily and in public favor, while the mother of all —King's College—remains to this day comparatively weak and helpless, and yet doing good work and conducted under far more liberal auspices than formerly.   It may be asked here why if King's College did not succeed under " the church," how comes it that the Methodist and Baptist and Presbyterian Colleges have advanced so rapidly when they likewise are strictly denominational and flourishing ?   The reason is obvious.   When the charter was obtained for King's College. the population was only adequate for the support of one high school of learning ; and had there been prescience enough among our fathers to see that as the population increased, embracing all denominations, and had they spread their nets to catch all the people alike, without creed or doctrine—in a word, opened the doors of a non-sectarian college, all might have been gathered in, and the one institution would have answered for all, even to this day. Instead of having half a dozen Colleges at work in the lower Provinces, one grand University would be amply sufficient for all purposes. While jealousy operated against King's College at the beginning, and kept it back, today there is an *esprit de corps* among the several denominations, each vieing with the other for prominence, or the laudable endeavor to make their College a success and a praise among the churches and throughout the land.

Still, there is no reason why King's College should not now be advancing in students, in funds, and in the confidence of the people. If there is still church about her, there is not enough to keep back those who can attend with all their scruples, and gain an education in Arts equal to that provided by any other college. If it is the want of funds, then it is a reproach upon the Churchmen of the Province, especially the wealthy ones, that they do not lend a helping hand, and take a leaf from the books of members of other churches, who feel a pride in carrying on their own distinctive denominational work. "By their fruits ye shall know them." Let Churchmen lay this text to heart and do their duty.

With regard to the failure of Dalhousie College in answering the expectations formed on the opening by the Earl of Dalhousie, I am unable to assign a cause, unless it be due to the old school of politicians, who did not only neglect to send their sons to it, but threw in its way all the discouragements

within their reach at the time, to render it inopera-
tive. I can account for the failure in no other
way. Its large class rooms stood idle for years.
Nobody but the Janitor occupied the premises,
except that part in the basement which was let for
storage.   During the summer of the cholera (in
1834) the building was used as an Hospital, whither
the sick and dying were carried daily in large
numbers to be treated, and from whence many a
dead body was conveyed for interment, scarcely
coffined and without ceremony.   It was a terrible
scourge, upwards of 1.500 persons perished
within eight weeks—it was an epidemic far worse
than the small-pox. which visited Halifax in
1825, and carried off upwards of 800 of the inhabitants.   In the midst of the worst part of the
cholera plague the Lieut. Governor, Sir Colin
Campbell, performed heroic service, attending the
patients day after day, and ministering to their
wants, thus setting an example which did good
and induced the attendants to likewise persevere in
their loathsome work.   Although His Excellency
in a few years afterwards was one of the bitter
opponents of Responsible Government, and for
whose recall the Reformers in the House petitioned
the home government, still his memory must ever
be held dear by the people of Halifax, for the
humane services rendered by him during that terrible visitation when the soul of every one was
stirred to its utmost depth, and the courage of His
Excellency tested in its sublimest form.

This old College Building is no more. As soon as the present Board got possession new life was infused within its walls, and in time its capacity not being equal to its patronage, the property was sold to the City, and a new College erected in the suburbs, in every way fitted for its increased and increasing numbers and popularity. Upon the old site stands the new City Hall, fronting which on the south is the Grand Parade. which presents a fine grassy parterre, with walks, and on the upper side west. a steep terraced slope margined with forest trees. The stone enclosure of the Parade ground is massive and highly creditable to the City.

Although never a financial success as already stated, Windsor College has sent forth into the world men who in after life distinguished themselves in the service of their country, by land and sea. and in the field of letters, reflecting upon their Alma Mater perhaps more lustre than can be said of any other Colonial Institution. For example —the hero of Kars, General Williams, who during the Crimean War held the Russians at bay for months, in the dead of an Arctic winter, amidst great suffering and privation, when beleagured in the fortress of Kars. a most strategic point. against which the enemy incessantly battered, at the sacrifice of human life and ammunition ; and when at last a breach was made in the walls, the heroic band was forced to surrender from sheer exhaustion. The Russian General on entering, highly

complimented Williams for his bravery, endurance
and skill. Then General Inglis, son of the late
Lord Bishop, who heroically distinguished himself
at Lucknow during the Indian Mutiny. Inglis
on that occasion was outnumbered and outflanked
by the enemy, and his little band of followers cut off
from the main army. He accordingly sought shelter in the Fortress of Lucknow—among this little
band there were many women and children. Day
and night, with demoniac yells and menaces, the
Sepoys bombarded the lonely garrison on all sides,
and as often as breaches were made in the walls
they were quickly repaired by the defenders.
During the wars of Cromwell's time, the Countess
of Derby defended her Castle called "Latham
House" for weeks against the besieging army,
which came upon her unawares, and when the
Earl was on the battle field at a distance. Her
little garrison consisted only of her household
servants and retainers, and her children ; and all of
these were brought into service in loading the
muskets while the Countess herself and her able-
bodied men fired from the portcullis and windows of
the Castle, and so the siege was finally raised by the
enemy as abortive. Here, then, was a counterpart
of that old heroic performance. Inglis knew the
fate of his dependents if the Sepoys once gained
an entrance, in his knowledge of the Cawnpore
massacre a few weeks earlier, when men, women
and children were thrown into a deep well and
there murdered, many of them being buried alive.

As the days went on the enemy around Lucknow increased in numbers—so that at length it became apparent to Inglis that if succour was not soon at hand, he would be compelled to capitulate, or the walls would be blown up from the outside, as the Sepoys now began to sap and mine at several points. But it was not to be so—a kind Providence stood by them—for just at the moment when despair had taken possession of every heart, from days of exhaustion, trial and hunger, and all hope of being rescued had fled, the sound of the bag-pipes was heard in the distance—every nerve of the watchers was strung to its utmost tension to catch the welcome signal. On fully realizing that the Campbells were coming indeed, one shout of frenzied joy went up from that little Fortress, the like of which perhaps had never been surpassed. It was the excitement of the moment—the shout of victory—the renewal of life, after weeks spent, as it were, in the agonies of death.

The relieving army was under the command of General Havelock, while Sir Colin Campbell, Outram and other Generals were on the march, enfilading in the same direction. It did not require the Sepoy dogs long to get out of the way when the British came up. But they still held possession of the Residency until the English Generals concentrated their forces round about, when after several hours of desperate fighting and terrible slaughter the capture was fully effected (21st March, 1858) and an awful retribution was visited upon the rebels. The back bone of the rebellion was now pretty well broken.

The wife of Nova Scotia's hero, (daughter of Lord High Chancellor Chelmsford—Sir-name Thesigar,) was with him in the Fortress of Lucknow, and shared with him all the sufferings of the garrison. The long trials and anxieties of Inglis told upon his health, and he died at a comparatively early age. His portrait hangs in the Legislative Council Chamber, Halifax.

KING'S COLLEGE, WINDSOR.

PROVINCE BUILDING, HALIFAX.

CHAPTER V.

Sir Wm. J. Ritchie, late Chief Justice of Canada.—Rev. Dr. Crawley and the Disruptions in the Church of England.—Bishop Inglis and Rev. Mr. Twining.—Church Families Turning Baptists.—Thomas C. Haliburton (" Sam Slick").—His Career in the Imperial Parliament.

Another graduate of King's College, (if I mistake not, at all events a Nova Scotian,) was the late Sir Wm. J. Ritchie, Chief Justice of the highest Court in the Dominion, who rose to his eminent position from sheer force of character and talents, united with industry and great judicial skill. As a lawyer, Ritchie held first rank at the bar of New Brunswick before he ascended the Bench in succession to Judge Street, who died in England in 1855. Shortly after the confederation of these Provinces, he was elevated to the Bench of the Supreme Court of Canada, and succeeded Judge Richard to the Chief Justiceship, the duties of which he continued to discharge with dignity and impartiality up to the time of his death. Young Ritchie went to St. John in about 1836, from Annapolis, where he and several brothers, who all became men of distinction, were born, their father being one of the Judges of the Court of Common Pleas of Nova

Scotia ; and although the whole family were Conservative in politics, from generation to generation, through all changes of Government, William J. Ritchie struck out on the Liberal side from the day he landed in St. John, and adhered to the principles of liberalism through all vicissitudes, as well before as during his legislative career. As a representative he distinguished himself and helped to bring about the system of Colonial party government,which we enjoy at this day. Judge Ritchie will therefore be historically known as one of New Brunswick's early Reformers.

Another graduate of King's College was Rev. Dr. Crawley, of Wolfville College, who in 1825, together with a number of other first class churchmen, seceded from the Church of England in a body, on account of the inconsiderate conduct of the newly created Bishop—John Inglis—by appointing to the Rectorship of St. Paul's the then Rector of St. John, instead of the Rev. Mr. Twining, the favorite, who should have been the person. This gentleman had been Curate for many years, while Dr. Inglis was Rector—both were very much liked—and it was but reasonable and fair for the congregation to suppose that he would be the Bishop's choice as it was the universal desire. The Bishop's act caused a wound to the Church which it took many years to heal, notwithstanding the fruitless attempts at cauterization. Numerous families locked their pews and left the Church—so that the new Rector was obliged for a long time to preach to empty seats. [It was not that the congregation had objections to Mr. Willis as a man and preacher—it was the action of the Bishop that caused the difficulty.]

Mr. Crawley, as just stated, withdrew from the Church of his fathers, and with others, representing some of the leading families of Halifax, set up an independent establishment, but for want of an *independent* Church minister, the building in Granville street, which they had erected, was turned over to the Baptist body, they themselves going with it, and so the descendents of those families continue to be good Baptists up to this day. Mr. Crawley was bred to the law, but shortly after the disruption he studied for the ministry, and became an able preacher. He died about six years since, at the age of 86, having been President of the Wolfville College for some years. Although Mr. Crawley entered Windsor College in 1816, he only received his degree of D. D. from his old Alma Mater about seven years ago, the tardiness for which I suppose is hardly worth canvassing. Dr. Crawley was a very able man, second to none of his College compeers for literary and scholastic attainments. The late Pastor of the Fredericton Baptist Church, Rev. Mr. Crawley, is a member of the same family. Indeed all the Crawleys rank high among the social and intellectual and religious forces of Nova Scotia.

Thomas C. Haliburton ("Sam Slick") was another graduate of Windsor, and who as a literary man has reflected lustre upon his Alma Mater and native Province.　In 1826 he published two volumes of the History of Nova Scotia, in the *Novascotian* office.　This was long before the author intended to devote his leisure hours to literary work; and it is a question whether Haliburton would ever have become an author had it not been for Howe, both of which gentlemen were on terms of the most intimate friendship.　In 1836 Mr. Haliburton wrote several letters which appeared in the *Nova-scotian*, entitled "Sam Slick of Slickville," and they were so amusing, and contained so many practical lessons calculated especially to work upon the dormant energies of the rural population, that Sam soon became a universal favorite, and the extra demand for copies of the *Novascotian* could scarcely be supplied.　Mr. Howe advised the author to have his letters re-printed in a new and less perishable form, which was done, and as soon as the book appeared it obtained a rapid circulation all over the Province, and a second edition was called for.　This then was the beginning of a very successful career in the literary field by the first Nova Scotian author and graduate of King's College.

Having thus planted his feet upon solid ground and considered his reputation for literary work fairly begun, Haliburton devoted his talents and time thenceforward more to the cultivation of letters than to the dry subtilities of the law.　The progeny of this once popular author may thus be summed up—after Sam Slick the Clock Maker

JUDGE HALIBURTON (Sam Slick.)

came Wise Saws—Nature and Human Nature —Bubbles of Canada—The Letter Bag of the Great Western, &c. These works all took well with the reading public, but some were considered better than others. As in the case of Dickens' first production—"*The Pickwick Papers*,"—which was thought by many to be his *chef d'œuvre*—so with Haliburton's first venture. In other directions he made no improvement upon the originality and popularity of "Sam Slick." His "Bubbles of Canada" was in my humble opinion a mistake, and brought out in conspicuous relief the Tory proclivities of his nature, and furnished an inkling of the political school in which he had been reared. The work was written about the time of the Canadian Rebellion in 1837, and designed to show that the Canadians in their struggles for Responsible Government had but little of which to complain. It was demagogues who made all the trouble, and that their grievances were imaginary, founded more upon the discontentment of their nature, especially their French nature, than any tangible presentment of well grounded political grievances. That every time the British Government yielded to their importunities, the more they felt encouraged to renew their demands. [The further consideration of this part of our subject, however, will come on later.] In short, our author was a Conservative of the first quality, and could see nothing unless through imperial spectacles—quite the opposite of Howe, although personally they were the best of friends, even companions. Like many other Colonists who get tired of the country of their birth and associations, and where perhaps they had made their money, and then leave all behind them for " *home*," there to reside and sink into ordinary mortals, our author finally quitted his native land and took up his abode in England where he married a rich lady, his second wife, and through whose influence he found his way into the British House of Commons ; but as a member of Parliament he was not in my opinion a success. On one occasion in particular he displeased the Government and House, by insisting at an inopportune time upon the consideration of some Colonial question, thus bringing down upon himself rather caustic remarks from several leading members. Authorship in the House of Commons goes but a short distance among men of great statesmanlike qualities. You must not only speak to the point and at the right time, but *say something* in order to be listened to and not coughed down. In our Local or Dominion Parliaments, it is different. Here, as at Ottawa, a member is personally known to the whole house, and has the sympathy of a large proportion of its members, his powers are well known, and though he may not be a " heavy weight," he is listened to, at all events, no matter to what side of politics he belongs. Now I do not mean to say that Judge Haliburton would not be a power anywhere and under any ordinary circumstance. I refer more to the exacting and arbitrary arena presented by the British House of Commons, and the wonderful tact as well as abilities requisite to meet its demands. No doubt had our author lived long enough he would have found a better place among British statemen.

CHAPTER VI.

*Residence of " Sam Slick."—Persons leaving their
Native Homes to Reside in England.—A Late
Rector of Trinity Church, St. John, and a Late
Rector of St. George's Church, Halifax.—Bishop
Inglis' Horse.—Admiral Sir Provo Wallis.—
Battle between the Shannon and Chesapeake.*

In another place we give a picture of the old
residence of " Sam Slick," in Windsor, as well as
his portrait. This once famous spot now resolved
into " the Classics," but also dissolved of late years
into very disproportionate proportions, is occupied
by a small family from the interior, whose
name is unknown to me. Forty years ago as a
stranger I wandered about those once beautiful
grounds, intersected by winding roads lined with
locusts and acacias. Last summer I witnessed the
scene again, but woefully changed—the roads were
almost blotted out, the foliage matted and tangled,
and half the shade trees gone. The Windsor and
Annapolis Railroad has also laid a sacrilegious
hand upon the place by cutting through the middle
or towards the back part of the property, so that
the peace and repose once enjoyed here, are
changed for the screech of the locomotive and the
roar of traffic. The old house is in a good state of

preservation ; but the *home* of the author has departed. *Sic transit gloria mundi.*

The memory of Judge Haliburton is kept green in Windsor by its spirited inhabitants. A Club called "the Haliburton Club" was started in 1884, (the President of which was Charles G. D. Roberts, Author, who was then Professor of Classics in Windsor College,) which meet together periodically to revive and discuss the merits of their once "Patron Author," and in other literary ways pass the time profitably and pleasantly, no doubt heightened by the exhilarations which wait upon good appetites and gentle indulgences. Long may they live to meet and have a good time—and help to keep alive the name of Haliburton.

With regard to persons abandoning their own country for "*home*," I remember listening to a University Oration delivered at one of the New Brunswick Encœnias by a distinguished son of Halifax ; and in the course of his able remarks he expatiated grandiloquently, even vituperatively, upon the conduct of so many rich men after making their money in our large cities, turning their backs upon their native land and going abroad to spend it, and live the remainder of their days in England, ostracising themselves from old friends, exchanging the pleasures of the social circle in which they were reared, for the dry conventionalities of a new existence, one to which they are strangers—while the positions which they before occupied are unknown and uncared for by

OLD RESIDENCE OF "SAM SLICK."

their new acquaintances. What followed this patriotic expression of fervor? This very same gentleman a few years afterwards "went and did likewise." Perhaps he will see this and remember the circumstance?

But to enumerate all the graduates of King's College, who in after life became somewhat famous in professional ways, would occupy more space than is necessary. But before closing with this college, reference to two more of her graduates might not be uninteresting, viz: the Rev. J. W. D. Gray, Rector of Trinity Church, St. John, and Rev. Fitzgerald Uniacke, Rector of St. George's Church, Halifax, both of whom graduated at the same time—1814—studied together—were close companions, almost inseparable—the one appeared to be necessary to the existence of the other—and in death they are not divided. In the centre of the little grave-yard, foot of "Dutch Village" hill, surrounding the church, two sarcophagi built side by side, may be seen covering the dust of these once very able divines. As theologians and pulpit speakers, both rose to eminence in their respective churches and towns. As a polemical writer, Dr. Gray excelled. and was recognized beyond the bounds of his own Province as a force. Rev. Mr. Uniacke held his congregation in increasing numbers, growing in strength until his last days. His sermons were sound and evangelical and well delivered. His memory is held sacred to this day by the old residents of St. George's Parish. Bishop

HALIBURTON CLUB ROOM.

Inglis and Bishop Suther, who recently died a Bishop in Scotland, were also graduates of King's.

[On one occasion when Bishop Inglis as Patron of the College was on a visit of examination, and having spent the night with the President, he was greatly chagrined next morning when preparing to leave for Halifax, on being informed by his groom that the tails of both his horses had been shaven clean off, not a hair scarcely left upon the stumps. The Bishop lost no time in going out to see for himself the outrage that had been perpetrated upon his horses and his own dignity ; and when he came in sight and beheld the awful spectacle, if he did not actually anathematize he talked very loudly against the guilty sinner, and if he could only catch him he would give him "the benefit of clergy " in such a way as the culprit would remember to his dying day. The Bishop had to get other horses to take him to town, for his own presented a picture worthy of a Hogarth. The Bishop's son, afterwards the famous General, got the credit among his College chums of having been the culprit on this occasion.]

Although in no way connected with King's College, while upon the subject of distinguished Nova Scotians, the opportunity is here improved of introducing to the readers of this Book, Admiral Sir Provo Wallis, who died in England a few years ago at the age of 101. He was born in the Naval Yard, Halifax, in 1791, his father at the time

being Chief Clerk in that interesting and very
active department. When 14 years of age young
Wallis entered the Royal Navy as a midshipman
on board the frigate *Cleopatra*, and from that time
forward, until the crowning victory on board the
Shannon, he was, so to speak, continually under
fire ; for in the early part of the century England
and France under Napoleon, were seldom out of a
broil. Space or the intention of this work, will
not permit even a reference to the many engage-
ments in which our hero took part—whether in
single combats or squadrons—until we come down
to the time of his participation in the engagement
between the *Shannon* and *Chesapeake*, which took
place off Boston Harbor in May, 1813. The United
States and England then being at war, a number
of naval duels were fought along the American
coast, with varying success on both sides respectively—sometimes the Americans were the victors,
and at others the English. The American ships
were largely recruited by deserters from the
English Navy, which fact was the main cause of
the war. Still, to lose an English frigate in battle
was a galling humiliation to a nation whose
prestige upon the high seas was great and sublime,
since Nelson a few years before at Trafalgar had
destroyed a French fleet far superior to his own.
Whatever may have been the disproportionate
armaments or strength of any two of the English
and American vessels which had met and won
or lost, Captain Broke of the *Shannon*, which

was lying at Halifax, resolved in his own mind to find a solution for this problem by ascertaining what men-of-war were lying in any of the American ports, and to satisfy himself of one of his own size and metal and number of men. Hearing of just such a vessel—the *Chesapeake*—lying in Boston harbor, he despatched a challenge to Captain Lawrence to meet him on the high seas—and to test the prowess and gallantry of each vessel—after explaining to him in his letter the exact size of the *Shannon*, number of guns and men, in order that Captain Lawrence might prepare himself accordingly, and that it should not be said afterwards that any disguised or unfair means had been taken, or trap laid. The challenge was accepted—the *Shannon* by this time was cruising off Boston harbor, awaiting an answer, when the *Chesapeake* was descried from the mast-head bearing down with all sail set and flags flying, in the direction of the English sea dog. The two vessels soon afterwards met, when the engagement began—it was over in fifteen minutes, but terrible while it lasted—the number of men killed and wounded in that short time was said to surpass what might have been expected from an action of several hours' duration—and among those who fell was Captain Lawrence himself; and among the wounded was Capt. Broke, while his first Lieutenant was killed—so that upon his second Lieutenant Wallis (the hero of this sketch, then only 22 years of age) devolved the duty of taking charge of the ship.

Before Lawrence died the last words he uttered were "Don't give up the ship," which, like Nelson's signal at Trafalgar, "England this day expects every man to do his duty," will last forever in the annals of naval heroism and epigrammatic significance. It may be somewhat interesting to quote here Captain Broke's own version of the battle: "The enemy," says Captain Broke, "came into action in very handsome fashion, having three American ensigns flying ; when closing with us he sent down his royal yards. I kept those of the *Shannon* up, expecting the breeze would die away. At 5.30 P. M., the enemy hauled up on the starboard side, and twenty minutes later the battle began, both ships steering full under topsails." Three broadsides were exchanged between them, and then the ships fell on board each other, the mizzen channels of the *Chesapeake* locking with the *Shannon's* forerigging. Captain Broke instantly gave orders for boarding. "Our gallant hands," he writes, "appointed to that service immediately rushed in under their respective officers, driving everything before them with irresistible fury. The enemy made a desperate, but disorderly resistance. The firing continued at all the gangways and between the tops, but in two minutes' time the enemy were driven, sword in hand, from every post. The American flag was hauled down, and the British Union Jack floated triumphantly above it. The whole of this service was achieved in fifteen minutes from the commencement of the action."

[The revival of this story is not at all pleasant, since the two nations are now interlaced in the most friendly, peaceful embrace, it is to be hoped forever (notwithstanding the Venezuelan trouble); but it is unavoidable while the person who performed such an important part in the tragedy is the subject of this sketch, and so identified with the history of Halifax that it cannot very well be passed over.]

Lieut. Wallis set sail for Halifax with his prize so crippled that it took many days to reach port, while he was in constant danger of being overtaken by the enemy and himself and prize retaken. It was on Sunday morning when the vessels were descried in the offing. The news soon spread through the town. The churches were all *in* at the time, but were *out*, emptied in a trice when the news reached the different congregations—nor did they "stand upon the order of their going," or wait for the benediction, but rushed out helter skelter and quickly down upon the wharves. [This I learned from "one who had been present."]

Captain Lawrence was buried in the old Church-yard, his funeral was attended by all the pomp and ceremony due to a British General, while minute guns were fired from all the ships in the harbor and from the Citadel. As soon as the war was over application was made by the American to the British Government for the remains of the gallant Lawrence. They were accordingly disinterred and conveyed to New York, where they

SIR PROVO WALLIS.

now repose in Trinity Church-yard, just at the head of Wall Street ; the sarcophagus may be seen near the left or lower entrance door to the Church.

Wallis' promotion was rapid from that time forward—now Commander, then Captain, Admiral, and so on in regular gradation. But our limits forbid further references. At the time of his death his name stood at the head of the British Navy as "Admiral of the Fleet," a mark of distinction conferred upon him some years since by the Lords of the Admiralty, in recognition of past and gallant services, a mark never conferred upon any other officer in the British Navy. He stood at the head of the list as Vice-Admiral, and bore all his honors and full pay as if in active service, until the day of his death. Her Majesty took great interest in him. On the anniversary of his centennial birth, she manifested her concern for his health by not only sending cheering words, but more solid tokens of her regard.

Mrs. Lawrence survived her husband many years. A person of my acquaintance was intimate with her at Newport, R. I., where she then resided, (say 60 years ago) and describes her as being an interesting lady with flowing silvery hair, and the traces of early beauty, which still lingered on in her declining years. And the old lady spoke in fine terms of Captain Wallis, who frequently visited the United States since the war, and always called upon Mrs. Lawrence.

CHAPTER VII.

*St. George's Church and the " Old Dutch Church."
—The Pew System and Jealousies Therewith.—
Old Mirey.—" The Club " writers in the Nova-
scotian.—Howe's Friends and Contemporaries.—
Imported Officials.—The Countess of Blessington
and " Gore House," London.*

St. George's Church (Round Church) already
referred to, is the outcome of the little Dutch
Church, situated near the upper end of Brunswick
street, which was built between the years 1758
and '60 by the German settlers in that part of the
town. It does not stand up to this day as an
enduring monument of the architectural skill and
enterprise of its founders, so much as it does of
their piety and zeal as a God-fearing people. The
grave-yard about it contains the last of many of
its original worshippers, some of the dates go back
to 1775 or 120 years ago. The building is of
wood—probably 40 by 30 feet in size. The steeple
surmounted by a " Rooster," which denotes the
trend of the wind, is the most imposing part of the
edifice. In this little temple then, the Lutherans
were wont to congregate at least once a week. The
pews were of the high back pattern, as in many
of the old churches of the present day, so that not

much more than the heads of the occupants were
visible. I suppose so long as the preacher could
be seen the fashions in the next pew were of no
consequence—the flower bed of bonnets were sure
to be noticed, no matter what else the ladies wore
behind the partitions. Thus was the pew system
in full vogue in those days. The innovation of
free sittings—(which allows every-one to occupy
the same seat regularly and statedly without
paying pew rent for the support of the church)—
had not then become part of the Dutchman's
creed, and so they were very jealous of their
pew rights. so much so that if an outsider, not
belonging to themselves, happened to stray into
the fold and within the sacred precincts of one of
these pieces of private property. his chances of
remaining till the end of the service was somewhat
doubtful. On one occasion, so tradition saith, a
South-ender (persons belonging at the lower end
of the town, then called Irish Town) happened to
take a seat in Hans Sourkrout's pew, and when
that worthy citizen (whose occupation was that of
a truckman) arrived, he was taken all aback at
what he considered to be an impertinence, and on
recovering his breath, he thus interrogated the
intruder: "I say Friend, who does your trucking?"
Reply—"John Rex." "Den you jist go and sit in
John Rex's pew." The congregation having out-
grown in numbers the dimensions of the church,
the site upon which the present Round Church
stands, was secured and a more suitable edifice

commenced, and fully completed in about 1826, although the foundation was laid in 1800. As soon as the congregation took possession of the new church the little old historic one was closed, but afterwards opened for school purposes, and it still continues as such I believe. As a connecting link between the German and English worshippers—by this time the tongues of the former had become pretty well Anglified—it was deemed expedient and proper to continue the services of the old Clerk—known as Old Mirey—for it would never do to ignore one of the standards of the little old Church ; it was enough to abandon the building itself.

The Clerk in those days occupied a seat directly below the Minister and made all the responses on behalf of the people. Now Mirey spoke more broken English in one sentence than any Dutchman that I ever knew, and were it possible to convey to the reader in print the modulation of his voice, his emphatic manner, the twist in his words,—in a word, a verbal fac-simile of the whole man while following the Minister, and the effect he produced upon a stranger in attendance for the first time, it would be more than comic. Had the phonograph been among the discoveries of the day, as now, and a few passages from the voice of Mirey been secured, it would be worth a good many nickels dropped in the slot for a person now to listen to the interesting tones of the Clerk of the Round Church seventy years ago. But after hearing him a few times people got used to him. Then again he felt the importance of his position by his affectation when off duty. The strut in walking to and from church (he lived directly opposite) was a study of itself amongst us youngsters, who loitered about "Stairs' Corner." This distinguished individual was finally superceded by another Clerk, who spoke better English. The interior of St. George's Church has undergone several great transformations since I first knew it. The singing gallery, or "choir," formerly occupied the Eastern bulge facing the pulpit. Now the singers are behind the pulpit. Before the Rectorship of Mr. Uniacke, the Rev. Benjamin Gray officiated, and was thence transferred to Trinity Church, St. John, where in a few years afterwards his house was destroyed by fire and his wife burned to death. The house stood on Wellington Row, the site about where the late Dr. Botsford resided.

In 1827 a series of articles appeared in the *Novascotian*, under the heading — "THE CLUB," written in a colloquial and somewhat satirical vein in the nature of dialogue, the object of which was to criticise the acts of public men, especially the family compact officials. These were written in such a good natured way and so wittily that no one could get angry — it was the iron hand masked under a silken glove, and its weight was felt by those assailed, but no retaliation was possible unless at the risk of being laughed at. The articles continued from time to time, extending over a long period, once a week, and became as popular as the sayings of Sam Slick before referred to, which came out later. The authorship of those " Club" articles was as profound a secret as that which enshrouded the Junius letters ; and these articles although long since forgotten, were very useful in their day, and it is doubtful if any one outside the printing office ever knew the writer, or writers. Sixty years have since passed away, and all the contributors likewise. Those writers formed a sort of literary *guild*, and held their meetings beneath Mr. Howe's roof, to which also belonged some of the ablest and "smartest" men in Halifax, such as Laurence O'Connor Doyle, and Dr. Gregor : and casual attendants like Judge Haliburton (Sam Slick,) S. G. W. Archibald, one of the ablest and wittiest lawyers of his day, afterwards Master of Rolls, the Jotham Blanchard of Pictou, when in town, Beamish Murdock, the publisher of several volumes entitled " Epitome of the Laws of Nova Scotia," and the " History of Nova Scotia," Thos. B. Aiken, of antiquarian research, (pretty much like Joseph W. Lawrence of St. John,) and a well read gentleman, Thomas Forester, who will come into more prominent notice hereafter. Then outside of this coterie was another circle of clever men, whose visits to Mr. Howe were very frequent, and of an intellectual character—such as Titus Smith, known as the Dutch Village Philosopher, a man of varied attainments, a standing referee in cases where parties disagreed in their astronomical discussions for example, mathematical problems, hydraulic and other scientific topics. He made the astronomical calculations every year for one of the Almanacs; and he frequently lectured in the Mechanics' Institute. Then there was Andrew Shiels of Dartmouth, afterwards Stipendiary Magistrate of that town, a very well informed person and poet. Shiels, although in manner very unpretentious, was a fine conversationalist and was thought a great deal of by Howe. Another was George Thompson, a good writer, and ' good fellow."

Probably the last named gentleman developed into the most important of all those named, in having been the innocent or accidental cause of Howe's after greatness as a Politician and Statesman, as Howe himself was the cause, as before shown, of Haliburton's brilliant career as an author. This will appear hereafter. Then there was the Rev. Robert Cooney, who was educated for the Priesthood, but turned Methodist. He published in Halifax a brief history of New Brunswick, written when a resident of Miramichi. As an eloquent Pulpit Orator he was thought highly of by the Methodist worshippers in both Provinces. But Doyle was the witty man. He and Howe were " trump cards"—indeed a complete pack, and equal to a theatre. Their conversations corruscated with flashes of wit, sallies of mirth, and clever hits— while the burst of laughter, in accompaniment,

might be heard across the street. Howe called
Doyle the wittiest man he ever knew. Space will
not permit me repeating some of his anecdotes
bonmots, repartees, epigrams, &c., let off in private
and on the floors of the House of Assembly, of
which he afterwards became a lively member. I
will endeavor to do so at the end of this volume.

These then were some of Mr. Howe's prominent
literary associates, materials for all of whom would
be abundant enough to supply an interesting
biographical work well worth preserving.

The writers then of the famous Club articles
were: Joseph Howe, Dr. Gregor, Laurence O'Con
nor Doyle, Capt. Kincaid, whose Book on the
"Adventures in the Rifle Brigade" at Waterloo
was widely known in England and America. His
regiment was then stationed in Halifax. These
were the gentlemen who set the heather in a blaze
once a week in the columns of the *Novascotian.*

The subject matter treated in some of those Club
articles may be here noticed by way of specimen.
As these Provinces once upon a time were held as
a nursery and feeding ground for the scions of
influential place hunters in England, it was no
uncommon thing when a vacancy occurred in some
lucrative office, for the Governor to inform his
superior at the Colonial office, when forthwith one
of those favored youths would be sent out to fill
the gap, while our own people loyally acquiesced.
The names of some of those outsiders will readily
suggest themselves to "the oldest inhabitants."

In New Brunswick the old folks have a vivid recollection of those transplanted exotics. In 1835 a Judge was required and its own bar was considered to be so poor in material, or perhaps so uninfluential, that a young man was sent out from England to fill the place ; and although he proved to be an excellent upright Judge, the legal gentry continued to smart for some years under the wrong done them. But so decided a stand was taken on the occasion that the Colonies have been permitted to make their own Judges ever since. Then a Surveyor General was wanted, when lo, another official was made to order in England and sent to Fredericton to fill the gap and pocket all the revenues of his department. The yield of the Crown Lands was not then what it is today ; the revenues probably amounted to ten or fifteen thousand dollars, and by the time the Surveyor General's and the other salaries were paid, there was very little left. But it was all right and dutiful in those days—for the heads of departments rode in their chariots, sometimes drawn by four horses richly caparisoned, with outriders and footmen. The business people of Fredericton were satisfied, because all this grandeur and big salaries brought wheat to their mills. As to the rest of the Province, no one seemed to care—it was too many hours before the dawn ere the people began to get their eyes open and compass the full glare of day. (Mr. Howe by this time had begun the dissemination of his reform doctrines.) Then again, a head clerk is wanted for the Crown Land Office; and if any one wants to know how this situation was disposed of, he will just refer to a work in the Legislative Library, called "The Life of the Countess of Blessington." "Gore House" in London about this time was the most famous resort for men of culture, great generals, poets and leaders of fashion. Among her ladyship's visitors was the Duke of Wellington, then the most influential man in England. Now the Countess of Blessington had a brother and she wanted the Duke's influence to procure for him a situation in New Brunswick. Sir John Harvey was Governor at the time, and when two such heads got together through letters of correspondence, it did not take long for the brother of the Countess to obtain a good soft seat in the Crown Land Office in Fredericton, next in position to the head of the department and over the heads of the native clerks.

Now, the *Club* articles dealt with such subjects as these—for the same injustice prevailed in Nova Scotia as in New Brunswick, and indeed in all the British Provinces alike. But the *Club* articles applied to Nova Scotia only and said nothing about New Brunswick; and great indirect good came out of their publication.

CHAPTER VIII.

Mrs. Howe, Wife of Joseph Howe.—Her Amiable Qualities.—" Rambles" Over the Province.— Natural Advantages of Nova Scotia.—Charles Dickens and Joseph Howe as Press Reporters.— Labour in the Gallery of the House of Assembly Reporting.—The Power of the Novascotian News-paper.—The System of Government in 1830 (Both Local and Provincial.)—Howe Destined to Become the Greatest Man in Canada.

Mrs. Howe, the wife of Joseph, was the daughter of Captain John M'Nab, Royal N. S. Fencibles, and was born in 1807, in Barracks, at St. John's, New-foundland, where her father's regiment was then stationed. Afterwards the family proceeded to Halifax where the regiment was disbanded. Her parents then removed to M'Nab's Island, a property which was owned by Hon. Peter M'Nab, brother of the Captain, he having obtained it from Gover-nor Cornwallis on the early settlement of Hali-fax. Here Miss M'Nab continued to reside with her parents until her marriage with Mr. Howe in February, 1828. Mrs. Howe died about six years ago, and reposes beside her husband in Camp Hill Cemetery. Ten children were the issue of this marriage, two only of whom survive, viz , Mr·

MRS. JOSEPH HOWE.

Sydenham Howe and Mrs. Cathcart Thompson,
both residing in Halifax or its vicinity. As some
of the wives of famous men have much to do with
shaping if not directing the lives of their husbands,
I have thought it not out of place here to introduce to the attention of the reader, a lady whose
superior qualities were highly adapted for the
encouragement of a man who had to pass through
many trying vicissitudes, during his checkered
political course. Mrs. Howe was a lady of fine
intellect, and her sound judgment and advice never
failed in producing wholesome results. She was
to her husband a help-meet indeed. Whenever
the clouds lowered upon his house, as they sometimes did, she stood beside him as his stay and
comforter, with words of cheer and consolation,
always making the best out of the worst features
of the trouble. She was fully aware of her
husband's great talents, of his ambition and of his
faults, which no man living is without, and she
knew how to minister to every necessity as a " guiding angel," and to lead by the hand, as it were,
beside still waters. Preferentially Mrs. Howe was
domestic in her habits ; but deferentially and in
obedience to her position, society claimed a large
portion of her time—indeed the time of the wives
of leading public men, like that of their husbands,
is regarded by the general public in the light of a
bill of exchange—to be drawn upon at sight—so
that during Mr. Howe's palmy days, extending
over a long period, there was very little repose

and retirement from the cares and responsibilities of official life. But such must ever be the penalty that waits upon popularity. On the death of her husband Mrs. Howe was considerately remembered by the Legislature of the Province, so that her closing days were passed in comparative ease at the home of her daughter, Mrs. Thompson.

In connection with his paper, Mr. Howe travelled all over his native Province, and thus made himself acquainted with " the people." and in this way laid up without calculation an amount of intangible and indirect political capital, which stood him in good stead in a few years afterwards. On his return home, he described his " Rambles." both East and West, in the *Novascotian.* in such a free, colloquial, conversational style, that his letters became highly popular. The fine agricultural districts, the facilities for trade in other parts, the natural advantages for carrying on large industries, the fine streams of water coursing from the hills and running to waste without turning a mill, and other natural beauties and advantages. he brought so vividly to the notice of his readers, that an enthusiasm was generally evoked. and the people everywhere were made to feel by the descriptions that they really had a country worth living in. and a prospective business in various lines worth prosecuting. Many of these journeys were made on foot. Being a good and tireless pedestrian, Mr. Howe would ramble into the lanes and by-ways off the main roads, and visit people who seldom went to town, and into whose homes the daylight seldom let in a ray of news as to what was going on in the outer world—[no railroads or telegraphs then]—while the whole literature of the house consisted of the Bible, Belcher's Almanac, and perhaps the *Novascotian*. Being of a highly jovial nature, Mr. Howe would soon win his way into the good graces of the family, especially the mothers, whose children he would dandle upon his knee in true Malthusian style. Those hardy yeoman were seldom visited by politicians, except at election times, when candidates for the House would find them out through information obtained from the nearest neighbor on the main road. In Mr. Howe's visits —they all saw that he had no political ends in view, there was no pending election, or in prospective— his business was that of a purely business nature and the future would take care of itself, as it did in time, very much after all to his political advantage. He was indeed unwittingly laying up in store " a good political foundation against the time to come."

Charles Dickens commenced his literary career by reporting for the London *Morning Chronicle* in the Gallery of the House of Commons. So with Joseph Howe. There was but one Gallery in the Nova Scotia House at that time, situated at the Eastern end of the Assembly Room. As the Press was of no account in those conservative and self-contained days, no provision was made for Reporters. It was all one to the highly distinguished

members of the House—for it was a great distinction to be a representative—whether or not their
speeches saw the light of day after delivery in the
august presence of one another. Here then in this
" pent up Utica,' hustled by a grimy crowd, our
future statesman might be seen day after day taking notes upon the crown of his hat—then, after the
House had adjourned at a late hour, and members
and the multitude had gone home to dine and
wine and retire to bed, Howe would go to work
to transcribe his notes for publication—for although
his paper came out but once a week, he had to
keep up with the day's work of the house, and so
he labored day and night, doing with very little
sleep. But there never yet was a self-made man
whose laurels were gathered by the wayside, unless
through hard up-hill toiling and determination.
Until Mr Howe's time reporting for the newspapers was a business seldom indulged in. Indeed
it was considered next to a breach of privilege for
a spectator to take notes in the House. Mr. Howe,
at all events, broke the ice, and wrestled in his
mind with all contingent probabilities, such as
going to jail or having his ears cropped, or some
other dire punishment, which it was at that time
in the power of the House to inflict. Without
reference to party—if there was any party at that
time, except one, " the Compact." — Mr. Howe
published his reports, without flattery on the one
side or acrimony on the other. His own views
were sunk in the respective speakers — every

member was allowed the full benefit of his own
utterances.   But then the Editor also appeared in
each day's debate under the editorial head, in
juxta position, as it were, with each of the speakers,
and expressed himself in no uncertain way upon
the questions before the House, and in so able
a way that the embryo or forthcoming member
had a better hearing in the country than if he
delivered himself orally upon the floor of the
House.   In looking over the debates, the reader of
the *Novascotian* was not swayed by the contesting
opinions of this or that member in the discussion,
but as a general thing was more or less influenced
by the Mentor of the country, instead of the House!
Yes, in 1830, six years before Mr. Howe "had
the honor of a seat in that House," his pen did
more in shaping and moulding public opinion than
most of the members—nor do I think it a stretch
of the imagination in saying this.   And he had
ample and congenial work for the exercise of his
abilities, in attacking the system of government
hat then prevailed.   The Executive and Legislative Councils formed one body—no two branches
as at present—and their discussions were conducted
with closed doors.   The public had no rights to be
respected in that "Star Chamber."   There was no
departmental government; and the sizes of the
salaries shared by the officials were measured and
meted out with no ungrudging hand, but in
keeping with the opportunities which the system
favored.   The City and County were governed

by a Board of Magistrates, appointed by the Crown, which in plain English meant the Lieut. Governor and Council, all firmly knit together by ties the most indissoluble—unanswerable to any other than their own authority, which was absolute, and so far as the people were concerned irresponsible. (Upon this branch of the subject more definite reference will be made hereafter.) City and Municipal Corporations were things unknown—not even contemplated as possible future eventualities. To these and such like measures Mr. Howe fearlessly addressed himself, and thereby was leading to his own entanglement—for his opponents left no stone unturned in their endeavors to work the coils of the law about him, as they well knew that the time was coming when such an outspoken fearless individual must commit himself, when his tongue through the law courts would be silenced forever. That time did arrive and his opponents were not slow to take advantage of it, as will be noticed hereafter in the great Libel suit; but instead of killing their tormentor, the course pursued resulted in his becoming the greatest man in British North America.

CHAPTER IX.

*Mr. Howe's Serious Illness.—Mr. Howe the Origin-
ator of the " Cunard Steamers."—The First
Atlantic Steamer, the Cyrius—Messrs. Cunard &
Co. Places the Steamers on the Ocean, 1840.—
The Halifax Hotel Fails and is Turned Into
an Officers' Quarters.—The Duke of Kent.—The
Prince's Lodge.—The Duke of Orleans (After-
wards King of the French) in Halifax.*

But the time now seemed to have arrived (1830)
for the end of Mr. Howe's career.   He was stricken
down with fever brought on by over-exertion and
over-heating in the Garrison Racquet Court, and
his death was hourly looked for.   Mr. Howe, like
his brother William before referred to, was a fine
player, but of course inferior to him as such.   A
game had been previously arranged ; the players
were Captain Canning, R. N., son of England's
great Premier, Captain Norcott, Rifle Brigade, and
another officer whose name I am unable to recall,
and Mr. Howe.   The day was warm, and the
playing was lively, both sides determining to win,
and it was kept up for several hours.   That night
Mr. Howe was prostrated, and the next morning
alarming symptoms supervened, and he steadily
grew worse as the day advanced.   Dr. Hoffman

and Dr. Gregor were his attendant physicians—both of whom pronounced his case very critical. His family and friends gathered around his bed anxious and expectant ; but having a vigorous constitution he rallied and gradually grew better. Had he passed away at that time it is questionable whether Nova Scotia would not have been doomed for many years longer, and not obtained the reforms for which Mr. Howe so stoutly contended. There was certainly no public man at the time, of equal nerve and ability, to cope with the existing state of things—or with his aggressive powers to storm the enemy in his stronghold, and do as Howe did. batter down the buttresses behind which the officials were so firmly intrenched.

It may be new to many persons when informed that it is mainly due to Mr. Howe that the line of Atlantic steamers known as " the Cunarders," came into existence in 1840. In 1838, in company with T. C. Haliburton (Sam Slick.) Mr. Howe visited England and many parts of the Continent. When off Ireland the steamer *Cyrius*, one of the pioneer steamers. came in sight, and the Captain was ordered by the man-of war's man, to come to him —for the sailing vessel (with Howe and his friend on board) was one of Her Majesty's ships, and her Captain was supreme on the seas. From the *Cyrius'* Captain much nautical information was obtained—regarding the behavior of the vessel in rough weather—(Dr. Lardner having predicted that steam in a storm was impracticable, as the rolling of the

vessel would prevent a steady generation of steam)
—the working of the compass—whether steam
could be depended upon without sails—the amount
of coal consumed in a day—how many days out
from New York, &c., &c. Messrs. Howe, Haliburton
and the Captain were attentive listeners, and prof-
itted by the information. The Captain returned
to his steamer and was quickly out of sight, while
the war ship floated like a log in a dead calm,
unable to move, with her sails idly flapping against
the masts. The thought struck Mr. Howe—why
not have steamers like this to carry the mails from
England to Halifax, and thus instead of being two
or three months making the passage from land to
land, cross over in one quarter of the time, as the
Cyrius had done ? Here was proof of the feasibility of the project. Accordingly, when in London,
Mr. Howe interviewed Hon. Mr. Crane, then on a
mission to the Colonial Office in the interests of
New Brunswick, upon a certain political issue
which had bitterly divided parties in and out of
the Legislature for many years. The result of
this interview was the drawing up of a Memorial
to the Colonial Secretary—(Lord Glenelg)—[whose
portrait, by the way, hangs upon the walls of the
New Brunswick House of Assembly, obtained at
the expense of the Province—1,000 guineas—in
commemoration of the services he rendered to
New Brunswick in connection with the "quit
rents" question, and through which the Liberals
—then known as such—gained a great victory]

setting forth in an able manner the great possibilities of steam communication between England and America, in the saving of time, &c., and these suggestions were enforced through the personal observations had on the high seas in the case of the *Cyrius.* To this Memorial his Lordship made a very encouraging reply. (I have all the documents before me.) The seeds thus sown soon began to germinate, for in a short time after this, Mr. Cunard (a most enterprising merchant of Halifax) having got a hint, proceeded to England, and in connection with Messrs. McIver, Burns and Co., of Glasgow, all of whom no doubt had considerable influence at the Colonial Office, a Company was formed to carry out the project of building a line of steamers for carrying Her Majesty's mails, and for which service heavy yearly subsidies were granted by the English Government. Over fifty years have since rolled away, and the Cunard Steamers and their officers are to-day looked upon with as much respect as those composing any one of the minor European Navies, if not England's Navy. So that it appears to me, if it was through Mr. Cunard's enterprise and energy that the world is indebted for this very successful venture, the meed of praise is no less due to Mr. Howe's foresight and advocacy in " setting the ball in motion."

In due time Mr. Cunard became wealthy and popular in England, and was created a Baronet of the Empire, which at his death passed to his son Edward, and is now worn by Edward's son, whose residence is or was up to a short time since in New York. Mr. Cunard's father was a native of Pennsylvania, and went to Halifax some time in the latter part of the last century, when or about the time the Duke of Kent held command there, and was in the Duke's employ at the Lodge for several years, occupying a good position.

When the Cunard steamers commenced their trips in 1840, it was supposed that the ports of departure and arrival would be Liverpool and Halifax. So satisfied of this were the people of the latter place, that a Company was formed for the erection of a Hotel large and grand enough for the accommodation of the great influx of trans-atlantic visitors calculated upon. Capital enough was subscribed and the Hotel was built—but alas "the best laid schemes o' mice and men, gang aft a-gley"—for after a few trips Halifax was regarded by the Company as suitable only as a *touching* place, while Boston was selected as the *stopping* point. The Hotel, if not its owners, at once took sick and languished, and hobbled along and finally succumbed for want of patronage. At all events its doors were closed, while the stockholders divided the profits and losses among them, "share and share alike"—and so it remained closed for years, when the next I heard of it was as an Officers' Quarters, a sort of barracks for Her Majesty's officers. On the retirement of the troops the building was rehabilitated as an Hotel, under the management of Mr. Heslin, and which since

SIR SAMUEL CUNARD.

his death has been conducted by his sons. The
first lessees in 1841, were two American gentlemen. Messrs. Parker & Hinckley, most excellent
caterers and managers. They left because the
calculations in regard to the great business to be
done through an increase of the Cunard population
failed to realize. Although the Hotel has of late
been renovated and modernized, so much changed
in fact in its interior and exterior fittings, that its
first patrons would now scarcely know it, still the
old dining room remains intact, or is occupied today
as it was fifty years ago, but much handsomer in
its appointments.

As near as I can learn Prince Edward (in a few
years afterwards created Duke of Kent) came out
from England in 1794 to join the Halifax Garrison,
prior to being appointed Commander in Chief of
British North America. He was a young man
about 28 years of age. His town residence was
afterwards converted into the Military Hospital,
situated at the base of the Citadel glacis, and nearly
on the edge of the road leading to the parapet,
after turning in from Cogswell street a short
distance. The present Military Hospital is a
modern affair. In the summer he resided at " the
Lodge," six miles above town, on the margin of
Bedford Basin. The house was built and occupied
by the Wentworth family some years before this,
but extensively enlarged and improved in every
way after the Prince became the lessee. Grottos
and mimic temples, artificial lakes and winding

walks through the woods in all directions and long distances, were built and laid out at considerable expense. To this end, and for work continually going on from year to year, there were carpenters' shops, blacksmiths' forges, stone-cutters' yards, painters' shops, and in short, such other facilities for doing everything upon the premises necessary, that the place represented a miniature town of mechanical industry. This busy hive was situated a few hundred yards above the Lodge, and from twenty to thirty men were employed at a time during six months of the year. Near the dwelling was the telegraph station, a wooden structure about 20 feet in height, supporting a flag staff and yard arms, for the purpose of communicating with the telegraph station on Citadel Hill, six miles distant, by means of flags and balls — at that time the only system of telegraph known — and yet the interchange of words was as correct though slow as it is at the present day under the electric system. The Prince spent most of his time at the Lodge, and went in and out among the workmen, clad in homely attire, with the same ease and freedom as any country gentleman who takes pleasure in the attractions of a country life, and interest in seeing his men busy at work, and making free with them in conversation without fuss or formality. As a disciplinarian in uniform, however, he was of the tartar persuasion among his troops, several companies of which he had quartered in a barracks called Rockingham, afterwards turned into an inn,

a short distance above the Lodge, on the margin
of the Basin, the foundation walls of which, I am
told, are still to be seen.   Between the Lodge and
the barracks it was a pleasant walk, and the Commander was often upon his men in the grey of the
morning, for he was an early riser, when they
little expected him, and woe betide the officer in
charge and his subordinates, if everything was not
in prime order, and ready for a march or parade.
Among his civilian workmen he was all affability,
but the troops had to stand clear if anything went
wrong with the Prince's digestive arrangements,
for at such times he would proceed to Rockingham
and there explode in real muscular language.   I
have the names of most of the leading workmen
who one hundred years ago toiled in the presence
and under the direct patronage of Royalty, but
like their royal master, they have long since gone
to their rest.   As their descendants now move out
of the tradesman's rut, and among "the fashion-
ables," it would not do to stir up burned embers
and fan them into a flame.*

During the Prince's residence at the Lodge, the
Duke of Orleans (afterwards Louis Philippe,
King of the French) paid him a visit.   The Duke
was in exile after the French Revolution in 1799,
and he spent a whole summer, going in and out

---

*It may not be out of place here to say that the above account
of the Lodge, &c., is made by me on the authority of "one who
was present" but now no more—a direct communication, as it
were, between the past and present generations.

THE PRINCE'S LODGE.

of town with the Prince, and moved about among the workmen on the grounds with all the ease and politeness of a Frenchman. When his son, the Prince de Joinville, visited Halifax in the *Bella Poule,* just after conveying the remains of the Emperor Napoleon from St. Helena to Paris, upon advice of his father and in company with Lord Faulkland, then Governor (1841,) he drove out to visit the ruins of the old Lodge, where the King (Louis Philippe) had spent so many happy days ; and when the Prince of Wales visited Halifax in 1860, he did likewise, to take in the old home of his grandfather, the Duke of Kent. Then again, every royal visitor to Halifax since has done the same—viz : Prince Alfred, Prince Arthur and Princess Louise. Truly this has been a royal spot, and is deserving of careful preservation In fact I believe no other spot in the world outside of Princely residences, is so much associated with royalty as this.

Our engraving represents the Prince's Lodge as it appeared in 1820—it is taken from a picture in the possession of a lady residing in Halifax, and is said to be good —the building gives evidence of decay, the grounds are somewhat rugged, and the front paling requires props to keep it up. But the building is now all gone ; and in its place, or near by, I am told there is a small residence. The Rotunda or Band House opposite, has been separated by a deep railway cut, completely dividing the two properties ; and it will be seen by the engraving that this Band House is boarded in as if used for a dwelling, or stable, or store house, or something of that sort. The dust of Alexander, says Shakespeare, might be traced to a bung-hole. Here we have a slight illustration of the conceit, viz : in the Band Stand of Royalty being turned into the ignoble purposes of a stable.

CHAPTER X.

*The Last of the Old Lodge.—Ruins of the Building.
—Remains of the Old Flower Beds.—The Hermit's Cell.—Departure of the Duke of Kent from
Halifax.—Some of His Furniture Still in Halifax
and New Brunswick.—Suggestions for Renovating
the Lodge.—Accession of William IV. and the
Dramatic Display in Halifax.—Public Lotteries
in the Olden Times.— The Avon Bridge, Windsor.*

In 1828, I visited for the last time the Prince's
Lodge, and published in Halifax at a later date
my impressions of what I then saw, which might
be repeated here, as follows:

As a boy, I used frequently, with other boys, to
go up to the Basin in a sail-boat and visit the
Lodge, which at that time was left in charge of
the bats and owls—for it seemed to have no
regular care taker. The walls of the dining room
were papered with old-fashioned landscape scenes,
representing the English chase, in which deer,
foxes, horses and riders, green fields, hedge-rows,
trees, streams, and high barred gates, formed the
picture. At this time the paper was hanging in
tatters upon the walls, the doors were open,
creaking upon their rusty hinges, and the sides of
the building were in a state of decay. The winds

and storms of winter were fast destroying all that
remained of this once regal residence. On one
occasion we filled the boat with the paper we
pealed off and confiscated to our own use—quite
enough to decorate both sides of the proscenium
of an improvised amateur theatre. which we boys
fitted up in an old barn on Water Street, and
where Mr. Rufus Blake (subsequently an actor of
celebrity in the United States) was the leading
spirit and stage manager.

The Lodge stood about one hundred and fifty
feet from the road—in front of which grew Lom-
bardy poplars, tall and conical, overtopping all the
other trees of the forest ; and skirting the road to
the full width of the property was a paling fence
with the scattered remains of what was once a
well kept hawthorn hedge, after the English style.
The grounds about and in rear of the dwelling
gave evidence of having in their prime been well
cared for. The formation of the beds in the garden
was still visible. The walks or paths through the
umbrageous forest were in a good state of preservation. I have gambolled away a summer afternoon with other boys, winding through those
sequestered and deserted avenues—one running
into another—away back into the dense forest.
I suppose there must have been over a mile of
these walks, if placed in continuation. There was
an artificial lake a few hundred yards in rear of
the dwelling—on one side of which was a wooden
Chinese temple, which afforded a cover and shelter

to the sportsman, who might throw his line out of the door or window, in his angling propensities, upon a hot summer day. On the walls of this little structure were hundreds of names carved with a knife or pencilled by visitors who, as it is customary on such occasions, wish to leave some impress behind them of an event so important to themselves, but not to others, in carving their names. Then there were other ornamental houses and grottoes scattered about the grounds here and there, inviting leisure and repose to the wanderer in search of the picturesque, especially when the hospitalities of the place brought together large numbers of the gentry and their ladies from town. The Prince was known to be a liberal entertainer.

All these places, even in their decay, with rank vegetation asserting its supremacy everywhere about and within, afforded a fascination to my boyish fancy, in which I feel an interest to-day in recalling. The Prince himself, it is true, was, I think, still alive (in England) but far removed from the grounds in which he took such great delight, from his Acadian and ARCADIAN home; but how many of those who had shared in his board and once sat in those fascinating grottoes had at this time passed away from earth forever? I suppose to-day there is not a vestige of anything about the place denoting that it ever was a human residence, much less that of the father of the Queen of the greatest nation upon the face of the globe! And what were once pleasant walks

THE ROUND HOUSE.

through the woods, are now I judge, blotted out altogether.   The spruce, the pine and the fir, have long since disputed the right of science and cultivation to hold possession of the demesnes, especially since there was not one to follow in the foot-steps of the Prince and keep the woods back.

The "Round House" on the opposite side of the road, where the regimental band used to perform every evening, still stands a monument of the bygone.   Let the inhabitants of Halifax guard this remnant of the glory of other days, and suffer it not to perish !

As you approach the Lodge from town there stood in the midst of the woods what was called " the Hermit's Cell." I have frequently been at that place. The story runs that there was a soldier belonging to one of the regiments, who took it into his head to live the life of a recluse ; and the Prince indulging his vagary, provided him a place in the densest part of the forest, where he pitched his tent and lived solitary and alone ; and here he was found dead, after a separation from the world of three years and upwards.

There is not a vestige remaining (1891) of the old resorts to indicate where pleasure once held high carnival ; even the once deeply cut fish pond, I am told is scarcely traceable. The whole landscape is as aboriginal in appearance as if it had never been cultivated, much less once a picture of rural grandeur and the highest landscape gardening, performed by artistic hands.

In 1800 his Royal Highness left for England.
Just previous to sailing he laid the corner stone of
the old Masonic Hall on Pleasant street, and was
presented with 500 guineas by the inhabitants for
the purchase of a star, and an Address in the old
Court House (since removed.)   Such of his furniture* which was not sold in Halifax (several pieces
of which the writer of this possesses) was shipped
on board the *Princess Amelia*, and she was cast away
on Sable Island and lost together with every soul,
numbering 200 persons.†

The day of his Royal Highness' departure was
one of great sorrow among the inhabitants,—I
suppose it was a somewhat sentimental sorrow,
enhanced no doubt by the high rank of the Prince
—the King's son—to say nothing of the lavish
expenditure of money for which he had for six
years been most famous at the Lodge and in town
—and for the associations which clustered around

---

*Since writing the forgoing, I observe in Progress, a letter
signed " A. F. Falconer, Sherbrooke, N. S." in which the writer
states that he has in his possession the identical piano, used by
Madame de Lausent at the Prince's Lodge in 1800. I am well
acquainted with the lady's position at the lodge during the
Prince's residence, and have several interesting anecdotes and
memoirs connected with the society's gatherings, and of the
lady's very interesting and agreeable manners. It was for her
that all the winding pastoral walks were made by the Prince
through the umbrageous forest. But as I had already extended
the limits, perhaps too far, in dealing with the lodge, I thought
it better not to go into this part of the subject. My information,
with regard to all I have said and might say, is strictly accurate
as I received it directly from a once living witness who resided
at the lodge during the five or six years residence of the Prince.
But with respect to the very kind and liberal offer of your cor-
respondent, viz: to present the historical piano to a restored

his every movement, and the prestige which was
given to Society by his presence—and all of this
was about to be severed forever.   Hence this more
than ordinary parting.   [See Appendix.

We read of the renovation of Cathedrals and
old Castles, and restoration of old historic places
after having been in ruins for centuries, even the
excavation of long buried cities, upon all of which
large sums of money have been lavished.   Might
not Halifax then with propriety and even profit,
undertake to restore the Prince's Lodge and surroundings to their pristine grandeur—erect upon
the very same spot a second edifice precisely after
the old architectural style, preserving inside the
same form, lineaments and size as regards rooms,
and the outside the same filigree adornments—
then set the gardener to work upon the lawn and
grounds and there reproduce the old flower beds,
walks, grottoes, lakes, temples—in short render
the whole place so complete and *lifelike* that it

---

lodge, I (G. E. Fenety) beg to add that I will be pleased in such
case to supplement the gift by offering a pair of mahogany
arm chairs, once used in the Prince's drawing room, purchased at the time of the auction sale by the father of the
writer.   Indeed, I have no doubt that if the lodge were
restored there would be as many relics of the Prince forthcoming as would furnish quite a large portion of the Mansion,
for I am aware myself of several such memoirs lying about.
In this way Mount Vernon contains relics of Washington.
It only requires an effort to be made by some one or more of
the spirited citizens of Halifax to take hold of the project and
the work of restoration may be carried out.

†I may here remark that I am not quite sure whether this
calamity happened when the ship was on her way out to Halifax or when returning to England.

would puzzle the "oldest inhabitants," were they to revisit the earth to know any difference between the past and the present. The house could be used as a summer hotel and the grounds for pleasure purposes. The old band-house could again be brought into requisition and music once more float upon the summer air. Is there a pleasanter site in all Halifax for the purpose mentioned—to say nothing of the historical associations which would spring to the minds of visitors through means of this recreative enterprise?

I never witnessed anything more dramatic and beautiful than on the occasion of the accession of William IV. in 1830. George IV. had been dead six weeks and his brother in his place, ere the news reached Halifax. To-day such an event would be known in an hour. There were six men-of-war in the harbor at the time, one of which was commanded by the new King's natural son, Captain Fitz Clarence, a ruddy faced, compactly built man, seemingly fond of a jolly life. The Governor gave a large dinner party in honor of the occasion—the King's accession. According to a preconcerted arrangement, when the King's health was proposed at nine o'clock in the evening, that moment a piece of artillery placed in front of Government House, gave the signal shot, when every ship in the harbor, including the Citadel, let bang their big guns, each firing a Royal salute—so that 168 guns were fired at the same time, as fast as they could be loaded and discharged. The night was dark, and the lighting up of the heavens and reverberating peals of thunder echoing among the hills, produced such a noise and weird appearance, that to use an old phrase, it would be easier to imagine than describe. It was perhaps the loudest response to a toast ever heard, and it came immediately as the words fell from his Excellency's lips—truly in a voice of thunder.

Lotteries nowadays are reckoned as uncondonable legal offences and justly so. The Government of the United States has within the last few years placed its iron heel upon the greatest abomination of the age—the Louisiana Lottery—by prohibiting the circulation of its literature through the mails. The morals of Halifax in the early part of this century must have been considered by the Legislature of the Province as somewhat dubious, and required legal restraints to keep the conduct of the people within due bounds—for an Act was passed many years since prohibiting horse racing, on the ground that such sports led to gambling, to which the tender susceptibilities of "the wisdom of the country" were stoutly opposed. Yet, strange to say, in 1819, another Act passed through the Legislature granting a charter to a Company, accompanied by an authorization to raise *by lottery* the sum of nine thousand pounds ($36,000)—for the purpose of building a Bridge across the Avon River at Windsor. Of course, the old law in opposition to horse racing must have been repealed, or its antithesis could not possibly have been recognized—but what a perversion of ideas among our fathers at different periods, not very distant apart, when laws so contradictory and sublimated in character, could find their way upon the Statute books of the Province! The Company commenced operations under the law in the ensuing Spring. The tickets were placed at one pound each, and the whole town soon became lottery-struck, rich and poor alike invested, all feeling that as times were hard in Halifax, very little work doing, there was at least one chance in a hundred, and that one chance every one felt was his, in getting a hundred pound prize for one pound risked. The amount realized by this Lottery I am unable to state, but it was large enough to warrant undertaking the work, if not to finish it. I remember well the day of drawing—in the old Court House, Market place —the room was crowded with anxious expectants, holding their tickets, and watching the numbers as they came out of the pandora box, and were called out by the presiding official. As a matter of course there was blank dismay depicted upon the countenance of the luckless one whose number drew a blank ; but then as misery likes company then as now, there were many others besides himself who suffered that day from the bitter pangs of disappointment. This, I think, was the last great public lottery held in these Provinces. The old Avon Bridge has gone, and another more substantial has taken its place.

CHAPTER XI.

*Trial of One of His Majesty's Officers for Murder
—The Hanging of John Leigh.—Halifax Industries in the Olden Time.—"Fish, Flesh and
Fowl."—The Dockyard.—Peculiarities of Intellectual Men.—William IV. a Great Babbler.*

In this same old Court House, the only one at
the time, took place the trial (in 1821) of Lieut.
Cross of one of His Majesty's Regiments stationed
in Halifax, on the charge of having murdered an
old man from the country who by chance found
his way into the Officers' Quarters, a long wooden
building one end of which stood on Cogswell street
leading out to the Common. The man was found
lying in the corridor in front of Lieut. Cross'
room, having been run through the body, and
from this and other circumstances suspicion fell
upon this young officer. He was accordingly
placed under arrest and put upon his trial. The
Court Room was densely packed, many of the
officers of the Garrison also being present; the
occurrence was so exceptional, one of His Majesty's
officers on trial for murder, that the whole town
was greatly excited, and the general sympathy
felt for one so young and high in society, found
expression among all classes—for be it known that

hanging in those days was not looked upon with the same abhorrence as at the present time, so that if brought in guilty, poor Cross would have to submit to the penalty of the law, no intervention of friends, or petitions for commutation, would have availed him.

As an example of the rigorous mercilessness of justice in those days, it may be here mentioned that two persons were on their way from Margaret's Bay, on foot—one had money on his person ; and when darkness overtook them, John Leigh, the other person, dropped behind, took out his knife, and drew it across the throat of his companion, robbed him of his money and made for town under the impression that his victim was dead. The wound, however, was not fatal—the man struggled all night in his agony, and when daylight came a person going to town saw him and conveyed him in his waggon, and on reaching town the news of the attempted murder soon spread, and before he had time to escape Leigh was in the manacles of the Police. He was tried on a charge of having attempted murder and for highway robbery. The victim by this time was able to attend Court, and give evidence against his old friend. Leigh was found guilty and sentenced to death, and the day of execution fixed. Petitions were got up and signed by hundreds if not thousands of the inhabitants for a commutation of punishment, in which many of the clergy joined, while the prisoner's own clergyman (Rev.

Mr. Cogswell) interceded as earnestly as if his own life stood in the balance. The Governor of the Province being absent in England, Hon. Thos. N. Jeffery occupied his place for the time being, as President. This gentleman was as hard as adamant ; under a sense of justice, no doubt, he thought it would be a violation of trust to interpose his authority in arrest of judgment ; and so he was immovable to every entreaty and call for mercy. The principle of *lex talionis*, and drastic measures, seemed to form a part of his religious creed. Leigh was executed on the Common, East side, near the Citadel railing. Before this time the place of execution was on Camp Hill, near the Cemetery.

Coming back then to the subject at which we broke off, viz., Lieut. Cross—after a long day's trial, the jury retired and in a short time brought in a verdict of " *Innocent*," which decision at once broke the spell and Halifax again breathed freely.

Halifax was never famous for her great enterprise, except in one case to be referred to hereafter. Unlike her sister City, St. John, her living dependence was upon resources more sure and lucrative. In the one case the fickleness of the English market rendered the sale of St. John's staples in the shape of ships and timber, always a matter of uncertainty. A constriction of trade on one side of the Atlantic was sure to produce a recoil on the other, so closely wrapped together were the interests of St. John and Liverpool ; and when those reverses came

St. John had nothing else to fall back upon in the
way of trade, and general stagnation and no money
always followed. The trade of Halifax on the
contrary was more sure, or less liable to fluctuation,
as it was dependent upon what may not inaptly be
called—" *Fish, Flesh and Fowl.*"

1st. *Fish.* Walking along Water Street a
stranger on casting his eyes towards the harbor,
would be impressed by the immense buildings,
large as churches, presenting themselves on almost every wharf, called fish stores, and acres of
the finny tribe (basking) drying in the sun, on
stages, barrels and on whatever or wherever a
vantage spot could be obtained, after having been
brought to town in their green state, by the fishermen, and in this way manufactured, it may be
called, for the West India market. The business
in this article (before the emancipation of the
slave, and the trade restrictions were removed by
England on the foreigner in her Colonial ports)
was immense and highly remunerative to the
Halifax merchants, whose vessels were many, and
brought return cargoes of West India goods, most
of which were reshipped to all parts of the Province, Halifax being the only *entrepot*—the free port
system as understood now, was a term which had
not then entered into our mercantile vocabulary.
When a change came (through the emancipation
of the slave) the trade of Halifax in the fish line
fell off considerably—so that her great warehouses
to-day stand only as memorials of her former

great West India business. But, then, unlike St.
John in such dilemmas, Halifax has always had a
substantial prop to support her, which may be
explained under the second head of "*Flesh*"—viz :
the MILITARY—which for a century or more have
not only been the flesh, but the bone and sinew
and muscle of the town, in the immense sums of
money that have been spent on her fortifications,
the support of the troops, barrack works, engineer-
ing operations—which if counted would amount to
millions—all of which have gone to enrich the
inhabitants, or keep them from the distresses of
St. John on the failure of their industrial crops, or
rather in the trade of their staple resources.
Then, thirdly, the *Fowl* part of the business, (the
term fowl is here used for the purpose of maintain-
ing the euphemism, although perhaps far fetched)
—by this I mean the NAVY, including the Dockyard.

We sometimes hear of "*flying* squadrons," but
mostly in time of war; and this may almost be
said of the North American fleet. which is on the
wing at least twice a year—now at Halifax (in
summer) and now at Bermuda (in winter,) the
respective headquarters during the two seasons.
Some half-dozen men-of-war lying at Halifax at a
time. representing at least 2,000 men, must necessarily expend large sums of money in the interests
of the butcher. the baker. the storekeeper, and in
fact all classes of the community. Then there is a
little town in itself—a town within a town—known

as the Dockyard, which affords another vast source
of income. Whatever be the business carried on
to day within its walls, seventy years ago and
later, thousands of workmen might have been seen
passing in and out of the gates daily on their way
to and from work—all the recipients of British
gold. So that the advantages possessed by Halifax
over St. John, as set forth at the beginning of this
head, have been such as to secure to her a strong
bulwark against the pressure of the times, whenever overtaken by commercial cataclysms. But in
spite of all these differences, the latter city has kept
pace with the former ; and it is a question whether
St. John would have been any better off to-day
had the cases been reversed. While the one city
has been obliged to work hard, the other has not
felt herself compelled to do so to the same extent.

I now come to the great stepping stone upon
which Mr. Howe entered public life as a speaker
and Statesman. Great writers and great speakers
are not always convertible terms in the same
person. A man may write well but be unable to
place his thoughts upon paper in felicitous or
equally forcible style In the one case the tongue
delivers the words as fast as the brain conceives
them—and the reverse of this is the case when the
same active brain attempts to give expression to
ideas through the comparative slow process of pen
upon paper. The great lexicographer Johnstone,
whose wise sayings are apt to this day, could talk
by the hour sitting, but when called to his feet, as

he sometimes was, although in the company of his boon companions—Beauclerk, Thrale, Langton, Reynolds, Goldsmith, Boswell and others—could speak only a few words at a time, and in such a hobbling, ricketty manner, that it was a relief to him when he resumed his seat. Byron, with all his genius, made but one speech in the House of Lords, and that so worked upon his nervous system, before and after, that he declared he would never make another. The putative author of the Junius Letters, Sir Philip Francis, was a poor speaker, and stammered and hesitated when addressing the House of Commons, and yet was full of information. Dr. Franklin's longest speech in Congress never occupied more than twenty minutes, but he travelled over more ground in that time and to the purpose than any one of his ordinary contemporaries did in travelling over a five acre field in as many hours. One of the most polished writers in the English language (Washington Irving) with whom I came in contact, on many occasions in 1835, invariably shirked the responsibility of making a speech. He had been known to stay away from a public dinner on the plea of illness rather than encounter the opportunity of hearing himself talk. Dickens, on the other hand, was more of a dual character in these respects—for as a *post prandial* speaker he was inimitable and effective. According to the Greville Memoirs William the Fourth was an incessant babbler—at all his banquets he thought it no less his kingly office, to make speeches than to entertain his guests with the rarest vintages; but he seldom spoke without making a fool of himself, or saying something which it would have been better for his Ministers had he left unsaid. Brougham could speak—the greatest torrent of words would flow from his lips, even a Niagara in volume, and in chaste and appropriate language, abounding in metaphor, tropes and figures, and classical and historical references; but place him at his writing desk with pen in hand, and he was only an ordinary mortal, as his autobiography attests. But the cases that might be cited of illustrious men not always succeeding in both departments of literature, are too many to be recalled here. Now Howe could write well, and his speaking talents, as they afterwards proved, were no less effective. But as a speaker in public, his attainments up to this time had been unrecognized because unknown. The opportunity, however, had now arrived for the testing of his marvellous powers in this respect as well as the real versatility of his genius.

CHAPTER XII.

*Magisterial Corruption.—Howe Indicted for Crimi-
nal Libel. — Howe Reading up Law to Defend
Himself. — He Speaks for Six Hours — Amidst
Great Crowds and Great Excitement.—Verdict
of Acquittal.*

Mr. George Thompson (an old friend of Mr.
Howe) addressed a communication " to the Editor
of the *Novascotian*," (1835) setting forth the
state of the Magistracy, and how the City and
County of Halifax had been governed for a long
series of years—how extravagance and waste of
the public moneys had been the rule—how men
grew rich, while the poor starved (especially in
regard to the management of the Poor House)—
and that the whole system was rotten to the core,
while there was no responsibility to the people, or
proper accounts and vouchers demanded by the
Government for the expenditures from year to
year. The charge was certainly a grave one, and
none the less libellous in the eyes of the law, as
understood or administered at the time, even if
the statements were true. The people generally
knew the condition of affairs, but were helpless,
prostrate, as it may be called, at the feet of their
rulers, if not oppressors. Howe was not the man

to quail when the fitting opportunity presented itself, and so he published the communication, which no doubt, as was suspected, he had to some extent inspired. The effect of this publication was like one produced by a bull in a crockery store from the havoc created. The whole town was in a blaze of excitement. The Government, the Magistrates and their friends, did not for a moment stop to deliberate whether or not the statements set forth might be true, but to fulminate as to the amount of punishment which should be meted out to the culprit for daring to slander the King's Justices, and bringing into contempt the great rulers of the land.

This was a more terrible storm for Howe to pass through than that occasioned by the Rigby vs. Cathcart letter some years earlier, before referred to.

But then the day of retribution had at length arrived, when Nemesis could have her revenge, and so the magistrates and their sympathizers and abettors, had the opportunity long wished for, to crash by one fell blow their persecutor and slanderer. There would be no more cakes and ale for poor Howe once they got him into Court, where justice, they thought, would all be on one side, on their side—and the meshes of the law would do the rest, by holding the offender in their iron embrace for a long term of years. The people generally looked over the shoulders of one another, tiptoe, wishing in their hearts success to the Editor, but hopeless that all would go well with him, as they were under the impression that the Bench, the Bar, the Church, and every official and man of influence, and hanger on, were all alike (to use a vulgar but apt expression, which may be allowed here) *sweetened with the same stick.*

An indictment for Criminal Libel was accordingly brought before the Grand Jury by their Worships and a true Bill found, and a day appointed for placing Howe upon his trial. I here cite his own words made to a friend just before the trial, as to how he himself viewed the situation:

"I went" he says, "to two or three lawyers in succession, showed them the Attorney General's notice of trial, and asked them if the case could be successfully defended? The answer was, No. There was no doubt the letter was a libel. That I must make my peace or submit to fine and imprisonment. I asked them to lend me their books, gathered an armful, threw myself on a sofa, and read libel law for a week. By that time I had convinced myself that they were wrong, and that there was a good defence, if the case were properly presented to the court and jury. Another week was spent in selecting and arranging the facts and public documents, on which I relied. I did not get through before a late hour of the evening before the trial, having only had time to write out and commit to memory the two opening paragraphs of the speech. All the rest was to be improvized as I went along. I was very tired, but took a

walk with Mrs. Howe, telling her, as we strolled
to Fort Massy, that if I could only get out of my
head what I had got into it, the magistrates could
not get a verdict. I was hopeful of the case, but
fearful of breaking down, from the novelty of the
situation and from want of practice. I slept
soundly and went at it in the morning, still har-
rassed with doubts and fears, which passed off,
however, as I became conscious that I was commanding the attention of the court and jury. I
was much cheered when I saw the tears rolling
down one old gentleman's cheek. I thought he
would not convict me if he could help it. I
scarcely expected a unanimous verdict, as two or
three of the jurors were connections, more or less
remote, of some of the justices, but thought they
would not agree. The lawyers were all very civil,
but laughed at me a good deal, quoting the old
maxim, that 'he who pleads his own case has a
fool for a client.' " Thus spoke Mr. Howe.

So great was the excitement that the Court
Room was crowded, even on the outside passages
leading to the room. It was truly "a day big for
Cæsar and the fate of Rome," as the question at
issue was the freedom of the Press.

Mr. Howe spoke for six hours and a quarter,
and delivered the ablest speech, so stated by good
judges, ever heard at any Bar on this or the other
side of the Atlantic by a layman. The effect upon
the vast audience was little short of that recorded
of Burke at the great Warren Hastings trial at

Westminster, when so powerful was the speaker's arraignment and eloquence, that the prisoner himself, was so overwhelmed and carried away, that he really thought he must be guilty of all the charges laid upon him. I here quote again from one who was present at the trial :

"The delivery of this speech occupied about six hours. The defendant was frequently interrupted by expressions of popular feeling. The Attorney General rose to reply, but was interruped by the Chief Justice who said, that as the hour was late and the jury had been confined so long, it would be better to adjourn the Court. Mr. Murdoch remonstrated ; Mr. Howe. he believed, had brought his defence to a close much sooner than intended, in order to avoid the necessity of adjourning the trial. It would be unfair, therefore, to allow the other side the advantage of the night to reconstruct their case. Mr. Howe begged the Court to believe that he did not wish to shut out anything that could shake his statements ; all he wished was to have the matter off his mind. The jury were consulted, and the foreman expressed their wish to remain ; it was therefore determined to do so, but the crowd and the excitement being so great. and the difficulty of preserving order evident. His Lordship adjourned the Court. On Tuesday morning the trial proceeded, when the Attorney General (Archibald) rose and addressed the Court, followed by the Chief Justice, both ably and fairly—after which the jury retired for ten minutes, when they

MR. E. G. GREENWOOD.

returned with a verdict of *Not Guilty.* The breathless silence in which it was heard, was broken by shouts of applause by the immense crowds in and around the Court House. After receiving the congratulations of his friends who were immediately about him, the defendant begged leave to return thanks to the Court for the kindness and consideration which had been extended to him throughout the trial. He trusted he had taken no liberty to which a British subject was not entitled, but he felt that the court might, as had been done elsewhere, have broken his arguments by interruptions, and tied him up within narrower limits. On leaving the Province building he was borne by the populace to his home, amid deafening acclamations. The people kept holiday that day and the next. Musical parties paraded the streets at night. All the sleds in town were turned out in procession, with banners; and all ranks and classes seemed to join in felicitations on the triumph of the press. The crowds were briefly addressed by Mr. Howe from his window, who besought them to keep the peace; to enjoy the triumph in social intercourse around their firesides; and to teach their children the names of the TWELVE MEN who had established the FREEDOM OF THE PRESS."

We give the picture of the only surviving Juror on that memorable occasion—viz: Mr. E. G. Greenwood—who was born in Water street, Halifax, 1st April, 1803, so that he is now about 93 years of age. He was a merchant during his early

years in the hardware business ; and in 1865 was
appointed to the responsible office under the Corporation as City Treasurer, the duties of which he
continued faithfully to discharge up to 1890,
when he resigned and was placed upon a pension.
His picture represents him as hale and hearty, and
I am informed that his mind is as clear and his
faculties as unimpaired as they were twenty years
ago. Long may he continue to live as a reminder
to the rising generation, of an occasion so preg-
nant to Nova Scotia and the Sister Provinces of
the great political freedom we enjoy this day, for
which he himself is largely credited. The last of
the fifty-six signers of the American Declaration
of Independence was Charles Carroll, of Carrolton,
State of Maryland, and when he died some years
ago, the whole nation shrouded itself in mourning, flags at half mast, minute guns, orations
eulogistic of the Patriot's virtues, and the great
services rendered by him to his country, if in no
other way than by subscribing his name to that
immortal document. No such tribute as this can
be expected at the obsequies of the gentleman now
before us when the time arrives ; but during the
remaining years of his life grateful Nova Scotians
cannot fail to keep before them the name of the
last survivor of that resolute band, who in 1835
declared that the Press of their country should be
free.

CHAPTER XIII.

Service of Plate Subscribed to Mr. Howe by Nova Scotians in New York.—Its Presentation and Address in the Old Court House, Halifax, by the Late Thos. Forrester, Esq. — Great Crowds Assembled.

As soon as the news of the trial and its result reached New York, upwards of one hundred Nova Scotians doing business there called a meeting to express their sympathy and jubilate over the victory. Patriotic speeches were made and resolutions passed pertinent to the occasion—one of which favored an Address to Mr. Howe and the presentation of a piece of plate, which afterwards took the form of a Silver Ewer, at a cost, as near as I can remember, of $120. subscribed mostly by those present. It may not be out of place here to state that the writer of this book was present on that occasion ; and little thought had he then, when requested to write the Address and the Inscription upon the Cup, that in *sixty years afterwards he would feel himself called upon* to refer to that occasion historically, as he is now doing.

Thomas Forrester, an extensive dry goods merchant (then doing business opposite St. Paul's

Church) and afterwards member of the Legislature, was requested by letter to make the presentation, which took place at the Exchange in the old Court House building, Market Square. According to the newspapers of the day the room was crowded—speeches were delivered by several of the leading Liberals, all highly complimentary to the contributors and the occasion. Mr. Howe of course accepted the present in a modest, becoming manner.

I am indebted to the *Acadian Recorder* of June 6th, 1835, for the following account of the presentation of the Cup :

" Agreeably to a notice issued on Saturday morning last the committee of presentation met at 12 o'clock in the Law Room of the Exchange, amid a very large assemblage of the people of the town, when Mr. Thomas Forrester took the chair. Shortly after Mr. Howe appeared the Chairman addressed him as follows :

" Mr. Howe—On Friday Captain O'Brien and Mr. John Fenerty put into my hands this letter :

" To Thomas Forrester, Esq.,

" Sir :—We the undersigned, together with our fellow countrymen now residing in New York feeling a pride and a pleasure in remembering the independent and upright men in Halifax, and knowing you to be one of this class, it was unanimously concluded to select you as the head of our committee together with Beamish Murdock, and Lawrence O'Connor Doyle, Esquires, Captain O'Brien and Mr. John Fenerty, for the purpose of presenting to the noble champion of our country the accompanying piece of plate.

"JAMES PIRNIE, Chairman.

"JAMES TALBOT, Secretary."

"NEW YORK, May 18, 1835.

[General Committee—Alexander Ross, James Pirnie, Geo. E. Fenety, James Marsters, James Talbot.]

"These gentlemen cheerfully accepted the trust reposed, and the public presentation was arranged in order that you might receive, in the midst of your townsmen, for whose benefit you labor, this token of respect and approbation of a large and respectable body of your countrymen in a foreign land. In their names, Sir, we beg your acceptance of this valuable piece of plate, purchased by their joint subscriptions and transmitted to our care, by the Brig Halifax, together with this letter addressed to yourself and by which it was accompanied.

" The letter, signed by the Chairman and Secretary, set forth, that at a meeting held at Crowley's hotel, New York, for the purpose of taking into consideration Mr. Howe's trial and defence before the Supreme Court at Halifax, it was resolved that a piece of plate should be presented as a token of esteem and admiration for Mr. Howe's noble defence of the freedom of the press, and exposing irregularities that had so long existed in different institutions of our country. In conclu-

PITCHER PRESENTED TO JOSEPH HOWE.

sion the letter said : "The names of the twelve
men who so nobly discharged their duty on that
ever memorable occasion, are indelibly engraven
on our minds; and may the tribunals of Nova
Scotia ever have as competent jurors to decide
upon the fates of their fellow men when undergoing the scrutiny of the law."

"The Chairman then said, that the piece of plate
being inscribed to Mr. Howe he would read the
inscription to the meeting, and it ran thus:

PRESENTED TO

JOSEPH HOWE, ESQ.

BY

NOVA SCOTIANS, RESIDENTS OF NEW YORK,

as a testimony of

THEIR RESPECT AND ADMIRATION

for his honest independence in publicly exposing
fraud,

IMPROVING THE MORALS,

and correcting the errors of men in office,

AND HIS ELOQUENT AND TRIUMPHANT DEFENCE

in support of

THE FREEDOM OF THE PRESS.

CITY OF NEW YORK,

1835.

[Thus, sixty years afterwards, I had the pleasure last year of
handling this cup once more—which is in the hands of Mr.
Howe's only surviving son.]

"Mr. Howe then said :

"MR. CHAIRMAN :—I accept with feelings, which
I can very inadequately express, the handsome and
costly present which a large body of Nova
Scotians, resident in New York, have thought
proper to bestow, and beg yourself, and the other
gentlemen of the committee, to transmit to the

donors this letter, in which I have endeavored to convey to them, my acknowledgements for the honor they have done me, and to thank them in the name of our countrymen for this substantial proof, that absence has not weakened their sympathies with those from whom they have been in some degree separated by the spirit of adventure, or perhaps the storms of life."

" HALIFAX, NOVA SCOTIA, May 30. 1835.

" GENTLEMEN :—I beg to acknowledge the receipt of your letter of the 18th inst., written in behalf of a general meeting of Nova Scotians, resident in the city of New York, and accompanied by a handsome piece of plate which has just been presented to me in the midst of our fellow-townsmen, by the committee selected for that purpose. Though conscious that I have done but little to merit the kind and complimentary expressions contained in your letter and inscribed on your gift. I should be sadly deficient in sensibility, if I did not feel gratified for sentiments so unexpected yet so flattering, and for a present which, though costly in itself is rendered doubly valuable by the circumstances in which it originated ; and by the proof it exhibits of the possession of feelings honorable to the donors, and to the country which gave them birth. The trial to which you are pleased to refer, I did not seek, but could not shun.—that it ended in the triumph of sound principles is to be attributed more to the firmness and sagacity of an intelligent jury, than to any ability displayed in the defence. They took a rational view of the responsibilities and duties of the press, and determined that their children should enjoy a blessing which their gallant fathers had bequeathed. Their verdict was hailed with satisfaction not only from end to end of our province, but in the adjoining Colonies; and they will no doubt be pleased to hear, that it has been so highly approved by the Nova Scotians residing at New York.

"The conviction forced upon my mind by your generous conduct on this occasion, and by the assurance conveyed in your letter, that Nova Scotia still possesses the sincere regard and unalienated affections of her absent children, is more delightful to me than even any personal share I may have in your esteem. That an individual should do his duty is but a small matter — that Nova Scotia should be loved and honored by her offspring at home and abroad, is of vital importance. Though comparatively insignificant in extent of territory and population, if she be rich in the affections of her sons and daughters — honor and prosperity must still be her portion. Those who remain upon her soil endeavor, even in the midst of her greatest trials, to cultivate and strengthen this feeling, and it is cheering to find that while sharing the blessings, and enjoying the pleasures of countries more advanced, those who are seeking their fortunes elsewhere are still mindful of her interests and proud of her name.

" In conveying my best wishes for the health and happiness of the Nova Scotians, resident in New York, be pleased also to assure them that a sense of their kindness on this occasion will never be effaced from my heart,—but shall constantly stimulate to a zealous pursuit of those objects which they so cordially approve.

" I have the honor to be, Gentlemen,

" Yours truly,

"JOSEPH HOWE."

"To Mr. James Pirnie, Chairman, and Mr. James Talbot, Secretary, of the public meeting of Nova Scotians held at Crowley's hotel, New York."

"The Pitcher is of silver, about twelve inches in height, and holding nearly three quarts, with a handsome gilt stand four inches high. And we understand the number of subscribers to it were about fifty to sixty—all Nova Scotians."

CHAPTER XIV.

*Mr. Howe Elected a Member of the Legislature.—
The Able Men He had to Encounter.—His Great
Abilities.—His Ambition Compared with that of
Other Great Men.*

The House of Assembly was dissolved by
Proclamation in 1836, when Mr. Howe for the first
time offered himself as a candidate for the County
of Halifax, and was elected by a thousand majority
over his next competitor, which showed that the
popularity he had achieved in his libel suit did not
only continue, but was growing every day. Instead of the elections being conducted in one
day and simultaneously throughout the Province
as at present, they lasted for a whole fortnight,
during which time there was much rioting,
debauchery and drunkenness, and the friends of
the respective candidates frequently collided, and
broken heads, not a few, were the order of the day,
and the night too. The Cork elections, a few years
ago, where the Parnellites and the M'Carthyites
found a battle ground for the *political expression* of
their feelings on both sides, emphasized with good
sound hickory bludgeon whacks, will convey to
the reader an idea of the great interest attached

to elections at the time of which we are writing—
when Howe was elected in 1836. Every party or
faction had its shibboleth by which it was recognized far and wide. On the banners of the Howe
party were inscribed "Joe Howe, our Patriot and
Reformer." The sobriquet "Joe Howe," now became a household word, not only in the County of
Halifax, but throughout the Province. It was
"Joe Howe" here, there and everywhere—nothing
could be done without Joe Howe's presence. He
was the Jupiter Olympus on all ordinary as well
as extraordinary occasions. By one leap and bound
in the course of a single year, he cleared all obstacles and became the most prominent man and
loudest talked of in all Nova Scotia.

Having thus been elected to the Legislature at
the early age of 32, Mr. Howe now had his feet
firmly planted in the stirrups, with a fine hobby
to ride, over a wide road, upon which he could
give reins to his ambition, no matter what the
character of the *pacers* he might encounter upon
the highway, and these were not a few nor less
fast or full of fire than himself. "The mills of
the gods grind hard" and Howe in his novitiate
must expect nothing but hard pressure between
the upper and nether millstones of the House, so
that he must depend altogether upon his own
resources and mental powers. It is true Howe
had the mettle and the bottom, but a mishap, or
slip, or stumble, a mistake, an error of judgment,
might at any moment precipitate him to earth;

for those "old stagers" he would be required to run with. well versed in all the technicalities and practices within the Parliamentary arena, and of great experience. from their long service in the Legislature, would have no bowels of compassion for poor Howe, "the upstart" and obnoxious intruder upon the rights and franchises of the old *noblesse* and monopolists—so that if he tripped or got himself into a hard place, he might as well have expected sympathy or mercy from the Turks. had he been bold enough to have gone into their midst and disputed the tenets of the Koran.

For be it known that at this time the House of Assembly contained a number of men who for their talents and abilities. and speaking powers, would have shed lustre upon a much more pretentious Parliamentary body—such men as Alexander Stewart, James B. Uniacke, William Young (late Sir William,) Mr. Marshall, Mr. Dodd, Martin Wilkins, J. W. Johnston, the great lawyer, and several other brilliant men—all of whom (except Young) were in opposition to the young Reformer and inexperienced beginner.

Before we go with him into the House of Assembly, where after all Howe's great *trial* was to begin, let us for a moment or two inquire why this young man should take it upon himself to wage war upon a system of government which had stood the strain of upwards of one hundred years, and no one till now had any complaints to utter, and thus incur the enmity of nearly the whole community—for every strand in the great political cable was compactly knit and bound together without the possibility of a break. Was it ambition to shine? No doubt this had something to do with it, but ambition cannot stand alone—to succeed in any great undertaking ambition must have something more than the vain hope of success to rest upon, even great talents allied to great courage and great natural resources. Howe well knew that if there were laurels to be gained, it was not by peaceful walks through green pastures. Briars and thorns. and hidden hornet's nests, and pitfalls, lay along his path. The highway to success with him was one beset with immense difficulties. No—his ambition was that of John Bright, who, to provide the people of England with cheap food, and that the wings of commerce might expand to breezes more favorable to trade, boldly encountered the hostility of the great landed gentry and aristocracy of the Nation. It was the ambition of John Hampden, who, with Selden and Pym, was determined to resist the unwarrantable encroachments of the Crown upon the privileges of Parliament and the rights of the people. (Indeed the cases of Howe and Hampden are remarkably alike. Charles vented all his spleen upon Hampden, as Lord Falkland did upon Howe, because each resisted their official superiors — but the Falkland embroglio will come up hereafter.) It was the ambition of Kossuth, who, to free his country, Hungary, from the tyranny of Austria, led his people into hostility, and when success was near at hand the bloody Muscovite came down upon them, and by his interference crushed out all hope of emancipation. It was the ambition of the great and good John Howard, the English philanthropist, who during the latter part of the last century spent his life in the reformation of the Prisons and Hospitals of England and the Continent, and in the pursuit of which he travelled continually throughout Europe spending large sums of money from his own private purse. Wretched, noisome prisons and cells, where the suffering of the unfortunate and helpless were terrible, were exposed and their management altogether reformed. Finally he fell a martyr to his own zeal, having contracted a fever in the Crimea, while pursuing his noble work. It was the ambition of Wilberforce, who as soon as he entered Parliament, when quite a young man, devoted all his talents and energies for the suppression of the Slave Trade. This accomplished by Act of Parliament, he next turned his attention to the abolition of slavery throughout the British Empire, and lived just long enough in 1833, to see this accomplished, and to receive the thanks of the Nation for his philanthropic zeal. It was the ambition of Cobden for his devotion in the cause of Free Trade, and having succeeded in England, next addressed himself to the Continental Powers, with the desire of indoctrinating his views upon all its respective governments, and brought France over to his faith, while it lasted at all events, and doubtless had he lived a little longer would have succeeded with other nations. While the memories of two such statesmen as Cobden and Bright live in the hearts of Englishmen, what is called " Imperial Federation," must be reckoned among the political impossibilities—for England can never go back upon a record which occupied thirty years to bring about through fiercest agitation. It is the ambition of Gladstone (for many years the leading statesman of Europe) who at the age of 86, is full of fervor for Armenian retribution upon the Turks. In short, it was the ambition of a great heart and a great mind so essential to all great patriotic undertakings that actuated Howe throughout.

This then was our hero, and this was his mission, on entering the Parliament of his native Province in 1836 ; and in nearly everything he undertook he succeeded.

CHAPTER XV.

*Opening of the Legislature in 1837.—Commence-
ment of the Reform Movement.— Howe's Maiden
Speech.—Attack Upon the Closed Doors of the
Old Council.—Howe at Close Quarters with an
Old Antagonist.*

The Legislature convened in January, 1837.
The Reformers commenced to show their hands
almost immediately. Laurence O'Connor Doyle
moved a series of resolutions, one of which was in
opposition to the doors of the Legislative Council
being kept closed to the public. Mr. Howe delivered his maiden speech on this occasion, and in the
presence of all the great guns of the House
awaiting an opportunity to discharge their heavi-
est metal upon him. It might be here stated,
that however much the "compact" of Nova
Scotia assimilated in all its essential particulars to
that of New Brunswick, indeed as was the case in
all the Provinces alike, the Council doors of New
Brunswick had been thrown open to the public
some years before this, which went to prove how
hard and tight was the grip which held so many
of the old school together in Halifax, and did not
care to have the light of day let in upon their

business doings. Doyle's resolutions passed unanimously, and were sent to the Council for its
concurrence—for even the obstructives in the
House could not resist that which everybody
knew was reasonable and sure to come about.
They would rather reserve their fire for an opportunity more momentous to the party with which
they were identified and would require all their
talents and speaking energies to defend.

The Council in its reply to the House spoke in
this wise: "His Majesty's Council denies the
right of the House to comment upon its modes of
procedure. Whether their deliberations were open
or secret was their concern, and their's only."
This is a mere specimen of the language employed,
to which taunts were added to open defiance.
Here then was the commencement of a fierce
wrangle between the two branches which lasted
for several years, before the Council doors were
forced open by the Reformers.

Then the duration of the House was for seven
years as in England today. In order to get the
time reduced to four years the Reformers had
many a hard up-hill fight. "Annexation" was not
then one of the war cries—the Reformers were
dubbed "Republicans." Had any politician in 1837
been bold enough to suggest "Independence," he
would have been throttled by both parties alike,
and probably have the tongue cut out of his
mouth in a figurative or disfigurative sort of way
and been silenced forever. We understand those

things better now-a-days. We are at liberty to
discuss any question that affects the interests of
the people, so long as we keep within judicious
bounds, not excepting "independence."

When the Bill came up for reducing the term
of the House to four years, a leading politician,
(afterwards Master of the Rolls) one of the old
school advocates led an attack upon Mr. Howe.
This gentleman had a sharp tongue, good voice,
and was an effective speaker; but like many of the
legal gentry of whose fluency of speech and the
reading of the same speech in print, are as dissimi-
lar as though two distinct individuals had been
concerned in the production, he appeared more
formidable than he really was. He took occasion
—now that he had Howe before him, and a chance
to pay him off, or give him what is not inaptly
called a good dressing — to resent the Editor's
old newspaper criticisms upon the conduct of the
last House, and he did this with great bitterness
and severity, and there and then challenged Howe
to a discussion of the points involved and to a
defence of his opinions upon that floor. This
speech occupied over an hour, three-fourths of
which was devoted to pouring cayenne pepper and
vitriol upon poor Howe's head, whose friends in
the House and gallery were numerous, and felt for
their representative, and that an impromptu reply
was impossible from so inexperienced a youth.

When Howe rose there was a breathless silence,
while his enemies chuckled in their sleeves over the

last speaker's supposed victory as they were sure
Howe's friends on the other hand trembled as it
were at the awkwardness of the situation—viz:
their man to be flayed alive in their presence,
after he had been in the House only four days
and never before engaged in a public encounter.
But once on his legs, and his feet firmly planted,
he stood forth like "a giant refreshed with new
wine," and as soon as he began his reply all doubt
of the man's powers and ability to accept the gage
of battle and do himself justice disappeared. He
did not only defend every political statement he
had ever made, but in turn defied his antagonist
to contradict any one of them. He did not only
argue all the points but elaborated upon them,
showed up the evils of the system of Government
that existed, and bore down upon them with even
greater vehemence, by his voice, than his pen was
even capable of. Having thus disposed of the
charges made in the challenge, and carried the
House with him by storm, Howe next went at his
adversary personally, the man who was to crush
the political life out of him at the outset, not like
the bull dog who feels he has his victim within his
power, but like the feline with poor mousey, who
plays with and worries it before making a meal of
it. He turned the tables so completely upon his
adversary, by anecdote, sarcasm, and gentle hits
a little below the *mental* ribs, that the whole
House was convulsed with laughter, nor could his
able opponents refrain from joining in, and all at

his victim's expense. I know of nothing like it, unless it be like "Webster's reply to Hayne," on the floors of Congress once upon a time, so familiar to all American readers.

Howe's enemies from this time forward knew the quality of their man, and what to expect from him and how to govern themselves accordingly. No man had greater power of sarcasm, and the faculty of holding and pleasing an audience than Joseph Howe. His humor was inimitable.

I propose in another chapter to make an extract from one of Mr. Howe's speeches, delivered a few days after his reply above referred to, that the reader may judge for himself his style of composition and force of language.

CHAPTER XVI.

Series of Resolutions Moved Against the System of Government.—To be Forwarded to the Colonial Office.—Anger of the Council.—Mr. Howe's Final Reply on the Closing Debate.

The Legislative Council having defied the House of Assembly in its reply to Mr. Doyle's Resolutions for opening the doors of the Council Chamber to the public, Mr. Howe next moved a series of twelve Resolutions in which the opinions of the Reformers were fully set forth—to two or three of which particular reference might here be made.

" 1. *Resolved,* That a Committee be appointed to draw up an address to His Majesty to embrace the substance of the following resolutions :

" 2. *Resolved,* That in the infancy of this colony its whole government was necessarily vested in a Governor and Council ; and even after a Representative Assembly was granted, the practice of choosing Members of Council exclusively from among the heads of departments, and persons resident in the capital, was still pursued ; and, with a single exception, has been continued down to the present time. That the practical effects of this system have been in the highest degree injurious to the best interests of the country ; inasmuch as one entire branch of the Legislature has generally been composed of men, who, from the want of local knowledge and experience, were not qualified to decide upon the wants or just claims of distant portions of the Province, by which the efforts of the representative branch were, in many instances, neutralized or rendered of no avail ; and of others, who had a direct interest in·thwarting the views of the Assembly, whenever it attempted to carry economy and improvement into the departments under their control. "

The subsequent Resolutions narrate seriatim all the political grievances asked to be reformed. The 11th and 12th provide a solution for His Majesty's consideration, from which I quote a portion :—

* * * " They know that the spirit of that Constitution—the genius of those Institutions—is complete responsibility to the people, by whose resources and for whose benefit they are maintained. But sad experience has taught them that, in this colony, the people and their representatives are powerless, exercising upon the Local Government very little influence, and possessing no effectual control. In England, the people, by one vote of their representatives, can change the ministry, and alter any course of policy injurious to their interests ; here, the ministry are His Majesty's Council, combining Legislative, Judicial and Executive powers, holding their seats for life, and treating

with contempt or indifference the wishes of the
people, and the representations of the Commons.
In England, the Representative branch can compel
a redress of grievances, by withholding the supplies; here, they have no such remedy, because
the salaries of nearly all the public officers being
provided for by permanent laws, or paid out of
the casual or territorial revenues, or from the
produce of duties collected under Imperial acts, a
stoppage of supplies, while it inflicted great injury
upon the country, by leaving the roads, bridges
and other essential services unprovided for, would
not touch the emoluments of the heads of departments in the Council, or of any but a few of the
subordinate officers of the Government.

"12. *Resolved,* That, as a remedy for these
grievances, His Majesty be implored to take such
steps, either by granting an elective Legislative
Council, or by such other reconstruction of the
Local Government, as will insure responsibility to
the Commons, and confer upon the people of this
Province, what they value above all other posses-
sions, the blessings of the British Constitution."

As these Resolutions contain the gist of the
Reform " platform," and which led to an agitation
of many years ere the principles contended for in
their entirety were brought about, and through
which Mr. Howe greatly distinguished himself as a
leader, I feel that I shall not be trespassing upon
the time and patience of the reader by dealing with
this part of the subject somewhat more diffusively

than in treating of other matters. In support of
his resolutions Mr. Howe delivered a speech which
occupied him eight hours—in the presence of a
crowded house, and alongside of most critical
compeers, more than three-fourths of the latter
clearly opposed to him—for although this was a
new House and there were many able Reformers in
it, it was not a *reform* House, for the majority of
members returned, *fresh* from the people, were
still bent upon an obstructive policy at the beginning. The debate lasted for nine days, and when
the division came the Resolutions were changed
and barely carried. All the able men of the House
spoke and bore down upon the mover with relent-
less and unsparing fury—such as James B. Uniacke,
who led the Government party, a most splendid
debater and orator, Martin Wilkins, Alexander
Stewart, and others of good talents and great
experience. [Here it might be as well to say that
Mr. Uniacke finding that Responsible Government
was destined to come sooner or later, subsequently
left his party and joined the Reformers like Sir
Robert Peel in abandoning the Tories to carry
the Corn Laws repeal when Prime Minister. But
more of Mr. Uniacke hereafter.] The staple arguments of the Tories may be summarized thus—
Responsible Government and Colonial dependence
were not only irrelevant but incompatible in practice—how can a Colony govern itself without
conflicting with the Imperial authority—co-exist-
ent Governments under one Empire, each in its own

way and distinctive in its operations, could not be carried on without continually clashing and would ultimately lead to Republicanism. And a great deal of nonsense like this. These vaticinations, as we all know today, have long since turned out to be mere will-o-the-wisps, while many of those who fought against the principles were among the first to profit by the change when it came about. After all the speakers had borne down heavily upon Howe, six to one as it were, that gentleman's right to reply, he being the mover, gave him a fine opportunity to pay back to each individual much more than he had received plus compound interest. Now, as Mr. Howe was an expert stenographer, a system he had acquired as a Reporter, it gave him a great advantage, for he noted down in shorthand all the utterances of his opponents and could answer them each in detail. In his reply therefore he handled the gentlemen in turn with bare hands, and caused the welkin to ring every time he made a point or a hard hit or a joke. Finally, when the general question on the Resolutions was put to the House it was sustained, as above stated, for the proofs frunished of the necessity were obvious and irresistible. On being sent to the Council, against which one of them bore heavily, that body became angry and repelled the charges contained therein, as being untrue and anything but courteous. However, the war was commenced in earnest and was by this time carried far into the Interior, no matter who was likely to be wounded. As the Council was in possession of power, and in the enjoyment of its rights to hold on, and in control of the purse strings, the battle necessarily raged between the two ends of the building—or the North and the South—and to bring the Council into terms of capitulation was the great desideratum, for however much the two parties at the Northern end of the structure, or belonging to the House of Assembly, might pepper each other, both were powerless to upset the chairs occupied by the old folks at the other end, especially while they had the Governor on their side and the countenance of the Tories everywhere.

The final result of this important debate was an Address to the King, embodying the substance of the Resolutions, when the Legislature was shortly after prorogued.

CHAPTER XVII.

*Extracts from Mr. Howe's Able Speech in Closing
the Debate Referred to in the Last Chapter.—
He discusses His Opponents Separately.—The
Great Effect Produced by his Reply.*

I have thought it worth while to copy here a
portion of Mr. Howe's speech after being assailed
by the whole Tory combination, day after day, as
before stated—in order to show the man's force
of language and infinitude of resources—and how
he handled his opponents, embracing the ablest
men in the Legislature at that time :

Mr. Chairman— There is a good story told of
an Irishman, who was put in the pillory for saying that the city authorities were no better than
they should be. He bore the affliction with ex-
emplary patience, and severe enough it was : for
every silly fellow who expected an invitation to
the Mayor's feast—every servile creature, who
aspired to a civic office, strove to win favor, by
pelting him with conspicuous activity. When
the hour expired, and a goodly array of missiles
had accumulated upon the stage, the culprit,
taking off his hat, and bowing politely to the
crowd, said : " Now, gentlemen, it is my turn, and

commencing with his Worship, pelted the crowd with great dexterity and effect. The Irish, who always relish humor, were so pleased with the joke, that they carried the man home on their shoulders. I have no expectation that my fate will be so triumphant, but no gentleman will question my right to follow the example. I have sat for ten days in this political pillory; missiles of every calibre have hurtled around my head; they have accumulated in great abundance, and if my turn has come, those by whom they were showered have no right to complain. As first in dignity, if not in accuracy of aim, perhaps I ought to commence with the learned and honorable crown officers; but there is an old Warwickshire tradition, that Guy, before he grappled with the dun cow, tried his hand upon her calves; and perhaps it would be as well, before touching the learned Attorney General, that I should dispose of the strange progeny his political system has warmed into existence. The eagle, before he lifts his eye to the meridian, learns to gaze with steadiness on the lesser lights by which he is surrounded; and "as Jove's satellites are less than Jove," so are the learned leader's disciples inferior to their master.

I confess that I am a little at a loss with whom to begin; but following the order in which they have spoken, the first favor is due to my honorable friend from the County of Pictou (Mr. Holmes.) That gentleman and I have long been opposed in this Assembly ; we never agreed but once or twice, when I was in the Government ; and then, I fear, I owed his support to his habitual reverence for the powers that be.   But I confess that I received it with strange misgivings ; finding myself seated beside him, once or twice, in the edge of the evening, I half fancied I must be wrong, for during a very long experience I had rarely known him right.   He told me there was " nothing in my speech ; " I will not pay so poor a compliment to his own, but may say it was very like a page of Ossian, smacking of " the times of old," but having nearly as much bearing on the practical business of life.   To my honorable friend's manliness and courtesy, I am willing to bear testimony ; but his reverence for the past makes him a very poor judge or expounder of the new principles : like old Mortality he delights in haunting ancient places and refreshing broken tombstones ; while the stream of life goes by and flowers bloom unheeded at his feet.   He fears that we dislike " the ungenial soil of opposition," but we stand upon it still, regardless of the example set us in 1842, when we found him, despite the admonitions of his friends, abandoning the " ungenial soil," and coming over to the richer mould of the administration.   *   *

My honorable friend found fault with me for my reference to David, and told me that that great and good man " raised not his hand against the Lord's anointed."   Neither have I.   I have not killed Lord Falkland, but I have shown him, as David did Saul, the folly and negligence of his advisers. When the drowsy guards left the master they should have protected, at his mercy, in the cave of Engedi, David cut off the skirt of his garment, to show the imbecility of the statesmen and warriors by whom he was surrounded. Again, when the crown officers slept in the trench, David removed the pitcher and spear from the King's side to prove their incapacity. These innocent contrasts between the vigilance of the man he had injured, and the parasites who inflamed his passions, had the desired effect ; for we find Saul exclaiming —and who knows but that His Lordship (Falkland) may follow his example,—" return, my son David ; behold I have played the fool, and have erred exceedingly."

The honorable gentleman (Mr. Holmes) reminds me that Lord John Russell supports good measures when Sir Robert Peel brings them down. We would do the same, if any were brought here. But our complaint is, that His Excellency conducts the government of this country with half a Council, who, in two sessions, have introduced no measures at all. But did my honorable friend ever hear of Sir Robert Peel complaining that he could not conduct the government on his own principles, because the Whigs would not help him? Did he ever offer them seats in the cabinet to sacrifice a leader, and then denounce him and abuse them, when the sage proposition was refused ? We are told that my friend Mr. Uniacke was not

the leader in the last House. He was ; if he bore
his honors with less ostentation than his successor,
he was acknowledged the leader of the government
from 1840 to 1843 ; and that rank was cheerfully
yielded by his colleagues. My honorable friend
tells us, that my popularity has declined. Perhaps
so ; but he forgets to add, that if it has, I lost it by
supporting Lord Falkland's measures, and Lord
Falkland's government ; by sharing the unpopu-
larity of those with whom I was associated, and
who have made so ungrateful a return. But is
this House the test of any man's popularity now ?
We all know it was returned before Mr. Almon's
appointment, before the retirements, before the
proscription. The people of Nova Scotia have had
no opportunity of pronouncing a judgment upon
these acts of folly ; when they have, we shall see
whose popularity and influence have declined. The
honorable gentleman gave us a lecture on decency,
but if he turns to my comparison again, he will find
nothing which the most fastidious taste would
reject. His name-sake was condemned by the
fanatics of Edinburgh, for writing the play of
Douglas ; the critics have perished, but the drama
still lives. I am surprised that the honorable
member reads no lectures to his learned friends,
who are greater transgressors than I ; and that he
should have forgotten that *The Pictou Observer*,
the organ of his own party, was remarkable for
disgusting obscenity. I must now part with my
honorable friend, whose joke at Mr. Uniacke's

expense might have been spared, had the member
for Pictou remembered that the reflection conveyed
on the piety and sincerity of the Presbyterians of
that fine county, was most undeserved : although
the wags do say, that, in his own person, by a
similar stroke of policy, the Antibugers lost a member. and the Kirk secured a deacon.

Let me now turn to an opponent of different
style of mind ; one with less originality but higher
" pretensions." That I should have lived to be
charged with " rapid declamation " by the honorable and learned member for Hants (Mr. Wilkins)
was most unlooked for. I had nerved myself for
everything else, but that quite overcame me. He,
whom I have seen day after day clear these
benches, until you, Mr. Chairman, sat like a
solitary victim ; he, whom the venerable President
of the Legislative Council assured that he was not
the only sufferer, when he complained of fatigue
after a long oration ; he, whom I heard thus
accosted by one of his own constituents at the nine
mile river : "Are ye never gawn to be doon, sir,
and let the ither man gie us a screed ?" Has it
been my misfortune to outherod Herod ? To appear tedious to the ears of him who wearies everybody else ? That gentleman and I met on
several occasions last summer, and although the
argument may have all been on his side, the free-
holders were generally on mine. He published his
speeches subsequently, and I was strongly tempted
to issue a new edition of them with this title :

Speeches of L. M. Wilkins, Esq., which did not convince the people." Vapid declamation! Oh, no, Sir, I cannot admit the learned gentleman to be a judge even of the article in which he deals. It has been said that language was given us to conceal our thoughts; if so, there has been sinful profusion in the case of the learned gentleman, who has one living language and two or three dead ones; yet so very few thoughts to conceal. He said I gave the House specimens of tragedy, comedy and farce. I regret that he has given us neither. The only character to which he aspires is the fine gentleman in the Vaudeville; but even that he dresses with too much pretension, and plays with little ease. His form wants the rounded symmetry; his features the dignified repose; his mind the playful energy which is essential to the character. He is too "fussy." He might pass for a scholar but for his pedantry, and for a fine gentleman but for his pretensions. The learned gentleman appears to have leaned over the Castalian Spring, not to slake his thirst, or arrange his robe to set off the harmonies of nature, but to fall in love, as Narcissus did, with his own image, and die with admiration of himself. The learned gentleman favored us with a lecture on good breeding, the gist being summed up at the end. One thing which he said certainly did astonish me : "I will not extend my hand to, or sit at the festive board with a man who lampoons a Governor." Here is a social proscription with a

vengeance !   How shall any man exist who has to
cut his mutton without the light of the learned
gentleman's countenance, and from whom his
gloved fingers are withdrawn ?   But is the learned
gentleman consistent in his reverence for authority
—with his virtuous hatred of those who write
lampoons ? This committee, this community, know
who was the reputed editor of *The Pictou Observer*, and they will judge by a very few passages
whether that gentleman's own near relative has
not committed the unpardonable offence. [Here
Mr. Howe read a variety of extracts from *The
Pictou Observer*, a paper said to have been edited
by Mr. Wilkins' brother, in which Lord Falkland
was accused of degrading his office by uncovering
his head, and holding the Prince de Joinville's
stirrup while he mounted his horse ; of going in
plain clothes to a ball on the Queen's birthday,
and having a foreigner for a secretary who might
purloin official correspondence ; of endeavoring to
concentrate all the powers of government and
legislation in his own hands, &c. He also read
several extracts reflecting on the House, the
Legislative Council and the Colonial Secretary.]
Now, Mr. Chairman, will it be believed that the
learned gentleman from Hants has maintained a
brotherly intercourse with the person who openly
countenanced, if he did not write these, and dozens
of other attacks upon the Lieutenant Governor ?
But, Sir, there is another passage in which it is
said Lord Falkland " has not only the bend sinister

on his escutcheon, but on his heart." Little skill
in heraldry is required to understand the malig-
nant indelicacy of that allusion ; and what shall we
think of the man who would introduce the slanderer, not to his own board, but into the bosom of
the Lieutenant Governor's family, after such an
outrage ? This was submitted to because the
learned member's vote could not be done without.
I leave him and his party to reconcile these facts
with their vehement regard for the honor and
feelings of the Lieutenant Governor. The people
of Nova Scotia will probably come to the conclusion that jokes and lampoons are very innocent
things when they come from the right side and
the right family.

All this has been forgiven and forgotten ; but I
am to be remembered even when a new Governor
arrives. Though he may "not know Joseph," he
is to be told of his misdeeds, though Martin's are
to be "cast discreetly in the shade." The learned
gentleman tells me that I closed the door upon
myself; but what are the facts ? That my friends
and myself walked out of the door because we did
not like the doings within the premises ; when
immediately a cry of burglary was raised. "Is
not the Governor to be the judge of his own
honor ?" the learned gentleman asks. Were we
not to be the judges of ours when false and de-
famatory charges were raised against us ? Were we
to shrink from necessary self defence ? It is said
that President Polk would not admit a man to his

cabinet who had laughed at him ; but what does
this prove ? The superiority of British to American institutions, making, as they do, the will of
the nation superior to that even of the chief
magistrate. The learned gentleman favored us
with the case of a gallant colonel, known to us
all ; but I intend to show that it was a most unfortunate illustration. His was an offence against
majesty ; against a lady and a sovereign, unpro-
voked, gratuitous, gross. But even that has been
forgiven and forgotten in the same reign ; the
officer is at the head of his regiment again, and
Her Majesty has one soldier the more, and one
sullen and discontented servant the less. But
what was said of the informer ? What does Sam
Slick say of him :

"Tho' I was born in Connecticut, I have travelled all over the thirteen united universal worlds
of ourn, and am a citizen at large. No, I have no
prejudice. Now, men that carry such tittle-tattle;
no, I won't say men nother, for they ain't men,
that's a fact ; they don't desarve the name. They
are just spaniel puppies, that fetch and carry, and
they ought to be treated like puppies ; they should
have their tails cut and ears cropt, so that they
might have their right livery.

"Oh, how it has lowered the English in the
eyes of foreigners ! How sneckin' it makes 'em
look ! They seem for all the world like scared
dogs ; and a dog, when he sneaks off with his head
down, his tail atween his legs, and his back so

mean it won't bristle, is a caution to sinners. Lord, I wish I was Queen!

" But without joking, though, if I was Queen, the first time any of my ministers came to me to report what the spies had said, I'd jist up and say, 'It's a cussed oninglish, onmanly, niggerly business, is that of pumpin' and spyin' and tattlin.' I don't like it a bit; I'll neither have art nor part in it; I wash my hands clear of it. It will jist break the spirit of my people. So, minister, look here; the next report that is brought me of a spy, I'll whip his tongue out and whop your ear off, or my name ain't Queen. So jist mind what I say; first spy pokes his nose in your office, chop it off and clap it over Temple Bar, where they put the heads of traitors, and write these words over it with your own fist, that they may know the handwritin', and not mistake the meanin', '*This is the Nose of a Spy.*' "

The member for Hants tells us, it is "the nature of his temperament to be excited." I should complain less if he had the power of exciting other people. The House decided, says he, "emphatically," that Mr. Almon's appointment was judicious; but as they only decided by a majority of one, even if the emphasis was in the right place, it was not very impressive. But we on this side, hold that there was a decided false quantity in the sentence, and prefer appealing to the grammarians in the seventeen counties of Nova Scotia, who, fortunately, have the power to correct our errors.

I must confess that nothing surprised me more
than the learned member's lecture on indelicacy of
expression ; he, Sir, who has every line of Ovid at
his finger's ends ; he who I have seen gloating over
the gross obscenities of *The Pictou Observer*. His
practice, even in that speech, was strangely at
variance with his principles ; though Angelica was
first introduced in the " cold abstract," gradually
she began to grow beneath the heat of his imagination, until, like Pygmalian's statue, she sunk
into his arms in all the freshness of health and
passion. She had not been long there, however,
before he began to give her a bad character, and
declared that he could not tell whether she was a
harlot or an honest woman. I will not undertake
to decide, but think that responsible government,
or Angelica—for that seems to be the fancy name
—will be very apt to be judged by the company
she keeps. Before passing from this topic, I may
as well caution the learned gentleman not to set
himself up for a moralist until he reforms a little ;
and when he preaches sermons on delicacy, to be a
little more choice of language, or we shall have to
apply the lines to him which Juvenal aims at
Creticus :

> " Nor, vain Metellus, shall
> From Rome's Tribunal thy harangues prevail
> 'Gainst Harlotry, while thou art clad so thin,
> That through thy cobweb robe we see thy skin
> As thou declaim'st."

The learned gentleman, with a solemn invocation
to Nemesis, asked me if I quailed before the " air

drawn dagger," the whirlwind, or the " false fire"
by which I was surrounded? He shall be my
judge. Three times I met him in his own county
last summer; he knows which of us shrank from
the encounter, or won the victory. He has seen
me here for the last ten days; he sees me now.
Do I quail? No, sir, I take my stand upon the
constitution of my country, and all the powers of
darkness cannot disturb my mind. But, oh! sir, I
should like to see him in my position, with an
armful of despatches heaped upon his head; with
a Governor and all his patronage to sap and mine
him; with two crown officers and half a dozen
lawyers in his front, and tagrag and bob-tail in
his rear; perhaps he might comport himself with
more dignity than I do, but I confess I have my
doubts. The reference to my pilgrimage to
Downing street, came with an ill grace from him.
When I went to Downing street, some years ago,
I went as a private gentleman, at my own cost and
charges. My Colonial character was my only introduction, and I received more courtesy and
kindness than I deserved. When that gentleman
went on his pilgrimage,—as my learned colleague
wittily reminded him,—the Province paid for his
staff and scallop shell; £500 sterling was drawn
out of the revenue of this country to furnish his
script; and his errand was hostile to the public
interests, and to the wishes of the people. The
learned gentleman cavils at my imagery, and tells
us that Lord Falkland stands like an English oak,

verdant and vigorous. I will adopt the figure, and admit that he stood so once ; but I fear that the insidious ivy, the parasite plant, and other creeping things, have so wound their tendrils around him, and though there is the outward semblance of a tree, the core is decayed, and the fountains of life withdrawn. But, Mr. Chairman, I lingered long enough with the member for Hants. In closing I may as well give him a line or two of plain English, in return for all his Latin. They were addressed by a great poet to a great king, but always come into my head when the learned gentleman draws towards the close of one of his "vapid declamations," and I long to exclaim—

> "At length proud Prince, ambitious Lewis, cease
> To plague mankind."

This was the strain in which Mr. Howe indulged in connection with all the gentlemen in succession who had attacked him ; and I have thought it worth while to copy the remarks that his powers may be understood better than by making a bald reference to them.

In future pages I will make quotations from Mr. Howe's Poetical works, for the purpose of exhibiting him in this line of literature. With respect to the piquant references to Lord Falkland, these will be explained hereafter when the grip is taken with his lordship by Mr. Howe, for his unconstitutional and undignified conduct as a Governor.

CHAPTER XVIII.

Howe Challenged to Mortal Combat.—He Accepts the Challenge and Fights.—His Magnanimity.— Challenged a Second Time, but Declines the Honor.— Former Duels. — Monsieur Tonson.— Howe and Keefler.—Uniacke and the Bull.

It was impossible to refer to a political abuse and comment upon it, without striking somebody. In the language of Shakespeare, it was like "throwing an arrow over the house and wounding a brother." In the course of debate Mr. Howe referred to the high emoluments derived by the heads of Departments and also by the members of the Judiciary, and in doing so no doubt he expressed himself somewhat forcibly—perhaps that the judges did not earn the large salaries they were in receipt of. The son of the Chief Justice (Haliburton, afterwards Sir Brenton,) John Haliburton, thinking that Mr. Howe had gone a little too far with his venerable father, challenged the ruffler of the domestic circle to mortal combat. It was all one who should kill Howe about this time, as he was in the midst of his revolutionary propaganda, and if not got out of the way the whole country would ere long be permeated with

the destructive seed he was sowing and fast ger-
minating and taking root.   John Haliburton,
then, was the man for the slaughter, no doubt
thought his "compact" friends.   Had Howe declined the challenge, it would have told greatly
against his courage, which was regarded in those
days as a necessary qualification in a leading public man ; and so he "joined issue," as the lawyers
say, with his challenger, and accepted the gauge
of battle at the hands of that gentleman's second,
whose name I have forgotten.   Howe's second was
his old friend Dr. Gregor.   It was on a fine bright
morning at 5 o'clock when the parties went forth
to battle—the one principal with deadly intent,
the other with harmless design.   When the word
fire was given Haliburton "let bang" at the
enemy of the "family compact."   Howe held his
fire, and when Haliburton's smoke had cleared
away he took deliberate aim at him—he had him
at his mercy—and then, shot into the air.   Howe's
courage was vindicated—his magnanimity com-
mented upon—both parties and their friends
marched off the field—all fully satisfied with the
morning's pastime—and no doubt enjoyed their
matutinal meal with far greater relish than they
did their potations the night preceding.

But Howe was not to rest here.   On a subsequent occasion, having made some reference to
the office of the Provincial Secretary and its ex-
travagances, the great head of that (irresponsible)
department — Sir Rupert D'George, — taking

umbrage, sent a challenge to Howe to meet him in mortal combat. If Haliburton missed his man, Sir Rupert, a better shot, would be sure to wing him and put an end to his agitations. This second challenge Howe very wisely declined, saying in reply that he could not think of making a target of himself for every one to shoot at, who imagined he had a grievance,—besides, he felt quite satisfied that his country just at that time could not afford to dispense with his services. This was about the substance of his answer.

While upon the subject of duels, it may not be out of place to refer to previous "affairs of honor," so called, in the olden time. In 1819, or '20, a Merchant in Halifax, named Bowie, had a case in court, and Mr. Richard Uniacke (afterwards Judge Uniacke) was the lawyer in opposition. Remarks were made of an irritating nature when a quarrel ensued. After the Court was adjourned Bowie sent a challenge to Uniacke, and the combatants and their seconds met in what was then known as the Governor's Pasture, about a mile above the present Halifax Railway Station— a place once containing a grove of trees, but now no longer recognizable, as it is well built up with dwellings. Bowie fell mortally wounded. His funeral was the longest ever seen in Halifax up to that time. A sort of trial was held—the form had to be gone through. Uniacke was acquitted.

About two years after this (1821) a very similar case occurred in Fredericton—the parties concerned were George Frederick Street (afterwards Judge) and Mr. Wetmore—father of the late Judge Wetmore—then a rising and very clever lawyer. A misunderstanding between these two lawyers occurred in the course of a trial, in which each was engaged on opposite sides—sharp words passed between them—then angry recriminations, then a challenge by Wetmore. They met on what is called the Maryland Road, just back of Fredericton, and a short distance off the road. Wetmore fell in the arms of death. A trial followed, as in the Halifax case. Chief Justice Saunders was the Judge on the Bench ; and an acquittal followed. In those days killing was no murder, when life was lost in duelling.

There is an old French play called Monsieur Tonson come again—the scene is laid in the Rue d'Rivoli, Paris—the story is, that a very popular politician by the name of Tonson occupied quarters on this street ; and he was beset day and night by callers—at length he moved out into a quiet quarter of Paris where he should not be disturbed by his friends. Another Frenchman moved into the vacated premises, and he came in for all the calls—the friends of the former gentleman not being aware that Tonson had moved away. The chief feature of the play is the annoyance to the new lessee, every time he received a fresh call— "Is Monsieur Tonson in ?" These calls came so often, the same query repeated, that it kept the tenant continually on the go, answering the door bell. At length he got cross and swore out of the window upon the head of the innocent intruder upon Monsieur Tonson's successor; and finally was obliged to move away.

Now the same story will answer for a modern occasion. Mr. Joseph Keefler (a gentleman well known for his urbanity and kindness of heart) was Sexton of St. Paul's Church, Halifax, a position he had occupied for many years—he knew everybody in town and everybody knew him, and he was much respected. Indeed he was regarded as one of the main pillars of the church. It happened that Keefler occupied a house on Spring Garden Road, and a few doors from Mr. Howe's residence. As the latter gentleman, like Monsieur Tonson, was in great demand about this time, he was called upon day and night at all hours, but his friends often mistook Keefler's house for Howe's—so that the former, like his illustrious Parisian predecessor in the same predicament, also began to get cross at the annoyance. "Is Mr. Howe in?" was the invariable query at Keefler's door. One night, being a little out of humor—and who doesn't get out of humor at times?—he made ready for the next comer, and to give him a bit of his mind for disturbing him. The usual knock at length roused Keefler and his ire at the same time.—"Is Mr. Howe in?" "No! —he is not—he don't live here—he is killing the Tories—Joe Howe slays the Tories, and Joe

Keefler buries them. I'm Joe Keefler, dang you—go to the next house, or to pot if you like!"

In the early days, and long before Railways were thought of, the gentry had their country summer residences some distance away from Halifax, generally occupying a full day and more to reach them. For example, the Collector of Customs (Hon. T. N. Jeffery) resided about a dozen miles below Windsor, the Lord Bishop at Aylesford, Hon. Mr. Robie and S. G. W. Archibald rusticated at Truro. So that they all spent a considerable portion of their time on the road; but having plenty of time and money at their disposal, this was nothing considering the healthful pleasures of a rustic life. Richard John Uniacke's country seat was at "Mount Uniacke.". Mr. U. was Attorney General of the Province—at that time a highly distinguished office, for the reason that great influence was required to obtain a leading public office independently of the people. "Mount Uniacke" was chosen by its owner on account of the fine lake on the premises. At the present day this lake fronts on the Windsor Railroad, and can be seen on passing, with the Mansion behind it. Formerly this lake was away back in the woods, where none could see it, unless they were visitors to the grounds. When first occupied as a country residence, "Mount Uniacke" faced on the old Windsor Road, and the main gates at the entrance to the grounds were very fine, resembling the approach to an English Park.

On passing in the stage coach those gates were greatly admired. In a few years afterwards, in straightening the road, the supervisors, without stopping to consider the grandeur of the gates, took the road about half a mile away from them, and so left the gates, as it were, in the midst of the forest once more, much to the annoyance and inconvenience of the proprietor. The Attorney General felt much interest in stock raising; more for his own amusement than from any pecuniary gain. Among his animals he had a famous bull which was raised upon the Farm, and between the two quite an intimacy was formed, so that Uniacke would always make up to his pet and fondle it in a familiar way. Now Uniacke was an early riser; and one morning, not making his appearance in the house at the usual time after his rambles, the servant man crossed over the fields, and in the distance discovered his master and the bull in deadly conflict, each struggling for the mastery. Both were so overcome and exhausted that they were down on the ground, Uniacke holding the bull by the horns in an iron grip. An ordinary man must have succumbed to the attack of the ferocious monster and been killed outright. But U. was a powerful six-footer of herculean proportions, in the midst of his manhood, and strong as a bull. It seems that as usual when Mr. U. made up to the animal that morning, the first thing he noticed was a bold disposition to attack him; and feeling the difficulty of the position, with no one within call, he made up his mind that he must either be killed, or overcome his antagonist. Both were so exhausted when the man came up that neither could scarcely move. The animal was shot, and Uniacke recovered from the shock and his wounds after some little time.*

---

*I give the story as it was told me when a boy, and not many years after the occurrence. I have frequently seen Mr. Uniacke in his later days and can call to remembrance his personal appearance very distinctly.

CHAPTER XIX.

Mr. Howe and Railways.—Public Meeting at Saint John Mechanics' Institute.—A Dinner Party.— George Bancroft's Gratuitous Remarks over the Death of President Lincoln.—The Late Civil War in the United States.—Mr. Howe in a Novel Field of Debate.—Howe's Speech at a Public Meeting at Birmingham, England.

During the great Railway movements in the Provinces (say in the forties) Mr. Howe was continually on the go between Halifax and St. John and Quebec, in advocacy of one line or another, sometimes accompanied by other delegates and sometimes alone—he appeared to be clothed with full powers to negotiate such measures as he considered best for all interests, especially the line from Halifax *via* St. John and the " North Shore." A public meeting was called at the Mechanics' Institute, where Mr. Howe addressed a large gathering of the citizens. There was great rivalry and even jealousy between the two capitals in connection with this project, Halifax in favor of the North Shore and St. John by the valley of the St. John River. On this occasion Mr. Howe was confronted on the platform by several of our ablest men, among whom was the late Chief Justice Ritchie and the late Judge Gray (afterwards of British Columbia)—but Howe held his own in his answers to all questioners. As an old friend, I had the pleasure of meeting Mr. Howe at this time at another friend's private table in St. John—the company numbered ten persons, all of whom are now dead, except two, viz.: Mr. John Howe and myself. It was a night ever to be remembered. Dinner was served at 7 p. m., and it was three next morning before the company retired to the drawing room, previous to separating. During all these hours Mr. Howe's stories and anecdotes of men and things never flagged five minutes at a time. He held that table in *silken chains* the whole night, and nobody seemed weary, sleepy, or desirous of getting away. Of course the "flowing bowl" went round in such a manner as would have furnished a thesis for a temperance lecturer to last him a whole year. I do not mean to say, however, that there was any one of the party " who was not entirely himself."

Again I met Mr. Howe on a subsequent occasion at the United States Hotel in Portland, Maine, when a number of Railway delegates were present, from different parts (if I mistake not it was the " European and North American Railroad," in which Portland, St. John and Halifax were interested)—Portland was represented by the great Railway magnate, well known at the time—John A. Poore—Hon. Hannibal Hamlin (afterwards

Vice-President of the United States) and Hon.
Judge Chandler of Maine. Our own people consisted of Mr. Howe—and if I mistake not the
present Senator Dickey of Amherst. Ex-Governor
Chandler, Robert Jardine, and George Botsford
represented New Brunswick. Although the meeting was in a public hotel, the dining took place in
private. The old bacchanalian refrain about
"good fellows" found full expression and amplifi-
cation on this occasion. The eating and (*I had
come nigh saying*) drinking occupied some five
hours of precious railway time. The Maine liquor
law (if there was such a law at the time) had no
terrors for the belligerents. It was eating, drinking, talking, laughing throughout this long *trying*
period of five hours. Howe, indeed, was never
happier or more brilliant than on occasions such as
these. I was the fifth wheel to the coach on this
occasion introduced by Howe.

On the assassination of President Lincoln by
Booth, the Honorable George Bancroft, the great
historian, was engaged to deliver an Oration before Congress, in commemoration of the illustrious dead. All the magnates in Washington
were invited to be present. Mr. Howe being
there at the time on business (of an imperial nature,) was, of course, provided like the others with
a seat of honor. Now, had the orator confined
himself to the subject in hand, instead of going off
at a tangent, and drawing comparisons between the
opportunities for rising into power in the United

States compared with those of England, all would
have gone well and in harmony with the occasion.
While in the Republic, said the speaker, a man
like Lincoln, with a humble beginning, rose to the
first office in the State, no such chance was offered
in a Monarchy, especially in England.   Here Mr.
Howe's nationality and patriotism were stirred to
their utmost depths, and if he only had had a
chance to make a reply at that moment, he would
have been in his element.   But this was impossible.
But he addressed a private letter to Mr. Bancroft
(which only found its way into print several years
afterwards) in which he contradicted his statements, as far as England was concerned, clearly
and unmistakably, by showing that some of the
ablest Statesmen that England ever produced
sprung from the loins of the great masses.   I do
not remember all the cases Howe cited.   There
was George Canning, the great Prime Minister,
whose mother was an actress—Lord Brougham of
humble parentage—Mr. Copley (Lord Lyndhurst)
son of a Boston Portrait Painter—Sheridan and
Burke, both of humble origin—to which might
be added among many more, a late leader of the
House of Commons and Chancellor of the Exchequer, Mr. Smith, a newspaper man and book-
seller.   In short, Howe showed that real genuine
talents had a better chance of coming to the front
and being universally recognized in England (in
spite of the accidents of birth) than even in the
great Republic—for it is patent to every one that

men of great genius and renown, like Webster, have never yet risen to the foremost place in the Nation. The Prime Minister of England, clothed with sovereign powers, stands upon the same footing as the President of the United States—aye, with even greater powers; and there have been Prime Ministers in England of as humble origin as even Lincoln himself.

Shortly after the Civil War had broken out in the United States, in 1861, there was a great deal of hard feeling expressed by the Northerners against Canada and England particularly, under the impression that they were in sympathy with the South, even affording it "aid and comfort." No doubt, there was everywhere outside the United States warm feelings and wishes for the success of what is now called "the lost cause," not for the upholdence of slavery, but on account of the political and economic grievances of which the South complained, and had been complaining ever since the days of Calhoun, and the "nullification" outbreak. Although this feeling in favor of the South was only shared in by a minority, it was somewhat excusable, on the ground that human nature is always on the side of the weak when in resistance to the strong ; and in no country in the world is this manifestation more pronounced than it is in the United States, as, for example, during the Canadian rebellion in 1837 and the Irish escapade in 1847, when public meetings were called in all parts of the country and resolutions passed, supported by some of the leading public men, against England and for the encouragement of the rebels.   All this was quite natural, if not justifiable.   Therefore it should be considered in all such cases, that what is sauce for the goose should be allowed to be the right sort of sauce for the gander.

At about this time (1861 or 2) Mr. Howe and a New Brunswick friend of his happened to be in London on some special business in connection with their respective Provinces, when one evening at a late hour they were walking through the Strand on their way home.   Now, there is situated in the Strand an institution called " The Free Discussion Forum," its membership consists of any one who chooses to enter and take part in the debate of the evening.   This club has been in existence for many years, and has proved to be a nursery for eminent statesmen and lawyers who have resorted hither to try their 'prentice hand at public speaking, and it has always been attended by the first people in the land—its proceedings are conducted with the strictest parliamentary etiquette, and here some of the finest and most brilliant speaking is to be heard, and yet the speakers may be unknown as the name is given under a pseudonym when the Chairman's eye is caught. When our Colonial friends entered the hall of this intellectual gathering, over a thousand persons being present, the subject of the evening's discussion was the President's Message just delivered to

Congress—an important topic at the time as England received a considerable share of attention in said message growing out of the civil war. When our friends entered there was a tall, lank Georgian upon his feet declaiming bitterly against the South, (probably he was then a resident in the North) and he was immediately followed by a Connecticut Editor who was death upon the slave-holder and the effete citizens of the South whose lives were spent in idleness and debauchery, a wretched lot the whole of them, residing South of Dixon's line. No doubt the Editor was under the impression that he was pouring out his talents on a sympathetic audience, since "slavery" was the principal plank he used in his platform. As soon as the last gentleman finished, Howe sprang to his feet, caught the Chairman's eye and went ahead on the side of the South—not that his sympathies were in that direction, but rather Northwards—as it was a sort of free lance, however, a man was at liberty to argue against his own convictions, *ad capitandum*, and so our hero improved the occasion in his own off-hand, nonchalant way, to the delight of his audience. Everybody was amazed at the speaker's powers, his minute knowledge of the subject under discussion, his mastery of language, his oratory—in short all felt that England's greatest man had the floor, but who that man could be was the great puzzle to them all. The arguments of the poor Georgian and Editor were turned inside out and they themselves mercilessly held up to the ridicule of the vast assemblage who enjoyed the " circus " heartily.

It was now after ten o'clock, the hour for closing, an hour rigidly adhered to, no matter who the speaker having the floor at the time ; but the audience was boisterous for Howe to go on—time with them on this occasion did not count for much, and so the more he talked and attempted to sit down the more they insisted upon his going on. It was after 12 o'clock when Howe finished, when suddenly a wiseacre in the audience sprang to his feet, none other than the irrepressible Citizen George Francis Train. Howe knew that he was caught, his individuality discovered, although he felt sure up to this moment there was not a soul in that vast assembly who could have possibly known him. Train's rising was to announce to the Chairman that he wished to reply next evening to the gentleman from Nova Scotia. [My informant who was present on the occasion said that that speech of Howe's was the most powerful he had ever heard him deliver, and he also remarked that the audience were so carried away by his eloquence and good humor that he believed they would have remained half the night had he kept on speaking.]

A few years after the above episode (I got my information from a gentleman who was in company with Mr. Howe) a public meeting was held at Birmingham—it was during the time of the cotton famine, when thousands of working men were out of employment, and the object of the meeting was for the encouragement of emigration to the Colonies. It had been previously announced that several Colonial statesmen would be in attendance and address the meeting. The hall was an immense one in size, but not half large enough to hold all who wished to gain admittance. The chairman announced that each speaker would be allowed twenty minutes to address the meeting. After several talented able gentlemen had spoken, "Mr. Howe from Nova Scotia" was introduced to the assemblage. He created such a powerful impression, by his speaking powers, that all the gavels within reach brought down upon the desk after the twenty minutes were up, could not have been heeded, so greatly was that vast audience swayed and carried away. Instead of speaking twenty minutes he held the floor for a whole hour, and even then had some difficulty in being allowed to stop. After the meeting was over, several persons, which soon became a little crowd, went up to Howe, with delight beaming on their countenances, to get further information about this Eldorado, Nova Scotia, whose charms and attractions Howe had so vividly portrayed—for its great agricultural capabilities, its mineral and mining resources, its magnificent climate, its fauna and flora, and in fact for being a land " flowing with milk and honey"—and so impressed were his hearers by the description that they had made up their minds, "there and then" to emigrate forth-

with, as there was nothing at home for them any
longer but starvation, the cotton mills all being
"shut down."   My informant says he never in all
his life saw an audience so worked upon as that
Birmingham gathering under Howe's magica
powers of persuasion.

CHAPTER XX.

Earl Grey's Tribute to Mr. Howe's Eloquence.— ".Joe Howe" Twelve Feet High.—George T. Phillis the Auctioneer.—Mr. Howe as a Poet.— Poems to Queen Victoria and the Hon. Mrs. Norton.

When Mr. Howe returned from England in 1851, after having secured from the British government a pledge of a loan of seven millions of pounds sterling at a low rate of interest for the construction of the Intercolonial railway, he delivered a speech in Mason's hall on the 15th of May of that year, which Earl Grey declared "one of the best that he had ever read." The following passage is quoted from it because it not only serves the purpose of giving a fine specimen of Mr. Howe's rugged eloquence, but also indicates his great breadth of view, exalted patriotism and keen political foresight; and for which information I am indebted to the *Halifax Mail:*

" England virtually says to us by this offer: There are seven millions of sovereigns, at half the price that your neighbors pay, to construct your railways ; people your waste lands ; organize and improve the boundless territory beneath your feet ; learn to rely upon and defend yourselves, and God speed you in the formation of national character and national institutions.

"But, sir, daring as may appear the scope of this conception, high as the destiny may seem which it discloses for our children, and boundless as are the fields of honorable labor which it presents, another, grander in proportion, opens beyond : one which the imagination of a poet could not exaggerate, but which the statesman may grasp and realize, even in our own day.

"Sir, to bind these disjointed provinces together by iron roads; to give them the homogeneous character, fixedness of purpose, and elevation of sentiment, which they so much require, is our first duty. But, after all, they occupy but a limited portion of that boundless heritage which God and nature have given to us and to our children.

"Nova Scotia and New Brunswick are but the frontage of a territory which includes four millions of square miles, stretching away behind and beyond them, to the frozen regions on the one side and to the Pacific on the other. Of this great section of the globe, all the northern provinces, including Prince Edward Island and Newfoundland, occupy but four hundred and eighty-six thousand square miles. The Hudson's Bay territory includes two hundred and fifty thousand miles.

"Throwing aside the more bleak and inhospitable regions, we have a magnificent country between Canada and the Pacific, out of which five or six noble provinces may be formed, larger than any we have, and presenting to the hand of industry, and to the eye of speculation, every variety of soil, climate and resource. With such a territory as this to overcome, organize and improve, think you that we shall stop even at the western bounds of Canada ? or even at the shores of the Pacific ? Vancouver's Island, with its vast coal measures, lies beyond. The beautiful islands of the Pacific and the growing commerce of the ocean, are beyond. Populous China and the rich east are beyond, and the sails of our children's children will reflect as familiarly the sunbeams of the south as they now have the angry tempests of the north.

"The Maritime Provinces, which I now address, are but the Atlantic frontage of this boundless and prolific region ; the wharves upon which its business will be transacted, and beside which its rich argosies are to lie. Nova Scotia is one of these.

" Will you, then, put your hands unitedly, with order, intelligence and energy to this great work ?

" Refuse and you are recreants to every principle which lies at the base of your country's prosperity and advancement ; refuse and the Deity's handwriting upon land and sea is to you unintelligible language ; refuse, and Nova Scotia, instead of occupying the foreground, as she now does, should have been thrown back, at least behind the Rocky Mountains.

" God has planted your country in the front of this boundless region ; see that you comprehend its destiny and resources; see that you discharge, with energy and elevation of soul the duties which develop upon you in virtue of your position. Hitherto, my countrymen, you have dealt with this subject in a becoming spirit, and whatever others may think or apprehend, I know that you will persevere in that spirit until our objects are attained.

"I am neither a prophet, nor a son of a prophet, yet I will venture to predict that in a few years we shall make the journey hence to Quebec and Montreal, and home through Portland and St. John by rail, and I believe that many in this room will live to hear the whistle of the steam engine in the passes of the Rocky Mountains, and to make the journey from Halifax to the Pacific in five or six days."

A bucolic gentleman having heard a great deal about "Joe Howe" and being a great admirer of his reputation, was very anxious to see him. He accordingly called one day at the secretary's office. He saw Mr. Howe as he entered, standing at his desk, engaged in writing. Our friend from the country soon felt himself at ease in the presence of the Nova Scotia wonder. On stating his errand, Mr. Howe said he was glad to see him, and talked with him as freely as though they had been life-long companions—so that our friend felt all over as if "Joe Howe" was not only the greatest man in the world, but the most agreeable that ever lived since Adam. Had Mr. Howe invited

him to dine which was no uncommon thing for him
to do, even with comparative strangers, our friend
would have gone off in a blaze of excitement and
perhaps never have got over it. At all events in
due time the gentleman backed himself out of the
office, and was soon afterwards on his way home
rejoicing.

Shortly after this he was asked by an acquaintance what he thought of "Joe Howe" since he
had had an interview with him.

"Think of him," was the reply; "there is no
room to think at all. He is the most wonderful
man I ever saw. When I entered his office he
seemed like a very ordinary mortal, about five feet
high. I had not been there more than half an
hour when he seemed like a man eight feet—but
before I left, to my astonishment, his head touched
the ceiling—twelve feet high."

[It should here be stated that I have read in
the papers a story something like the above, in
reference to another person; but who the original
was I am not prepared to prove. It is my opinion,
however, that it is applicable to the Howe case.]

Another great admirer of "Joe Howe" was
George T. Phillis, Auctioneer, whose business
establishment was on Water street, a short distance south of the "Ordinance." He was one of
the wits (after Doyle) of the times. Persons of
leisure from all parts of the town would make it a
point to pass along when an auction was under-

way, in order to be regaled with Phillis' stories, while selling goods. "Here's a fine box of dip candles for you, warranted to burn faster than any other dips in the town—by lighting them at both ends, you may have the protection policy (at this time the talk was English free trade and protection, both parties for or against at bitter variance) illustrated—you see, in this way, you make money by encouraging the domestic workman, and the faster you burn the candles the more light you have for yourselves, and the more money you save to the country." Again, "Here is a feather bed made upon a new pattern—[bed somewhat ancient but in the interests of good taste I omit the gentleman's intrusions, although they contain the pith of the joke.] Why, gentlemen, this Map if sent to the British Museum would bring its weight in gold — going, going—are you all done — gone. Some of you will feel sorry when you come to reflect that a feather bed Map of Europe should pass out of your hands, on account of two pounds ten"—[no cents then.] "Next, gentlemen, I have to offer you is a lot of India Rubber overcoats, warranted to keep the rain from penetrating the skin. These holes, gentlemen, [referring to several worn holes,] are intended to let the water out, when it rains too heavily for it to run off, made after a new pattern, and of great historic value, as they were used by the antedeluvians when coming out of the ark." Then, again, "here is a lot of old iron, the remnants of a Bankrupt Estate, the irony

of fate had a good deal to do with the articles
getting into my hands. Here you have tongs,
shovels, old scraps, nick-nacks, and here is the remains of a big gridiron of great historic value, as
it was used in the Masonic lodge for a great number of years, and is capable of broiling anything,
from a Free Mason to a tough beef steak."

As a Poet Mr. Howe contributed to different
Magazines, and also put to Press a volume of between three and four hundred pages. As a
metrical writer he stood high in the opinion of
capable judges—while his Poems and Songs and
Lyrics are highly felicitous in expression and
poetical fervour. Besides this volume, from which
I quote what follows, he has left in manuscript, a
number of fugitive pieces highly creditable to the
genius of the writer, and which may some day find
their way into print. The first selection I make is
addressed—To The Queen—and was presented to
Her Majesty by Lady Laura Phipps, at Windsor,
at the request of the ladies of Hants County, who
were greatly interested in the Poem when it appeared among private friends.

"Queen of the Thousand Isles."

Queen of the thousand Isles ! whose fragile form,
'Midst the proud structures of our Father Land,
Graces the throne, that each subsiding storm
That shakes the earth, assures us yet shall stand,
Thy gentle voice, of mild yet firm command,
Is heard in ev'ry clime, on ev'ry wave,
Thy dazzling sceptre, like a fairy wand,
Strikes off the shackles from the struggling slave,
And gathers, 'neath its rule, the great, the wise, the brave.

But yet 'midst all the treasures that surround
Thy Royal Halls, one bliss is still denied —
To know the true hearts at thy name that bound,
Which ocean from thy presence must divide,
Whose voices never swell the boisterous tide
Of hourly homage that salutes thy ear;
But yet who cherish, with a Briton's pride
And breathe to infant lips, from year to year,
The name thy budding virtues taught them to revere.

How little deem'st thou of the scenes remote,
In which one word, all other words above,
Of earthly homage seems to gaily float
On every breeze, and sound through every grove—
A spell to cheer, to animate, to move—
To bid old age throw off the weight of years,
To cherish thoughts of loyalty and love,
To garner round the heart those hopes and fears
Which, in our Western Homes, Victoria's name endears.

'Tis not that, on our soil, the measured tread
Of armed legions speaks thy sovereign sway,
'Tis not the huge leviathans that spread
Thy meteor flag above each noble bay,
That bids the soul a forced obedience pay !
—The despot's tribute from the trembling thrall—
No! At our altars sturdy freemen pray
That blessings on Victoria's head may fall,
And happy household groups each pleasing trait recall.

And gladly, with our Country's choicest flowers,
Thy son and heir Acadia's maidens greet,
Who shared thy roof, and deigns to honor ours
For moments rapt'rous, but alas ! how fleet !
And if in future times the thoughts be sweet
To him, of humble scenes beyond the sea,
When turning home his mother's smiles to meet,
And mingle with the high born and the free—
We'll long remember Him who best reflected Thee !

The next poem is addressed to the HON. MRS.
NORTON, whom Mr. Howe met at Lady Palmerston's Soiree in London, her ladyship being the wife

of the then Prime Minister. Hon. Mrs. Norton was a grand-daughter of the Right Hon. Richard Brinsley Sheridan and aunt of our late Governor-General, Earl Dufferin—now Marquis. At this time the lady's fame as a poetess extended to both hemispheres—she ranked as such with Mrs. Hemans, Mrs. Sigourney, " L. E. L.," and other bright female stars of the period. Several of her gems I have beside me—most beautiful pieces of composition, but not required here. Her husband was the Hon. Fletcher Norton, the son of a Viscount, from whom she separated, as there was inequality of dispositions. I remember his brother well in Halifax, as son-in-law and aide-de-camp to Sir Colin Campbell, Lieut. Governor. He was a fine-looking, tall young man of ruddy complexion, and was what the ladies, I suppose, would call—*handsome*—an adjective out of place, as it has always appeared to me, when applied to the stronger sex. At all events, this Captain Norton would be noticed in ten thousand for his good looks. When on duty in Halifax in the dead of winter he contracted a severe cold, which soon settled into congestion, and his death followed in a few days afterwards. He was buried from Government House with military honors. These matters, however, are only by the way.

A few days after his return from the Soiree in London, Mr. Howe sat down and indited the following lines, addressed to the Hon. Mrs. Norton, which will be found on the next page :

Hon. Mrs. Norton.

Lady, how eagerly I thread the maze
Of rank and beauty, 'till thy noble form
Stands full before me—'till at last I gaze,
In joy and thankfulness, to find the storm
That shook the fruit profusely, spared the tree;
To realize my dreams of time and thee—
To find the eye still bright, the cheek still warm,
The regal outlines swelling, soft and free,
And lit by luminous thoughts, as I would have them be.

Unconscious thou, how, far beyond the wave,
The lowest murmur of the softest strain
In early life articulate music gave
To thousands, who, when agony and pain
Shook every tremulous string, yet sigh'd again,
That ever sorrow should the notes prolong.
Unconscious thou, that 'midst the light and vain,
The stranger turns him from the glittering throng,
In Mem'ry's stores to hoard the graceful Child of Song.

How oft, in weariness, we turn away
From what we've sought, from picture, fane, or stream ;
But well dost thou the ling'ring glance repay
With full fruition of the fondest dream ;
The light that o'er the billows used to beam,
Lodged in a stately tower. The minstrel's smile
Is sweeter than her Song—the playful theme
Of early genius, even less versatile
Than are the matron charms that Soul and Sense beguile.

The Maple, in our Woods, the frost doth crown
With more resplendent beauty than it wears
In early Spring. Its sweetness cometh down
But when the Woodman's stroke its bosom tears.
And thus, in spite of all my doubts and fears,
I joy to see thy ripened beauties glow
'Neath sorrow's gentle touch that more endears;
To feel thy strains will all the sweeter flow
From that deep wound that did not lay thee low.

CHAPTER XXI.

*Mr. Howe on Colonial Changes.—Mr. Howe
Chosen Speaker of the House of Assembly.—
Charles Dickens in Halifax.—The Canadian
Rebellion of 1837.—The Disabilities of the Re-
formers.—Sir Francis Bond Head, a Failure.—
The Old Family Compact.*

In 1846 Mr. Howe addressed a series of letters
to the Colonial Secretary (Lord John Russell)
upon the re-organization of the Empire—a sort of
Imperial Federation idea of the present day—but
then politics were altogether different at that time.
Then the Reformers were struggling for Responsible Government and saw no chance of getting it,
unless through process of still heavier battles, the
success of which would enable Colonists to hold
seats in the Executive Council, and not to be kept
continually before the gangway by a small, narrow
exclusive circle in Halifax. It was to break these
bonds asunder that the Imperial Government was
asked to open the doors of Parliament to Colonial
talents. Again, there was at that time a Trade
Zollverein between England and her Colonies—the
great days of protection, when her colonies were
all but obliged to consume British manufactures.
The system was then something like what the

Imperial Federationists are asking for to-day, and their desire that the whirligig of time shall revolve backward—in other words, that in consideration of her Colonies, England shall re-impose a portion of the duties ancillary to her free trade days, and that foreign articles entering our markets shall be somewhat weighted—in a word, asking that the old boot shall be revamped and placed on the other leg this time. Ay, and there are combinations simple enough to believe, or are trying hard to make themselves believe, that the Bright and Cobden school of politicians are all dead and buried, and because Lord Salisbury is at the head of affairs John Bull is going down on all fours in order that the protectionists, or fair traders, as they now call themselves, may walk over his body. However, what I wish to convey is, that persons should not run away with the notion, that because Mr. Howe wrote in favor of the re-organization of the Empire fifty years ago, at a time when the circumstances were altogether different to what they are now, he would if alive to day entertain similar opinions. [Further remarks upon this subject in a later chapter.]

After the elections in 1847, Mr. Howe was chosen Speaker of the House. At this time the Great Novelist Charles Dickens, arrived in Halifax on board a Cunard steamer on his way to the United States. Now both these gentlemen had formed an intimacy in London when Howe was on a visit there a few years before. As soon as

WILLIAM LYON MACKENZIE.

Dickens landed Mr. Howe took him in charge and introduced him to honorable members, and had a chair placed beside that of the Speaker's for " the distinguished visitor." Now Dickens at this time was the lion of all English speaking leaders—for his works were just fresh from his pen, and the sayings of the elder Pickwick and Sam Weller, were in everybody's mouth. Dickens afterwards dined with Howe, and they kept well together during the remainder of the former's stay on shore. On his return to England Dickens described the occasion, and likened the Legislative Chamber in Halifax to that of London, by bringing the former into view looking through the big end of a telescope.

In 1837 while the reform agitation was in its full plentitude and the most bitter political feeling everywhere prevailing between the opposing parties throughout the Province, the excitement in Canada as then called, growing out of the same causes—viz., the Reformers against the Compact— was now about assuming a very aggressive shape —in short nothing less than the taking up of arms by the agitators for the redress of their grievances and ultimate independence. The leader of the Reform Party was Wm. Lyon Mackenzie, a man of good talents, force of character and influence ; but unlike the Nova Scotia leader, he lacked judgment and prudence, hence his failure at the critical moment and finally was compelled to flee the Province, when the patriotic army which he had organized and taken into the field was overthrown and routed by the loyalists. It must not, however, be supposed that the malcontents of 1837 were composed of the rag-tags of Canada, mere desperadoes, rough characters full of adventure, whose only aim was to destroy and pillage. Nothing of the kind. Some of the best blood of the country was either in participation or in sympathy; but in saying this a large proportion of Reformers, however bitter they were against the Tories and their oppressive practices of Government, were opposed to overt acts of treason—they rather counselled a continuation of agitation, and that a day must come when their wrongs would be righted through Constitutional means. Among this highly respectable class were Mr. Hincks (afterwards Sir Francis,) Mr. Bidwell, Mr. Baldwin, Dr. Nelson, and many other such dignified but moderate men. In Lower Canada the excitement was even greater than in the Upper Province. Louis J. Papineau was the leader of the Reformers. a man of great eloquence and talents, and of most commanding presence, and he was assisted by others of the highest respectability among the *habitans.* Public meetings were called in all the towns of both Provinces, at which the boldest and most defiant language was used by the respective speakers—not against the Constitution or Government, but against the " family compact," and what they called " the plutocracy." All they asked was a reform of the existing abuses—and as an alternative revoluntionary action and independence. It was the same in Nova Scotia, where the Governor and Council were banded together, and held in contempt as it were the remonstrances of the people's representatives. But the Nova Scotians would not go into rebellion.

This agitation in both Canadas as in the Lower Provinces had been going on for years, without producing the smallest effect upon the Government; and when in 1836 Sir Francis Bond Head was appointed Governor, it intensified the excitement, as he was quite unfit for the position. Brought up in the most straight-laced Tory school in England, had been one of the Poor Law Commissioners, his dealings hitherto mostly with paupers, so that his feelings and disposition were attuned to very common place observances at home. This then was the man sent out to govern a highly spirited, intelligent people; and he proved himself in the end to be no better than was prophesied of him at the beginning. Then the Tories, as in Nova Scotia, had ready access to the back stairs of the Colonial Office, and their side of the story was always listened to, whatever it was, and accepted as gospel truth—while the Reformers had no other way of making themselves heard than upon the floors of the House of Assembly, and that availed them nothing. In the elections in Canada in 1836, this Sir Francis Bond Head threw himself into the contest with all the ardour of a candidate, and this for the purpose of defeating the Liberals; and thus (as Mr. Charles Lindsey, Mackenzie's Biographer, observed) carried despair into many a breast where hope had till then continued to abide. The coercion of Lower Canada by the Imperial and Local Governments caused the most excited persons in both Provinces to look to a revolution as the only means of relief. Mr. Mackenzie was among those who came to this conclusion. But he only shared with a large class of the population a sentiment which was the inevitable outcome of the existing state of things, and which affected masses of men, at the same moment, with a common and irresistible impulse. The Toronto " Declaration," made on the 31st of July previous, was the first spark to kindle the flame of insurrection. It committed all who accepted it to share the fortunes of Lower Canada. The machinery of organization and agitation, which was created at the same time, became the instrument of revolt.

At one of the public meetings it was complained that " a bribed and pensioned band of official hirelings and expectants, falsely assuming the character of the representatives of the people of Upper Canada, corrupted by offices, wealth and honors bestowed upon their influential members by Sir F. B. Head, since they took their seats in the House of Assembly, have refused to allow a free trial to candidates ready to contest their seats —have refused to order new elections for members who have accepted places of gain under the gov-

ernment—have refused to institute a free and
constitutional inquiry into corruptions practiced
at the elections through Sir F. B. Head's patent
deeds and otherwise ; and although they were returned for the constitutional period which the
death of the King had brought near to a close,
they have violated the most solemn covenant of
the British Constitution, by resolving that their
pretended powers of legislation shall continue over
us three years longer than they were appointed to
act."

Now with regard to the conduct of the British
Government towards the Canadian Reformers, it
must be said that the former were kept in perfect
ignorance of the nature of the complaints of the
latter through. as just now stated, the secret
machinations of the Tories in their back stairs
access to the Colonial Secretary. This ignorance
was only removed by the outbreak and what followed, as will be shown hereafter. Mr. Hume
and others in the House of Commons used strong
language against the outrageous system of Colonial Government, and did not condemn the outbreak. Then there was a large body of Orangemen in both Canadas, well organized—so that to
them was finally due the suppression of the revolt
and restoration of peace, and relieving the Compact and the Tory Officials of their fright and
returning to them their offices and emoluments—
but, only for a time longer.

Although the "rebels" were meeting in public

SIR FRANCIS BOND HEAD.

everywhere, and great preparations being made
for an outbreak at an opportune moment; and
this going on for weeks in Upper Canada, Sir F.
B. Head took no heed of the situation—nor did he
make the least preparation for taking the field,
but listlessly played with the cat in his chimney
corner (figuratively speaking); let what might
come it was all one to him, as it appeared by his
apathy. There were very few regular troops in
Canada at the time, and those were under the
command of Colonel Gore (who had married a
Halifax lady, and finally settled down in England
as a knighted General.) The " patriots " or
" rebels " had mustered at different points in the
Province, and their object was to make a descent
upon Toronto and capture it. All told they had
probably 2,000 men to operate. But as Mackenzie
himself was the General in Command, and did not
know the first thing about military tactics, all his
movements were nothing but a series of blunders
and disasters. In one skirmish at St. Charles they
gained a victory, and that was all. Had they a
good General to lead them Toronto might have
been taken with ease. Not having a leader and
poorly armed and equipped, they advanced, were
repulsed and ran. Historically, they can only be
remembered in the same light as Falstaff's regiment marching through Coventry. Indeed, I
know of no such blunders in history, except they
be in the cases of Louis Napoleon in his descent
upon Bologne in 1845, with a handful of men to

overthrow the Government of Louis Phillipe ; or
the mad attempt of Aaron Burr, ex-Vice President of the United States, who in 1806, attempted
to seduce the Western States from their allegiance
to the union, and join with him to revolutionize
Mexico, then under Spanish rule, with the intention of having himself created Emperor of Mexico
including said Western States. On proceeding
down the Mississippi a flotilla of a dozen flat boats
with but sixty followers he was trapped a little
below Natchez, his forces scattered and himself,
after many hardships caught, and finally tried in
Richmond, Virginia, on a charge of high treason,
but he escaped conviction through a mere techni-
cality. Burr, though of brilliant talents, was
reported to be a great villain. Louis Napoleon
was imprisoned in the Fortress of Ham, but after
a year or two made his escape in the disguise of a
carpenter, and afterwards became Emperor of
France.

As before observed Mackenzie, the chief pro-
moter of the rebellion, although a very able,
honest and courageous man, lacked discretion and
judgment, which this outbreak fully demonstrated
—for he should have known that a man untrained
to arms was no more fit to lead an army into the
field, especially against the Tory forces and all the
Orangemen in all the Provinces, numbering many
thousands beyond what he could possibly muster
—had no more chance of success than hitherto he
had of convincing the Compact that they ought to

place their offices at the disposal of the people.
If there were but few troops in Canada, there
were several regiments in Halifax, and Militia
aglore in all the Provinces, all of which would
have been marched to the scene of action—so that
had the " rebels" taken Toronto, they could only
have held it for a short time. It was a vast, stupid
mistake for a civilian to attempt the conquest of
Canada, and bring into terms the Tory Compact
through force of arms.

CHAPTER XXII.

The Rebellion Crushed.—Bad Generalship.—Order Restored.—Lord Durham Sent Out to Canada.— His Very Able Report Showing the Causes of the Rebellion.—Tory Insult to the Governor General and Burning of the Parliament Buildings.—Effect of Lord Durham's Report.— Mr. Paulette Thompson Sent Out to Canada.—Coalition Government.

The rebellion was crushed at a single blow, although a number of lives were lost in the respective skirmishes. Mackenzie and Dr. Rolf, another of the active spirits, made their way to the frontier—as did all the other leaders of the revolt—and thus saved their necks but not their reputations in this direction of the " forlorn hope." Mackenzie after being in the United States a short time, obtained a good position in the New York Custom House, but even here the restlessness of his nature overmastered him, and he again got into trouble. He discovered something wrong in the management of the department — perhaps " boodling"—and instead of minding his own business and holding on to his office, he must needs take it upon himself to right matters by giving

information, accompanied by remedial proposals.
The consequence was, especially being a foreigner,
he lost his place. When the amnesty was pro-
claimed by the British Government a few years
afterwards, Mackenzie returned to Canada—a
broken-down man, health shattered and a sport
for Tory gibes and squibs, until the day of his
death, not long after.

The publication of the amnesty brought back
all who were concerned in the rebellion, with
some exceptions; and in not many years after
some of the leaders, for whose heads large sums of
money had been offered, were elevated to high
positions in the Provinces, and even honored by
the Sovereign with titles. All this came about
after the smoke of battle had cleared away and
the British Government could clearly discern the
real condition of affairs, and the cause of the differences between the parties, brought about by
Lord Durham, in his able " Report," as we shall
see hereafter.

Order having thus been brought out of chaos,
so far as the suppression of the rebellion was concerned, and Radicals and Tories agreed together
to live at peace, and yet holding to their respective
principles, it was after all only the calm that
presaged another storm; for when the Legislature
subsequently met in Quebec, a Bill was passed for
the idemnification of those loyal subjects who had
lost their property through the rebellion, which
loss should be made up by the Province; but of

course as the Liberals were not recognized as
LOYAL subjects, no matter what the innocent ones
lost, they should not be included. But at length
at a subsequent meeting of the Legislature, when
the Liberals were in the ascendant in the House,
they in common justice to their friends, brought
forward a similar measure, on the ground that as
those Liberals who also lost heavily were equally
loyal to the Crown, no matter what they thought
of the Compact, and equally opposed to the ex-
treme measures of the " rebels," why should not
they be compensated as well as those who after
all were virtually the main instigators of the rebellion ? This Bill was carried, and when the
Governor (Lord Elgin) came down to the Houses
of Parliament to assent to all the measures that
had passed during the Session, this among the
number, he was met at the door of the building
after prorogation by a howling mob, imprecating
upon him everything that was disgusting to hear
—not only so, but they volleyed upon him every
missile they could lay their hands on, rotten vege-
tables, rotten eggs, and even worse and harder
substances. The Governor, however, managed to
escape injury. After thus venting their spleen
upon His Excellency, the next course was to set
fire to the Parliament Buildings and burn them to
the ground, and this they accomplished appar-
ently without interference. Here was a specimen
of Spartan chivalry with a *vengeance* ! The " old

flag" loyalty touters were chiefly responsible for
this disgraceful proceeding.

But what came out of the rebellion ?   Let us
see.   We are told in the good book, "out of evil
good comes," but no one sows bad seed and expects profitable returns ; and yet, perchance, good
growth often springs from poor tillage. So in
life among men. The effect of the rebellion was
to arouse the attention of the British Nation, and
an inquiry into its cause was demanded ; and when
the people of England *speak* the Government have
to *listen*. There must be something serious at the
bottom of all the trouble to account for such a
terrible outbreak—besides the great sympathy
manifested by the United States on the side of the
revolters, had a very decided meaning.

Accordingly the British Government now saw
the importance of appointing a special commission
to go out to Canada and intelligently ascertain the
cause of the trouble ; and Lord Durham was the
nobleman selected as the intermediary, with that
end in view. On arriving in Canada he did not
allow himself to be taken in hand by either party ;
but resorted to the most studious ways possible to
get at the bottom of the whole story. His first
step was to ascertain the names of the leading
politicians on both sides and upon whose modera-
tion and judgment reliance might be placed. He
called just such persons together, and thus after
sifting all the evidence and making allowance for
the partisanship as exhibited on both sides, he was

LORD DURHAM.

enabled to reach the prominent facts, and strike a just balance between the disputants.

On his return to England he drew up his famous Report, which must forever stand in our Colonial Annals as the most important political document ever published by a British Statesman, in which is set forth in the most fair and masterly manner, the grievances of which the Liberals had for so many years been complaining, and which finally culminated in open rupture. But LORD DURHAM's REPORT must be read to be understood and appreciated by all fair minded persons. The effect of its publication in England upon the British public and Government was prodigious. Mr. Charles Buller, private secretary (since deceased,) a very able man, rendered no unimportant service in the composition of this Report—so said at the time.

What followed?—and now we return to our regular subject, after this long digression. Mr. Paulett Thompson, President of the English Board of Trade, was next sent out to Canada (1839) as Governor General, clothed with plenary powers, and as a pacificator, with a view of restoring peace among the contending parties and placing on a more equitable footing a system of Government, such as all parties might accept without prejudice. What was called " Responsible Government," a sort of mongrel affair, had been acknowledged by the Tories for several years back. Finding it impossible to stem the incoming tide any longer, they

made a virtue of necessity and accepted the new
order of things, but not with a very good grace.
The old Adam was still living in the Tory breast,
and Mr. Howe they thought was a dangerous man
to be in power in Nova Scotia. The heads of departments continued to hold on to their offices,
without reference to the people's representatives.
Responsible Government with the Tories did not
mean the surrender of a single privilege they had
always possessed—it simply meant a willingness to
do what the people wished, so long as their own
individual interests were not disturbed. To carry
out the new system in its entirety meant *party
government*, which in their opinion would never do
for the safety of the Province, because, suppose
the Howe party once got into power, British connection would be at an end, being sustained by
the Legislature they would some day bring in
such radical measures that a second edition of
the Canadian rebellion would be sure to follow.
As soon as the outbreak in Canada had commenced, an earnest endeavor was made by the
Tories to incriminate the Howites, because the reforms for which they were contending were precisely the same as those of Papineau and Mackenzie
—but with this difference, the action of the one set
of men was treasonable, while that of the other
was peaceful, constitutional, altogether within their
rights as British subjects. Then there was a
strange absurdity in the objection set up by the
Halifax Tories when they sought to show the

danger of *party* government ; and yet they were at that very time carrying on party government themselves ? None but those of their own opinions had ever been allowed to take part with them. As in Canada above so in the Maritime Provinces below—the Reformers everywhere were prostrate, so long as the Governors and Councils of the respective Provinces held the reins of power and were upheld by the Colonial Office, which until now had received all its information, *ex parte*, as before stated, surreptitiously, from behind, at the back door, through the many telephones (figuratively speaking) which the Tories had at command.

But now Mr. Thompson came out— he landed in Halifax and there commenced to lay his plans ; but before accompanying him further on his mission, and by way of episode, an amusing incident might here be recalled. In 1837 (or about that time) this gentleman being President of the Board of Trade and an active free trader in the House of Commons, was very active against the best interests of the Colonies, as so stated. Now timber from the Baltic entered sharply into competition with our New Brunswick staple, notwithstanding the high foreign levies. To remove this duty then as threatened at one fell swoop, it was thought would be death to the St. John trade. Accordingly the citizens (the noisiest part of them) turned out and got an effigy of the right honorable gentleman prepared and bundles of faggots and set them in a blaze on King Square, amidst derisive shouts and execrations by the motley crowd there gathered. The business of the Province, however, survived the threat and trade in timber went on as usual, or with perhaps some diminution. On arriving in St. John from Halifax, on his way to Canada, in a year or two afterwards, as Governor General, this same gentleman was received with open arms, and shouts of welcome. "Crucify him—crucify him," now gave place to *pæans* of rejoicing. Triumphal arches were erected at principal points for His Excellency to pass under. Nor was the irrepressible Address omitted, exuberant with loyal and devotional expressions of attachment to "our beloved Queen." The fickleness of public opinion so often spoken of now found expression in its most fantastic form.

To go back where we left off. When Mr. Thompson landed in Halifax, he called together the leading members of the opposing parties. Mr. Howe being the central figure in the opposition ranks, of course received the lion's share of attention. Lord Falkland was then the Lieutenant Governor, a nobleman of most fickle temperament, moulded pretty much after the Sir Francis Bond Head pattern (before alluded to,) and of whose subsequent actions we shall see more presently. His wife was the natural daughter of the King (Wm. 4th) through whose influence no doubt he obtained the position for which he was altogether by nature unfitted. The better plan thought Mr.

Thompson for cutting the Gordion knot, in a
tangle about both parties, was to call upon Lord
Falkland to form a coalition government—it would
not do to dismiss the present Cabinet, that would
be giving way too much to the opposition—nor
would it do to form an out and out opposition
government. As a compromise then, Mr. Howe
was invited by the Governor General to take with
him into the Cabinet two of his colleagues, and
this at the time was considered all round to be
the best possible arrangement that could be made.
Messrs. Howe, Uniacke and McNab accordingly
entered the Government—three in number—while
the old party retained six, so that the balance of
power was anything but fair, still it was an
acknowledgement of the claims of the Liberals to
a voice in the Executive. All went on well for
some time under the new dispensation ; and had
the Tory element possessed a little common sense,
this state of things might have continued for years ;
but No ! their old proclivities were too rooted and
grounded in their nature to enable them to keep
their eyes open to the dire possibilities of their own
fatuity. After the first year of the " coalition,"
the Liberals found that their colleagues were too
many for them—in numbers—they discovered
from time to time manœuvres of which they could
not approve, and to add to their annoyance they
saw that my Lord Falkland was playing into the
Tory hands. Now, if Falkland had no brains his
wife had. She was a person of remarkable talents

and accomplishments, a fine conversationalist, and
an excellent lady in all respects. She thought
that Mr. Howe was one of the most able and brilliant men she had ever met—so I was informed at
the time. No doubt, then, this lady was the
means of cementing the strong friendship between
her husband and Mr. Howe. But after a year
or so, perhaps finding his old boon companion
(Howe) getting too many for *him*, in his views,
his Lordship became jealous and more foolish
than ever, and so his pliable majority, willing
at any moment to drive the minority out, were
ready to welcome the first opportunity for the
fulfilment of their wishes. There were rumors
from time to time that all was not harmony within the Council Chamber at Government House—
in short, the mountain was in labor and the air
filled with sulphurous fumes, while other signs
were ominous of an eruption to take place at no
distant day, and a great smash-up all round.

And so it came to pass. At length the storm
burst—the small cloud which for a long time had
been gathering in volume over Government House,
startled the community one fine morning with a
crash. Without consulting their three Liberal
colleagues, the Tories advised the Governor to
appoint a gentleman of their own politics to a
seat in the Legislative Council, and his Lordship most stupidly consented. This was the last
straw that broke the animal's back. Messrs.
Howe, Uniacke and McNab immediately threw up

their seats—the "coalition" was at an end, the case with all coalitions, dissentions within and want of cohesion without among friends. The success, or rather want of it, in the Pitt and Fox coalition is familiar to the English reader. And as another instance of the want of harmony in such combinations, it may be mentioned what occurred in New Brunswick. About two years after the break-up of the Halifax coalition, the great Liberals over the way were wheedled into the committal of a similiar coalition blunder, when in 1845 Messrs. L. A. Wilmot, Charles Fisher and George Stillman Hill left their party as it were, and joined the Tory Government, and thus submitted themselves to a large majority of their opponents, and at the same time crippled what was left of the Opposition in the House. They did this with their eyes open to what had taken place in Nova Scotia ; and the same results followed in both cases.

While the coalition lasted in Halifax. the Tories in the House and the Liberals were at peace. Both sides slaked their thirst at the same stream. It was a sort of truce, but was immediately broken after the Tory treachery instigated or acquiesced in by Lord Falkland had taken place. And now the old Government was resolved once more into its original form, as " compact" as ever.

CHAPTER XXIII.

"Daddy Chalker."—Old Liquors in Halifax.—Peppermint and Shrub.—The Popular Minister who Stole Sermons.—Mode of Burials in the Olden Time.—Wine at Funerals.—Objections to the Hearse when Introduced.

About sixty years ago there resided in Halifax an old gentleman of respectability and good plain standing who went by the name of "Daddy Chalker." He was one of the characters of the time, and possessed what is called strong "individuality." His principal mental endowment was in the knowledge he possessed of the ages of more than half the town, from infancy to old age; and in this respect he was what might be called a walking chronologer. How he came by this wonderful gift of conjuration, was a puzzle to many, and he seldom made a mistake in singling out his victim. Now, to know the individual ages of half the members of a population (then of fifteen thousand) either required a strong memory or a system of mental arithmetic not easily to account for; but "Daddy Chalker" seemed to understand his business if nobody else did and seldom made a mistake. Of course, there were different theories advanced to account for the man's phenomenal peculiarity. But the fact is incontestable that the girls of Halifax knew their own ages, and that Chalker knew as much as they did. On the occasion of the anniversary of a birthday in any household, Daddy would call to compliment the individual, and his reward was generally a glass of wine. Now, as it is very likely that in a population of so many thousands, there must necessarily be several birthdays, taking one house with another, for every day in the year, our old peripatetic philosopher must have imbibed considerable wine in the course of his rounds—at all events quite enough to keep him going from one house to another; and as the wine in those days was pure he always managed to carry his head straight between his shoulders. We will suppose that Sarah Ann's birthday is at hand—to-morrow or next day. "Now, ma, don't let Chalker in, the nuisance." "But, my dear, he knows your age all the same, and you are aware of the penalty for closing the door against him?" Sarah Ann begins to think, and then withdraws her objections. She knows better than to hold out—for the penalty is, if Chalker is not properly received, he feels himself at liberty to tell Sarah Ann's age to all the boys. He is thus "boodled" with a glass of wine, which is the black mail he levies, especially after the girls have attained a certain age, and don't want to be classified among post mortem female bipeds. When Chalker died the prayers of all the girls in town went up for the repose of his inquisitiveness.

But how could the man drink so much wine and not become obfusticated? Easily enough—then "the pure juice of the grape" was the stimulating tonic—a bucket full would not intoxicate, for the stomach suffered worse than the head. Those were anti-temperance days, and dealers in wines had no temptation to adulterate their wares to make money.

But then if a person was fond of the real ardent sixty years ago, Halifax supplied any quantity of "Old Jamaica," also pure, but not to be trifled with. Then there was the old Schiedam, known as Holland's gin, white as water and purity itself, especially when it began to bite. The old codgers used to dilute their "Jamaica" with spruce beer and this they called calibogus. At evening parties the flowing bowl went the rounds among the ladies in the shape of peppermint, shrub, clove water, aniseed, and such other innocent decoctions. The manufacture of all those things has gone out with the lost arts—for I only know of them now as historical reminiscenses. The fine arts, however, have brought in something to take their places, (but these things too are destined to give way ere long to something less spooneriffic) such as Old Rye, Tom-and-Jerry, Pig-in-the-whistle, mint julep, hazel beer, and so forth. For which scientific beverages we are indebted to our uncle Jonathan, who in his progress of civilization takes care to provide means of irrigation, so that the land may not become parched, or suffer from undue thirst, and Canada is not far behind. Although they may appear trifling for a book, these remarks are made for the purpose of showing the habits of the past in order to contrast them with the finer qualities of the present period.

Some fifty years ago there was a young minister suddenly appeared in St. Paul's church, Halifax, and soon became the idol of the town for his eloquent sermons, his elocution, and oratorical powers generally. He held his congregation spellbound, as though he possessed a magic, magnetic influence over every soul present. His sermons were delivered extempore, the only effective method of holding an audience whether religious or secular. Long before the hour of service the church doors were besieged by many persons desirous of getting in after the pew owners had taken their places. The appearance of this young preacher in the pulpit was very fine, and his graceful gestures were not surpassable. During the height of his popularity he paid a visit to St. John, and preached in Trinity church ; and as his fame had preceded him, and his coming known to many of the congregation, the church was filled to overflowing. Everybody was delighted, and his praises were upon everybody's lips. In the evening he preached in St. Luke's church, Portland, the Rev. Mr. Harrison being rector at the time. Here the young minister's reception was equally imposing. The church was crowded to the doors.

Bye and bye it leaked out that this highly popular minister was preaching other people's sermons. In other words, he was a plagiarist, and the sermons not of his own composition. A reaction set in, and this famous young divine disappeared from the arena as suddenly as he came forward. From that time to this I have been unable to trace or fix him anywhere, and he may be under ground for aught I know.

The foregoing facts are brought to my recollection from reading in the newspapers a few years ago that an excellent speech delivered in the United States by Hon. Mr. Mercier of Quebec, was the production of a certain gentleman, whose name is given, and that the hon. gentleman was merely " the mouthpiece of another man's ideas ! "

" Vell, vot of it," as Jimmy Twitcher says in the play. To merely write a speech or sermon (I here desire to include the St. Paul Preacher) is a small matter. It is the *delivery* of either that tells. A mere writer is not to be compared with the speaker whose art is " listening Senates to command." Suppose the rev. gentleman in St. Paul's used other people's property as his sermon, so long as he was doing good, and no harm to the real author, is not such a man in the pulpit of far greater use than a dull, prosy preacher tiring everybody out even though his sermon may be full of brains ? The answer will be *dishonesty*—by appropriating the work of another as if it were your own, and not letting on to the congregation what you are doing.

There may be something in this, but the point I make is, as far as the people themselves are concerned, so long as good sound doctrine is preached in an attractive and telling manner, is it not better to ask no questions so long as you are receiving good from the preaching? But even taking the view of plagiarism, if history is to be relied on I have read of sermons having been written by lay-men hack writers as they were called, for the use of high dignitaries of the church, and for which they were but poorly compensated. If my memory serves me, I read of Johnston the great Lexicographer, earning many a pound by writing sermons. Nor did the ministers announce from the pulpit the names of their authors—this would be *infra dig.* But we come back to the starting point. It is the preacher or speaker who is entitled to all the credit for making good use of the material within his reach. In fact there is much more labour in memorizing a sermon or speech than in writing it for delivery.

Meeting Mr. Howe in the street one day, a gentleman visitor remarked to him—how very dull Halifax appeared to be—few people to be met with, while the stores and business places were quite idle. (No doubt the person so remarking had just come from some large bustling city, and noticed the great difference.) "O," replied Mr. Howe, "it may be dull just now—but you wouldn't say that if you saw some of our big funerals—then our streets are quite lively." But how changed

now is everything in regard to burials compared
with the olden time. Sixty-five or seventy years
ago a hearse was unknown in Halifax and I suppose all over Canada. The dead were carried to
the burial ground, sometimes a mile distant, upon
a bier, four men having it upon their shoulders—
no matter how heavy the weight, or warm or cold
the weather it was work that had to be done, and
the labor was immense. Over the coffin a black
velvet pall was thrown, with cords attached which
were held by the pall bearers ; the ministers and
physicians preceded the coffin. On one occasion I
was present at the funeral of a person who had
lived a long distance up town, and whose weight
was not less than 300 lbs. ; on this occasion the
coffin was placed upon three bars or long sticks, and
carried by twelve men—not upon the shoulders
but held directly in front of them at arm's length.
It was a long, wearisome, solemn journey, and the
day was hot withal. When the churchyard was
reached the difficulty of lowering the coffin into
the grave presented itself for the first time. The
usual means in such cases were here impracticable.
The lower end of the grave had to be dug out and
a long incline was made which extended some feet
outside—so that by this slanting process and
several rollers put down the coffin was finally
rolled into its last resting place. Outside coffins
or shells were seldom or never used—so that the
body found its level without any obstruction in its
passage.

The pall holders in those days—six in number—wore long crape scarfs looped up on one shoulder, and tied with a bow on the opposite side nearly touching the ground, while the hat band of the same material was fastened in the same way at the back of the hat and hung a foot or so down the back. For young persons the scarfs and hat bands were of white material. The mourners were also supplied by the friends of deceased with hat bands worn in the same way, the ends falling upon the back. It was customary for all the known friends to be invited—sometimes perhaps numbering 20, 30 and 40, and more. So that the more friends one had the more costly the funeral, as everyone invited was provided with the emblems of mourning including kid gloves. All this is now dispensed with ; and even pall bearers are not considered in most places as essential adjuncts to funerals, although still observed occasionally in some places. The coffins were usually made of pine wood, polished with lamp-black. Those who could well afford it had the wood covered with cloth, with trimmings or edgings of tin foil material, always on hand at the hardware stores, with breast-plate and handles of the same metal. What are now called *caskets* were unknown,—made of mahogany, rosewood, walnut, and other expensive materials. Nor were such things as coffins or other death accessories kept on hand by cabinet makers or undertakers, as at the present day. These had all to be made to order when wanted.

On assembling at the house of death the mourners and friends filling the rooms, sometimes to overflowing, were provided each with a glass of wine and a biscuit, which were always considered to be very acceptable, and perhaps in some cases this custom caused more mourners than were desirable. There were no flowers used on such occasions. This is a modern innovation. The presence of death, according to my judgment, was marked in a more becoming manner. At the present day we feel that we have not done our duty to the memory of our dearly beloved lost ones, unless we smother their bodies in flowers, and vie with one another in producing the most exquisite designs. Flowers may be considered, when used in this way by the pious and well meaning, as symbols of the resurrection, and I have no doubt it is all right enough—but it always seemed to me as a perversion of these beauties of nature, and I prefer to see death in its deathly form, according to the old ways, in sombre hue, in plain simplicity.

When the hearse was introduced, say 65 years ago, it was under great protest. Indeed, it was considered by many well meaning people a sacrilege to drag the bodies of their friends to the grave by horses. The clergymen, some of them at all events, went so far in their objections as to say that they for their part, would never walk before a horse at a funeral. It was, therefore, a long time before the town got reconciled to the hearse. Nor was it the custom for coaches to attend funerals, which now-a-days add considerably to the expense. But then the cemeteries were all in the towns and there was no need of them. Nor did the people place large elaborate monuments, or obelisks, and such like meretricious tokens over the bodies of their friends, as now, but contented themselves with plain headstones which told their grief just as well, and were as well recognized. Now there is rivalry in these things as in every other worldly thing no matter what the expense, or rather in my opinion the waste of money. Everybody wishes to be up to his neighbor, and we do not look in vain, although it is all vain, when in our cemeteries for such like fashionable observances. All right, however, to those who are of that way of thinking.

CHAPTER XXIV.

Lord Falkland's Pranks.—His Scribblers in the Press.—Howe's Fight with Falkland.—The Latter Shoots his Horses on the Common Before Leaving the Province.—The Johnstone Government Fast Sinking.—The Opposition Sticking Together.—Elections of 1847.—The Liberals Carry the Day.—New Brunswick Politics.—Mr. Howe as a Lecturer.—Railway Addresses.—Public Letters.—Appearance Before the House of Lords.

Resuming our direct subject. When the next session opened (in Lord Falkland's time) the old war of parties was resumed with more intensity than ever ; but the strength of the opposition was augmented by several abler men than it ever possessed before, such as James B. Uniacke, one of Howe's most formidable opponents and debaters, Wm. Young, and others. Lord Falkland, once so fair minded as was thought at the time, now identified and allied with the Tories, had made himself particularly obnoxious, not only by allowing his own *Royal Gazette* scribes to bitterly assail Howe in particular, but even had writers engaged to abuse him (so charged at the time) by communications in the New York *Albion*, then

the great English organ of Colonial Tory opinions,
and in short did his utmost in other ways to
humble Howe and give him his *coupe-de-grace*.
But foolish man, as he was, he was finally hoisted
by his own petard, and in a year or so afterwards
left the country like those other great mistakes—
Sir F. B. Head, Sir Colin Campbell, and at a much
later date Governor Gordon, of New Brunswick—
failures of the most pronounced type.

Under these repeated provocations Mr. Howe
again donned his war armour, and with more vigor
and abilities than ever measured weapons not only
with Attorney General Johnstone and his followers who stood as targets for his shots upon the
floors of the House day after day, and receiving
heavy shots in return ; but with the Governor
himself, who had by his own volition become a
conspicuous figure, and not only showed himself a
prejudiced partizan, but full of personal spite and
revenge, and thus fairly left himself open to all
that could be said about him. Having violated
the rules " which doth hedge a King," and by the
observance of which the King " can do no wrong,"
and descended from his high position and become
a political wrangler, he must now take the consequences of his fool-hardiness. This, then, was
Lord Falkland's case in 1845, when Howe took
him in hand to show him that although a lord by
birth, he was only a parvenue by nature. Volley
after volley had been fired at Howe by the Governor's organ, published by the Queen's Printer in

the official *Gazette* Office, when Howe took up the
cudgels not only upon the floors of the House but
in his old powerful newspaper the *Novascotian*,
now in other hands. Soon Falkland became the
butt of the whole town, from the published pas-
quinades and squibs of the Press under Howe's
control. The poem called "The Tale of the
Shirt," after the style of Hood, was especially
amusing, in which his Lordship was lampooned in
the most witty manner, and for having written
which Howe was taken bitterly to task in the
House by Attorney General Johnstone; Howe
turned the tables upon his opponents, Lord Falkland in particular, so that the whole scene was
like that of a play house—everybody laughed
and applauded, gallery included, notwithstanding
the Sergeant-at-Arms was ubiquitous, crying out
"Order" in all parts of the House, when Howe
took the floor. Said the chief actor and culprit,
"had I stated that his Lordship did not wear a
shirt at all—or that his shirt stuck to him when
he attempted to rise, the Hon. Attorney General
might feel justly indignant. But I cannot
imagine how the mere mention that his Lordship
wore a shirt like a mere plebian, although he had
no pants on at the time the poem was written,
and that he was not made up of mere frills and
collars—then, Mr. Speaker, I acknowledge that I
would be justly amenable, not only to the censure
of this House, but to the laws of outraged decency
as well."

In fact his Lordship scratched a Russian and aroused a Tartar ; and until the day he left the Province for *good*, he was not spared the lampoons and criticisms of the gentleman he attempted to destroy. When a Lieutenant Governor demeans himself and his high office, by " rushing in where angels fear to tread," he becomes the author of his own condemnation, and this gentleman, constitutionally speaking, richly deserved all that he received. A few days before leaving Halifax for England Falkland had his carriage horses, splendid animals, some three or four in number, sent out to the Commons and shot by some half a dozen soldiers engaged for the purpose, and this barbarity was committed in order that the horses should not fall into plebian hands—and so he put them out of the way. This shows the manner of man that he was. His wife having died in England, he subsequently married the Dowager Duchess of St. Albans. I believe that his Lordship is now dead.

But the warfare still continued in the House—the Government had a majority of three to keep their heads above water, so that matters were whittling down pretty finely. Attorney General Johnstone was the great Falkland leader and defender ; and although James B. Uniacke acted as leader of the Opposition, for prudential reasons, it was only nominal, for Howe was virtually the leader, as everybody knew at the time. With Howe it was *aut Cæsar aut nullus*. The Liberals were now gaining in strength every day, not in the Legislature, but in the country. Herbert Huntington of Yarmouth was a very able man on the Liberal side, and his influence was immense in all the Western Counties. At length the Government finding that their craft was sinking under them, made overtures to the leader of the Opposition—viz : that he (Uniacke) and several other gentlemen should come over and join them, *but not to include Mr. Howe.* Their object was to break up the party and at the same time destroy Howe, while the bait or olive branch held out was so many fat offices. Howe expressed a willingness to the arrangement, rather than be considered as an obstructive to a better system of fair play in government management. He felt that whatever patched-up arrangement might now be made, every thing would come right at the ensuing elections. Uniacke's reply—after consulting with his leading political friends—was in substance an emphatic " No ! As we have contended together in man fashion for principles which we think to be for the good of the country, none more so than Mr. Joseph Howe—we cannot think of such a thing as laying down our arms at this time of day and going over to your camp—but under any circumstances we shall never abandon Mr. Howe." This was the substance of the answer given.

But now came the day for a final settlement of old scores between the parties. The general elections which were held in 1847, gave the Liberals a large majority in almost every County of the Province. This was the final victory, the consummation of a struggle which had been going on bitterly since 1836, when Howe first entered the House—for it meant party government at the hands of the people—it meant a surrender of all government power by the Tories, and more than all the surrender of the departmental offices, with very large salaries attached to each, but which have been since considerably curtailed.

And this success did not only mean Party Government, but it meant RESPONSIBLE GOVERNMENT in its purity, to be conducted thenceforward precisely as it was in England. It was well understood, for some time past, that thereafter the parties in office must retire as soon as the majority in the next new House should declare a want of confidence in the Government. Until now, while backed as they were by the Governor and Council, the old party were safe; but all this was to be changed on the working out of the principles laid down in Lord Durham's Report, and which the British Government had recommended and declared through despatches should be the political guiding rule of faith, when the fitting opportunity should arrive. It had now arrived?

On the assembling of Parliament the Conservatives had to pack their trunks and move out, when the Liberals stepped in and took possession of their departmental offices—Mr. Uniacke as Attorney General, Mr. Howe as Provincial Secretary, and so on.

As before remarked, the Liberals of New Brunswick held together in a compact body, but in quite a minority several years, when their ranks were diminished by the secession of Messrs. Wilmot, Fisher and Hill. The bait held out (1845) was the Attorney Generalship, which the former gentleman had accepted, hook and all—which meant its hard conditions—viz : paralyzing their old *confreres* in opposition, and keeping the advancement of the party back for several years. And no doubt considering it was all for the best, the other two gentlemen went with Mr. Wilmot to keep him company, obtaining the usual prefix to their names. The Liberal Press at the time (or rather what there was of such an institution) denounced the movement with some ascerbity especially since the coalition in Nova Scotia before this had collapsed into a calamity—a smash up, politically, leaving more than a wreck behind, even the restoration of the old party to power and stronger than ever. So it turned out in New Brunswick. As soon as the Chief Justiceship became vacant on the death of Mr. Chipman, the Governor, Sir Edwin Head, with a head almost as hard as that of his cousin, Sir F. B. Head, but of more mental weight, overlooked his Attorney General (to whom the office was justly due, according to responsible government, which our Tory friends *pretended* to recognize at the time) and appointed Judge Carter to the vacancy, and then very reluctantly offered Wilmot a Judgeship, which he accepted, for the opportunity might not again present itself very soon ; besides the Governor's power remained unbroken, and the advice of his advisers went no further with him than it did on any former occasion. Then the office vacated by the Attorney General was handed over to an outsider, Mr. John Ambrose Street, instead of offering it to Mr. Fisher who was the next entitled to it in the order of promotion ; and this was done that the Tory element in the Government might remain intact and without diminution of strength. This was too flagrant a breach in the understanding that both parties should be fairly treated by the Governor, and so Messrs. Fisher and Hill *struck* and came forth out of the fiery furnace, to commence again *de novo* as Liberal agitators.

After several drawbacks through the arrogance of Governors and want of foresight and stability among the constituencies themselves, Responsible Government became a " fixture" in New Brunswick —1855 — when the *first Party* (Liberal Party) Government was formed, or eight years after Nova Scotia had been in full possession. And yet some of the small wheels in the new concern have from time to time become clogged for want of the right lubricating oil to allow of the machinery running smoothly, when the Chief Engineers (former Lieutenant Governors) have taken it into their heads to run the engine upon the high pressure principle, at a faster speed than the Constitution required—for example, when Mr. Manners-Sutton (in 1856) objected to the Prohibitory Liquor Law; and again when Governor Gordon played antics on the Confederation issue in 1866. But those are subjects that may be presented more fully in detail at some future time.

Having now obtained full power in the Government of Nova Scotia the Liberals set to work in right good earnest, not only to reform old abuses but to work out Responsible Government in a truly British way, by introducing new measures for the benefit of the Province, and standing or falling by them—such as giving to the Town of Halifax an Act of Incorporation and doing away with the old Magisterial body as a governing power—Opening the outlying Ports of the Province and making them free as shipping ports—Dividing the Executive and Legislative Councils and throwing open the doors of the latter to the public, and a number of other important measures of which the people of Nova Scotia are to-day in the full enjoyment.

As it was not the original design of the writer of these Memoirs to do more than refer to such matters and incidents in Mr. Howe's career as crossed his mind from time to time, it is deemed inexpedient to follow Mr. Howe in his political course since the formation of the first party government in 1847-8. To do so, even to take up the salient points, would fill several volumes—for all his principal political work really commenced after that year and lasted for ten or fifteen years longer, during all of which time Mr. Howe continued to be a *power* in the Legislature, in the Government, and throughout the Province.*

Mr. Howe's services in other fields of literature outside of the Legislature have not been more than alluded to—such as his Letters to Lord John Russell on the reorganization of the Empire—his Railway speeches in England, when the Halifax and Quebec Railway project was mooted—his appearance and the impression he made before a Committee of the House of Lords, on Colonial subjects—and also at the Colonial Office and before Earl Grey—his Letters to Sir Francis Hincks—to Mr. Charles Archibald—to Lord Falkland—his numerous missions to England and to the United States—his services as Fishery Commissioner between England and the United States—his correspondence with Sir John Harvey, Lieut. Governor, who died and was buried at Fort Massey Cemetery, (Halifax) following his wife, who passed away a few months earlier—his many lectures before Mechanics' Institutes and learned bodies — his great Trade Speech at Detroit, U. S., &c., &c. Indeed the labors of Mr. Howe were incessant from

---

*Still, even after this period, 1847, I do not fail to note any incident of minor importance that may have occurred in Mr. Howe's career likely to meet with popular acceptance—so that this book is complete in itself as far as the aim and object are concerned.

the day of his Libel trial until his death, thus proving that he was a man of great physical endurance as well as vast intellect, and all devoted to the interests of his country.

CHAPTER XXV.

The Old Liberal Party in a Minority.—Attack Upon Hon. James B. Uniacke and Mr. Howe's Able Defence.—Meeting of P. E. Island Delegates for a Maritime Union.—Its Failure.—Canadian Politicians with Other Plans.—Ministers of State and " Lords." — Titles. — Confederation Carried. —Bad Treatment of Nova Scotia.—Hon. Mr. Laurier's Opinion of Said Treatment.

The latter years of Mr. Howe's life are not altogether unfamiliar to the present generation—nor do they contain enough of interesting incident, suitable to the popular taste, to extend this work much more at length ; and yet one of the most trying episodes in this remarkable man's political career requires to be considered.

When Mr. Howe retired in 1863 from the Legislature—at the very height of his popularity—it was to assume other duties, having been appointed the year before by Her Majesty's Government—(in succession to Moses H. Perley, Esq., of St. John, who died on the shores of Labrador while in the discharge of his duties) as Imperial Fishery Commissioner—at the time the " Reciprocity" negotiations were in progress, which treaty. was abrogated in 1866 by the Americans. The Liberal Government in 1863 was in a minority, and Mr. Johnstone was Attorney General and Dr. Tupper Provincial Secretary. All the old members of the House—like Young, Doyle, Wilkins, Uniacke, Huntington, Stewart—had disappeared from the scene of former conflict, and Howe stood alone, as it were, like an ancient oak shorn of its living branches. And then there was quite a falling off in the mental calibre of the succeeding composition, although it contained some men above mediocrity who could talk well, if not soundly, and were not always responsible for the correctness of their utterances—such as those at a subsequent period, who, without scruple, handed over their country to the tender embraces of their neighbours—without " by your leave"--all of which will be explained presently. Nor were the men who composed the Government at that day strictly in line with the old reformers, but rather belonged to a school of their own, more ambitious for their own welfare than for the interests of their constituents—for at an earlier period, I read that the Provincial Secretary (Dr. Tupper) with another of his colleagues bore down heavily upon the memory of Hon. James B. Uniacke, Mr. Howe's close, bosom, political companion—for reasons which do not appear—and who at that time was upon the verge of the grave —when Mr. Howe turned upon his assailants and in defence of his friend delivered one of the most eloquent, scathing and severe philippics upon the heads of his traducers ever heard, it was said, in any legislative body—and from this I make a single extract :

" What shall I say of such foul birds as the Pro-
" vincial Secretary and the honorable member for
" Victoria, who have settled upon the reputation
" of my departed friend, even while his great heart
" was breaking and his noble spirit was winging
" its upward flight ? What need be said ? We
" all knew him and we know them. A serpent
" may crawl over the statute of Apollo, but the
" beautiful proportions of the marble will yet be
" seen beneath the slime."

In 1855 Members of the Governments of Nova Scotia, New Brunswick and P. E. Island met in Charlottetown for the purpose of working up a scheme for a union of the Maritime Provinces—a subject that had long been talked of, and to which the meeting of those gentlemen gave a practical bearing. No one for years doubted the feasibility of bringing about such an arrangement, and everybody seemed to be in favor of it. Had there been difficulties in the way, of an insurmountable nature, some of the critics of the day would not have been slow to discover and expose them. True, certain minor objections were suggested, such as the location of the seat of government, the tariff, &c., but all small in themselves, and not worth contending about.

As soon as the Canadians heard of this convention a happy thought struck their leading politicians, none other than to make a sudden descent upon the Maritimers and take the wind out of their sails, by getting them to make common cause with themselves and embrace all the Provinces into the one congeries. They "came—they saw—they conquered." The delegates from above were (as near as I can remember) Sir George E. Cartier, Sir John A. Macdonald, Sir Edward Galt, George Brown. It did not take these gentry long to convince our folks of the grandeur of their conception and the great possibilities that awaited all parties officially. Instead of being mere honorables in their respective Executive Councils, they would become Ministers of State, while our Legislative Councillors would be turned into Senators and men of great National importance—a back ground imitation of the House of Lords. It did not require much coaxing to bring our folks into line, especially our own Nova Scotia Representatives, one in particular, whose mental vision sometimes ran in the direction of an acute angle, and somewhat interfered with the ethical considerations of a political question. But certainly our Maritime delegates returned home with their views enlarged as to the future, and announced that there were so many difficulties in the way of a Maritime union that they were obliged to give it up! Like the King of France with his army, who went forth to do great things —he marched up the hill and then marched down again.

It was considered very questionable at the time whether the people above would have thought of us at all, had it not been for their own legislative complications. Parties were so evenly balanced— the French of Lower Canada and the English of Upper Canada—that often for days and weeks at a time there would be a dead-lock and all business brought to a stand still. It was Nationality and religion on the one hand, and Orangeism and political conservation on the other, which continually clashed and blocked the way ; and, therefore, if only the Lower Provinces could be worked into the lump it would be soon leavened and legislation thenceforward would flow on smoothly ? This then was the animating cause of our big sisters above visiting Charlottetown and patronizingly taking us by the hand and smothering our delegates with official kisses. And so it all turned out agreeably to the programme and promises made—our Executive Councillors were transformed into Ministers of State and our Legislative Councillors into " Lords," after a pattern ! More than this, our democratic view of things on this side of the water was next to be subjected to an unusual strain, by the introduction of titles, such as had always and only been reserved and dispensed by the sovereign for great services rendered to the Empire at large, whether in the field, in science, discovery, or some distinguished performance deserving of special recognition and reward. Since the union, knighthood, like the Nova Scotia

Baronetage of old, has become one of our inflated institutions ; and if we keep on in this way Knights will soon become as common as German Counts— for in Germany it is said 30 per cent. of the population are supposed to be thus stilted—or like the Magistracy of New Brunswick where every tenth man is deputed to be a Justice of the Peace, without reference to his chirographic handiwork, or acquaintanceship with Thomas Dilworth or Lindley Murray.

Having agreed among themselves at Charlottetown for this Confederation and the terms thereof, the delegates next conferred with the English Government with a view of obtaining its countenance and support, which were as easily to be had as Canada united would save an immense deal of labour to the Colonial office, for thenceforward, instead of dealing with half a dozen Provinces, the one Government and Governor, would only require attention. Accordingly what is called the " North America Act" was passed through the Imperial Parliament, and soon afterwards put into working order.

When the question for acceptance or rejection of " Confederation" was submitted to the people of New Brunswick, in 1865, it was defeated by an overwhelming majority, but in a year or so afterwards it was accepted by about the same majority, reversed—such a turn of the screw in a single year had never been known in any country, which showed that the Confederates had not allowed the grass to grow under their feet during the interval, while the Lieut. Governor (Gordon) was obliged by the English Government to make a meal of his own convictions (for he had all along showed himself hostile to the movement) and in swallowing them had to do all he could in his power on the opposite side, and have Confederation carried in New Brunswick, whether or not. Then again about this time the Fenians from the United States made a raid upon the New Brunswick borders with a view to a conquest, and this created a political diversion. The gallant Militia of that Province, however, met the enemy and drove them back ; but the Fenians helped to carry Confederation just the same, and they should not be overlooked on that account. The dire necessity for a union after that was not to be blinked out of sight. To be always prepared for such an emergency was an idea that took with the groundlings, and so to be loyal to the crown and save the country many of them changed their opinions and their votes. Confederation in New Brunswick was, however, accepted by the people of their own free will.

And now with regard to Nova Scotia. The air about this time was filled with strange sounds (Mr. Howe, the " father of his country," was absent on his fishery business)—loud mutterings by the people were heard on all sides, with singular unanimity against Confederation, even upon any terms ; but when it came to be known that it was already a settled thing and to be carried, through the audacity and machinations of certain unscrupulous Politicians, the temper of the inhabitants was aroused to fever heat. But let the people rage as they pleased, the deed was done—it was a foregone conclusion, and Nova Scotia was *forced* to submit.

This is the way it was done.—In the session of 1866 a resolution was moved in the Nova Scotia House (the Conservatives being in the majority) by Mr. William Miller (now in the Senate I believe) authorizing the appointment of a delegate to London to co-operate with those to be appointed by the other Provinces, in order to make arrangements with the British Government for the Confederation of the North American Provinces. The opposition to this resolution was led by Mr. Stewart Campbell, of Guysboro, who contended that it would be a gross outrage to pass such a resolution without first submitting the matter to the people at the polls as had been done in New Brunswick. But all of no use. The original motion was carried at half-past two in the morning and the people as it were put at defiance, in the solemn hours of darkness.

No such dastardly act was ever perpetrated upon a free people, except it might have been at the time of the union of the Irish and English Parliaments in 1800, and the attempt now being made (at this writing) to force Manitoba into a measure of which the people almost unanimously disapprove—and this is being done chiefly by the very same kind of man who coerced Nova Scotia in 1866. The leader of the opposition (Mr. Laurier) ventilated this subject pretty freely in the House of Commons in March last upon the Remedial Bill. It was no less an act of coercion of Nova Scotia than the attempt now being made towards Manitoba, with only this difference—while the Legislature of the former carried the Confederation Bill, the Legislature of the latter is in opposition to separate schools in any form, and the majority of the people is on the same side. The coercion in the former case (Nova Scotia) was the work of a base and brazen majority, regardless of the people —an act of " brute force," as Mr. Laurier called it. The coercion of the latter Province is threatened by an outside Legislature altogether. And yet the principle to be recognized in both cases are identical—differing only in form, but not in essence. It certainly required a bold and unscrupious man or men to " play such tricks before high heaven," as in the case of Nova Scotia, and the names of the perpetrators will forever be held in scornful remembrance.

What would have been the part of statesmanship (said the same gentleman) upon that occasion ? The part of statesmanship would have been to try and persuade the people of the grandeur of the idea, because they were a people eminently fitted to see the grandeur of such an idea—of Canadian Confederation. But such was not the course taken. Instead of applying himself to persuading his own fellow countrymen of the grandeur of this act of Confederation *he forced the project down the throats of the people of Nova Scotia by the brute force* of the majority of a moribund parliament, and the hon. gentleman must to-day bear the responsibility and the stigma that for a whole generation the great idea of Confederation was to the people of Nova Scotia synonymous with oppression and coercion.

CHAPTER XXVI.

Mr. Howe's Opposition to Confederation.—He is Delegated to Proceed to England.—He Goes and Lays the Complaint Before the Colonial Secretary. — Gets no Redress.—Returns to Halifax Broken Down in Spirit and in Health.—The Inhabitants Greatly Disappointed —No Inconsistency in Mr. Howe's Course.—Past and Present State of Things —Hon. Mr. Chamberlain's Speech on Imperial Federation.—Canadian Independence. —Why Mr. Howe Sought for Changes.—But Everything is Now Changed. — Too Much of Party at the Present Day.—Annexation to the United States Going On. — Mr. Howe on the Independence of Canada.—Mr. Howe as a Free Trader.

When Mr. Howe arrived upon the scene—to whom his countrymen had always looked for counsel, and to whom they were so greatly indebted for their political freedom—he naturally became indignant at the treachery of his old antagonist—of the very man who had so often crossed and annoyed him, (whatever Mr. Howe's proclivities might have been in the direction of Confederation of some kind,) and so he made common cause with his countrymen with a view of undoing, if possible, what had been so infamously perpetrated. The people of Halifax—certainly all the old Liberal party—three-fourths of the inhabitants—rallied around Mr. Howe, speeches were made and denunciation found expression upon the heads of those who had thus betrayed and surrendered them to the Canadians.

The conclusion finally arrived at was that Mr. Howe should proceed to England and lay the case before the British Government. But, alas, the mischief was completed; for when Mr. Howe on his arrival in England remonstrated with the Colonial Secretary and other members of the Government, he was answered in substance, " Mr. Howe, it is too late—the papers are signed—and the Act of Confederation will go into effect immediately— and you are requested to show no more opposition." The big heart of Joseph Howe was crushed by this answer, from which there was no appeal, and so he returned to Halifax a disappointed and broken down man. When his fellow citizens (the old Liberal party) met to receive the bitter announcement of his failure, it was like a funeral gathering and a most solemn day in Halifax, or like the conquest of the Province by a foreign enemy.

A short time after his arrival from England, I called upon Mr. Howe (the Hon. Mr. Randolph of Fredericton was with me) in a friendly way—he then resided in Dartmouth,—and he did not hesitate to freely express his opinions with regard to

the present and future prospects of his country
and the great wrong that had been perpetrated,—
the fire, however, no longer burned brightly in that
bosom, when he spoke of being forced to accept
the scheme—the absence of humour and anecdote
so common to Mr. Howe's nature was conspicuous.
He seemed to be transformed into the personifica-
tion of the strong man bowed down by a wasting
sickness; and I have no doubt that his years were
considerably abridged through the disappointments
of that the most trying event in his long political
life.   A man to have wielded supreme and healthy
power, as it were, over his countrymen for more
than a quarter of a century, to be jockeyed aside
by a man in whom Mr. Howe never had any faith,
and to see his country taken from under his feet,
was a terrible blow to Nova Scotia's greatest statesman and patriot, and he never after that was the
same man.

(Here I wish to pause for a few moments to
meet the charges of inconsistency preferred against
Mr. Howe's course in regard to Confederation.
The whirligig of time like the kalediscope, which
shows fresh prisms at every turn, brings about
many changes in a few years.   What would do
for to-day might not do for to-morrow.   Besides,
Mr. Howe, however great, was like some others
less gifted, not always successful in propounding
theories capable of being reduced to practice.
Saul among the Prophets was not always the
wisest.   Lord Durham in his famous Report sug-

gested a union of the North American Provinces
as a panacea for certain political ills, before referred to, and Mr. Howe had an inkling in the same
direction. But it is one thing to speak well of a
measure in the abstract, but altogether another to
deal with it in the concrete. I have no doubt that
Mr. Howe would have favoured Confederation in
1867, if he had been consulted on the subject, and
took an interest in the details; but to follow in the
footsteps of a man in whom he had no confidence,
was altogether against his nature, as well as
against the disposition of the people generally.

When his letters to Lord John Russell in 1846
were written, in which Mr. Howe suggested a closer
union between England and her Colonies, and for
the latter to be represented in the Imperial Parliament, "high protection" was the order of the day
—and the Colonists had a monopoly of trade in the
markets of the mother country—(our federationists wish to revive the principle to-day with their
"preferential trade" ideas)—the foreigner was kept
at bay to our great advantage, and England had a
similar monopoly in her Colonial markets. So
that had Mr. Howe's proposition been acceded to
in 1846, England, if disposed, had not to recede
one step to meet the case on commercial grounds.
How is it to-day? The ports of England are
thrown wide open to the whole world, and her
Colonies have to compete with the alien in the
sale of their products—not only so but by the
repeal of the Navigation Laws foreign vessels, to

our great disadvantage, may be built and sold in
her markets, and the whole of our coasting trade
is thrown open to the Americans, or any other
power, and so they have the whole of our North
American coast range—five thousand miles in extent, and fifty ports of entry—in which to ply
their trade and interfere with us, while the United
States denies the Colonies any such privileges !   If
it is to the interests of England to maintain this
unjust balance, as far as we are concerned, no one
can find fault—it is done in the interests of her
own people ; but when we see Colonists (mostly
on the Conservative side) trying hard to work
their way up hill with a view to induce the
mother country to come down in her tariff, in
order to meet certain new fangled and impracticable notions, yclept " consolidation of the Empire,"
it is enough to blanche the cheek of any high
spirited patriot *   Nor would Mr. Howe's representations in the Imperial Parliament at the time
have staved off any important measures the English people had set their hearts upon—for the
protests of our representatives would have been as
a mere whisper in the babel of six hundred English
tongues in the Imperial Parliament, the interests
of Colonists to the contrary notwithstanding.

---

*I discussed this subject of " Imperial Federation " at full
length in a Pamphlet three years ago, and perhaps exhaus-
tively ; and the last statesman-like utterances upon the subject
were semi-officially delivered in a late speech by the Hon. Mr.
Chamberlain, Colonial Secretary, wherein he shows, I think,
the impracticability of such a measure, although the diplomatic
utterances are well coated over with sugar. [See Appendix.]

But the advocates of Imperial Federation seem to take a deeper interest in this matter than the people of England,—at the same time unable to show in what way the Colonies are to be the gainers by such union. As remarked elsewhere INDEPENDENCE should weigh with such minds as the only possible change next in order, not that I consider it would be to the advantage of Canada, but otherwise—for independence would involve a far greater expense to maintain than we are now under, however great that is. But the independence of Canada must come in time according to precedent, the common nature of things, and the accretion of population. The Kingdom of Prussia had long been a Nation before 1806, when the population, overrun by Napoleon, was less than four millions—the population of the United States when her independence was declared, was only three millions—the same may be said separately of half a dozen European Principalities. So that Canada with its five millions to-day and the prospective millions fast coming along, according to Mr. Howe, and, of the old Confederate promises of twenty millions in twenty years, furnish almost absolute data that " cause and effect" are as applicable to Canada in this matter as to other countries. Do the federationists mean to say that a population of twenty millions, even twelve, can be kept on as a mere *Colony?*

While nobody wants such a change of policy the idea is nevertheless a strong buttress against the notion of " Imperial Federation," which is like asking the young lad, on the eve of manhood, in full growth and vigour, not only to remain on the old farm on which he had been brought up, but to work with his brothers and sisters, to dig and moil along as usual, while the old mother (Mrs. Bull) looks on and says " that's good children, but after all you have got to do as I say while you are with me—but at the same time you are at liberty to go off and set up in business for yourselves."

The notion of drawing the whole world together in a single tie of affection, and co operation—fifty Colonies divided by vast oceans, and having no sympathies in common, as regards trade or anything else, is so Utopian that the great wonder is that sensible men can entertain it for a moment! To compare the case with that of the United States, or the union of the German Principalities, is sheer nonsense—for in both cases there are no geographical divisional limitations—both are compact bodies like Norway and Sweden.

Then we are told that by Federation, the Empire consolidated, would be strengthened, even rendered impregnable. How?　Have not the Colonies always fought the battles of England on their own soil?　What more could Canada do if she sentimentally formed part of this grand " Federation," than she did on all former occasions when her soil was invaded, or the honour of the Crown threatened?　Did not the militia of Canada save Canada to England in the war of 1812?　Did not the volunteers of the lower Provinces as well as the upper, spring to arms on every such occasion ? During the Canadian rebellion in 1837, the Legislatures of Nova Scotia and New Brunswick voted all their revenues away, the former amounting to half a million, and the latter to four hundred thousand, to be called for if and when wanted. The same offers were made in the case of the North Western boundary difficulties in 1839. Why then talk of Colonial defence (as one of the great Federal planks) and thereby tacitly tell the people of England that the mother country alone fights for us, and that only by this visionary union can we be able to help her ? However, Mr. Chamberlain's last and great semi-official utterance upon this subject has given to the fad its *coup-de-grace* ; but even should Mr. Chamberlain wheel into line with the agitators, the people of England themselves will have something to say as the final court of appeal.

In 1846 Mr. Howe complained of the quality of the Governors sent out to the North American Provinces, mostly men appointed for their qualifications as soldiers in the field, or clerks in the great departments, or naval heroes; but seldom one of fitness to govern in the civil service of the Crown, as Governor, or with the least knowledge of what was due to Colonial ways and habits, or a free spirited people. In this Mr. Howe was correct, as any one may recall by brushing up his memory in reference to the Maritime Provinces.

But to-day this is all changed—we now make our own Governors, and when we do not like them, we have only ourselves to blame ; but it is my opinion that since we have had this privilege, we have had men placed over us who will compare favourably with even the best of " their illustrious predecessors."

Then, in 1846 many of our public offices, such as the Imperial Customs (and other offices named by Mr. Howe) were filled with English proteges. who had influence enough " at home " with influential friends to obtain for them such positions (for example as in the cases referred to in a former chapter when Messrs. Carter (Judge) and Powers (Crown Land Office, and Mr. Baillie) in New Brunswick were hoisted over the heads of the natives.) This is all changed in 1896. So that here again the cry for representation in the " Imperial Parliament " has lost another of its arguments.

Again, in 1846 Mr. Howe complained that Colonists had no chance to serve the Queen in her military service—or rather had no footing compared with the young scions of England, where commissions and promotions could only be had by purchase, and therefore our young men disposed to enter the army had no chance, for want of money and influence at the Horse Guards. In 1896 this is all changed—the system of purchase has been abolished, and merit alone gains the coveted position. Not only so, but our Colonial

Military Schools have the privilege of sending four cadets a year to join the "Royal Standard" of England free of charge.

Then, again, when in 1846, Mr. Howe addressed Lord John Russell for a voice in the Imperial Parliament, the honors of diplomatic appointments among Colonists, were never once thought of on either side of the Atlantic by men high in office. In 1896 this is also changed. We now send diplomats to Washington and to Paris, (and have we not a High Commissioner in London, although his duties have never yet been publicly defined ; for we certainly overlook him or think we have no need of his services, when our statesmen in Ottawa require to transact any special business in England, such as the raising of money, &c.) So that we are fast rising in the National scale of importance, and all this without representation in the Imperial Parliament !

In 1846 we were held so fast by England in leading strings, and our complaints so indifferently listened to at the Colonial Office, that any escape from this condition would have been preferable to the doubts and uncertainties by which we were surrounded ; and is it any wonder that a man with Mr. Howe's great capacity and talents should suggest some plan whereby Colonists might be placed upon a better footing, especially when he cast his eyes across the American border and saw how the same race of men, no better than we, enjoyed all the advantages of free men, and rose to become men of world-wide distinction? But this too is changed in 1896. We have now all that we require in the way of self-government. In fact we have too much of it—for the curse of party, and bad men and worse measures, promise to be our ultimate ruin, unless the intelligence and honesty of the land come to the rescue and teach men high in office, of whatever party, that public morality and private morality are synonymous terms.

But then if our friends copy Mr. Howe as an authority in one thing, he should be copied in others of equal importance.

Mr. Howe, in 1846 estimated that the population of Canada, would amount to fully 12,000,-000 by the end of this century, which has only four years to run—the prophets who brought about Confederation and the purchase of the great North West from the Hudson Bay Company, placed it at 20,000,000 in twenty years from the purchase—the time has long since lapsed, and here we are with 5,000,000 !—a small increase in twenty years—and our utmost endeavor is to hold on to what we have got. " Annexation" is going on piecemeal—our people are detailing themselves across the border every day, individually, or in family platoons. But with regard to Mr. Howe's opinions (as above stated) upon other great questions, if the reader will turn to page 189 (2nd volume of Mr. Howe's speeches and letters by Hon. Mr. Annand) he will see that the speech de-

livered in the Nova Scotia Legislature on "the
re-organization of the Empire," abounds in very
free and liberal expressions in regard to the independence of Canada, and that she is able and can
very well afford to go into business for herself.
He shows the natural advantages, the great re
sources, and the objects to be gained under a distinct nationality. But that he may be thoroughly
understood (and not by what is stated here) in all
his arguments, his speech must be read, as an extract or two would not be enough to represent him
correctly, but taking him in the abstract he certainly was not opposed to Canadian Independence,
even fifty years ago, under certain favouring circumstances.

Then with regard to his opinions in matters of
trade. He was an out-and-out free trader, a
follower of Huskisson, the great Palladium of
British justice towards the poor man in giving
him cheap food. In the course of a debate in the
House (see page 157, 2nd vol.) on Protection and
Free Trade, Mr. Howe remarked :

" Even were his arguments [referring to the
" previous speaker] sound, I represent Cumberland,
" and I ask myself if I am prepared to tax the
" farmers, lumberers, quarrymen, sawmen—com-
" peting, as they are obliged to, with all the world,
" —for the purpose of bolstering up certain
" artificial branches of industry, which cannot
" stand competition upon a fair and just basis?
" But the true reason why I am opposed to the

" imposition of the proposed duties is that I be-
" lieve they can stand on their own strength, while
" the fishermen and laborers would suffer. * * *
" I ask the hon. gentleman if he would increase
" the price of the articles they need, that a few
" manufacturers—who now live, some of them in
" affluence and splendour—may be better paid ?"

The same arguments are as applicable to-day
as they were when Mr. Howe spoke. Let his
utterances then be ranked among future quotations whenever the Imperial Federationists seek to
bring him into court, especially the National Policy
Protectionists !

CHAPTER XXVII.

The Closing Days of Mr. Howe's Active Life.—Indifference of Canada Above the Maritime Interests.—Still Ambitious for Public Life.—" Better Terms."—His Acceptance of the Situation.—His Countrymen Loud Against Him.—Runs an Election in the Dead of Winter and Succeeds.—His Introduction to the House of Commons.—Victory Inverted.—Mr. Howe Appointed Lieut. Governor.—His Death.—Concluding Remarks.—A Monument Proposed.

I now come to the closing chapters in this great man's eventful history. The afternoon of a life so brilliantly spent at its meridian, was now about to close somewhat in shadow. The evening of his days did not exhibit the rosy tints which fleck our summer horizon, while the great orb of day is sinking to rest. The shadows which crossed his path at this juncture, rendered his latter years very trying and even distressing. His old political friends who had always stood about him in a solid phalanx, now divided, and went into bitter opposition to him—presently to be explained.

We have seen how Confederation was *coerced* upon Nova Scotia ; and the reasons assigned by

the people for their objections to this union pure
and simple. I have already said that Confederation was instigated by Upper Canada from being
unable to maintain the balance of power with the
Lower Province in Legislative matters, and so to
overcome the obstacles they brought the Lower
Provinces in as a make-weight—more that than
from the pure love they had for the people by
the sea, or to strengthen the Empire in North
America.*

At this moment Mr. Howe was in the zenith
of his fame. His countrymen—his old political
friends to a man—saw that he was powerless to
right the great wrong that had been perpetrated
upon his country. He could do no more, and he
might then have folded his mantle about him, as
the great tribune of the people, and said :

> " I know myself now ; and I feel within me
> A peace above all earthly dignities,
> A still and quiet conscience."

Or with St. Paul he might have exclaimed : " I
have fought a good fight—I have finished my
course—I have kept the faith."

But the great soul of our subject, still having a
lingering ambition for public life, failed to measure the situation as his best friends did, and so he
committed himself to a course of action which in

----

*Instances might be cited of the indifference shown to our
interests even up to this day. especially in driving their Atlantic Steam Boat business through American Ports without regard to Maritime claims.

the long run did him an infinite amount of harm
and but very little good—in the estrangement of
old political friends,—in the turmoil through which
he had to pass, (at his advanced years)—in the
humiliating (in my humble opinion) circumstances
of his later surroundings—in the comparatively
insignificant position he held at Ottawa in the
Government, and among "statesmen," so called,
the chief of whom being a man of far inferior
mould and abilities to himself, and of such make
up as he had slain, politically, more than half a
dozen like him, in his own legislature during his
prime and palmy days. O. but this was sad !

Now, had Mr. Howe retired from active politics
at this time, no doubt his old political friends
would have stood beside him and up to the day of
his death. Even his former anti-responsible opponents had learned to respect and admire him for
his good and honest qualities, and that his former
politics after all had been a great service to the
country. As to the Governorship it would no
doubt have fallen to his lot had he not stirred a
finger, and by his retirement he would have been
saved all the drudgery through which he had to
pass, (costing him his life I may say,) while this
high reward (the Governorship) for long services
in his own Province, could not have been withheld
from him, if disposed to accept it at the hands of
his enemies !

Mr. Howe's first step towards making overtures
to the new Dominion Government—for terms of

 Life and Times of

capitulation as it seemed to me—was in the light
of a suppliant for " better terms" for the Province.
The insult had been given and the blow struck,
but there was a disposition here manifested to for-
give for a money consideration ! The Dominion
Government, seeing the opportunity as they thought,
of placating and reconciling Nova Scotia to the new
state of things, accepted the proposition, and accordingly Mr. Howe and Hon. Mr. McLellan, the
latter afterwards Governor of Nova Scotia, drew
up the necessary documents, embracing more
money in the way of annual subsidy, and so the
Province was thought to be all right after that—
but not so, for the old inhabitants are still cross,
altho' the present generation accept the situation
as all right—as our children have accepted Responsible Government, without knowing what it
cost their forefathers to obtain it.

Mr. Howe's next step was to obtain a constituency and enter Parliament. Hants was the
County which he chose for the trial. Here (1869)
Mr. Howe was met in opposition by Mr. Goudge, a
highly popular gentleman living in Windsor. The
election took place in the dead of winter, so that
to get about among the numerous constituents in
all parts, would be a serious undertaking for a
much younger man. Mr. Howe was about 67
at this time. The snow storms and drifts on
corduroy roads, sleeping in cold beds at night, and
speaking in public day after day in exposed
places, were all a terrible trial to him ; and when

he came out of the struggle barely victorious his
health was shattered—indeed the seeds of permanent disease and final dissolution, may be traced
to that election contest.

When Mr. Howe took his seat in the House of
Commons for the first time, he was, as is customary.
introduced to the Speaker, and his escort for that
purpose were two of his old Confederation opponents—a most remarkable and sorrowful spectacle. It was like the *capture* of the great Tribune
of Nova Scotia by two persons, to be laid upon the
altar of the new Dominion as an oblation for what
they considered to be the political sins of their
countrymen in their resistance to Confederation.
Here was victory inverted! Mr. Howe was taken
into the Government and appointed Secretary of
State. These were the honors, if such they can
be called, that awaited a heroic life, now drawing
to its close—after thirty years a leader of some of
the ablest men this country ever produced, now
allowing himself to become the follower of a man
(Sir John A. Macdonald) belonging to a school
whose politics had ever been at variance with his
own, and whose sympathies were *en rapport* with
those persons Howe battled against for so many
years of his prime! Alas, that such a man should
have lived to be the witness of his own fallen
greatness! He stood in that Assembly like a
majestic oak in the midst of a forest, denuded of
its foliage by the lightning's blast—or a Sampson
after being shorn of his locks by a Delilah—an

emasculated form and a taunt by his enemies—or
to use another similitude, he was like one who had
fallen from the Eiffel Tower, almost dead before
reaching the ground.

In 1873, Mr. Howe was made Lieut. Governor
of the Province he had so faithfully served ; but
his health was now so much shattered, that his
honors were but short lived, for he expired in a
few weeks after his appointment. He died (a
strong constitution suddenly broken down) at the
age of 69.

Mr. Howe's remains repose in the Camp Hill
Cemetery, and his wife and children rest within
the same iron enclosure. [See account of his
funeral in the Appendix.]

Thus, I have endeavored, though perhaps inadequately, to draw a living picture of the life of a
man who in his prime would have reflected lustre
upon any legislative body in the world. Considering the work he had given himself to do, commencing publicly at the early age of thirty, and
what he accomplished in the face of most formidable odds—at a time, too, when these Provinces
were sadly and unfairly governed, it must be admitted that Mr. Howe stands forth to-day on
record as the greatest man that British North
America has yet produced—if the term greatest
may be applied to one combining so many brilliant qualities. His abilities, his fearlessness, his
command of language, his sententiousness, his
speaking powers, his complete knowledge of men,

and his control (if the word may be allowed) of men—as a facile, trenchant writer, whether in prose or poetry (several volumes of his poems are in print)—his wonderful industry and aptitude, and on the whole the uses to which he devoted all these manifold natural gifts for the benefit of his country—I say considering all these things, no other public man, past or present, in British America, ever attained to the same political altitude as Joseph Howe; and it is doubtful if there will be one like him to come after. And then, *he died poor!* This implies more than can be written—for with all the opportunities he had for enriching himself, as other Nova Scotians have done, Mr. Howe would despoil a friend rather than touch unhallowed coin belonging to the State. He would not compound with his conscience and take advantage of his position to turn money into his own coffers, however excusable in certain cases, but rely altogether upon his salary for the allowance which the law made him. To connect such a man with what now-a-days is called " boodling "—in plain English, *stealing*—would have been an utter impossibility. " HOWE DIED POOR !" Let this be placed as a memento over the entrance door to the vault which covers his dust. He might have left his family rich had he been unscrupulous, or like some other politicians.

In private life, or among friends, Howe was a host indeed. He was full of life and humor and anecdote. No man ever laughed louder or en-

joyed the conventionalities of the dinner table
with greater zest than he. For him money had
no charms—it was come day go day ; while in public. (on the floors of the House and in his office,)
he was all accuracy and regularity ; and yet in
private in his own house, he took no heed of
system or domestic requirements—that is to say,
he would invite a friend to dine with him—the
same day—and yet cause no preparation to be
made at home for the occasion. He was hearty
in his friendship, trusty and steadfast. As a loyal
man in its real sense, and to British institutions, his
Sovereign never had a trustier Knight ; but then,
he was equally loyal to his country, to freedom
and the rights of man, whether political, religious
or social. There was no duplicity about him—
nor did he show the usual art and cunning of the
politician. If he made promises it was with the
intention of keeping them. Even a political opponent found favor in his sight—or rather he
would not step aside to throw a stumbling block
in his way, but rather aid him. In a word :   " He
was a *Man*, take him for all in all, we ne'er shall
look upon his like again."

MONUMENT TO MR. HOWE.

Four years ago, I suggested through the columns of St. John *Progress*, the following remarks, and I now repeat them, and am glad to find that a movement has been made in Halifax for the erection of such a monument to the memory of Nova Scotia's great benefactor :

The memory of great men is always perpetuated by their countrymen in monumental stone, or marble, or bronze. The Central Park in New York, for example, contains many such works of art, either in the way of statuary, or monolith, or mausoleum, or cenotaph—in short they are of every variety of expression, recalling the memories and performances of soldiers, patriots, poets and statesmen. But not alone Central Park—almost every public park or square, not only in American but European cities, contain one or more trophies to their great men. All these are the evidences of pride and gratitude and public spirit on the part of a people, for the services rendered to their country in whatever sphere, and who are unwilling that their benefactors shall pass out of notice or memory. Has not Joseph Howe done enough for his native Province, to render his name immortal in the hearts of a grateful people —yea as much so as any other man, dead or alive —*cæteris paribus*—in any city or country in the world, to whom monuments have been erected? It cannot be a mere matter of opinion as to the invaluable services rendered by Howe, not only to his native Province but to all British America as well. This is recognized and established beyond peradventure. Nor should a solitary mistake of a great life, stand in the way for a single moment, when placed in juxtaposition with the manifold acts and reforms which this able man so assiduously struggled for and brought about. I do not presume to suppose that a suggestion of mine would lead to anything being done in the way indicated. But I would express the hope that Halifax will some time in the early future see her way clear, to organize a movement, having for its object the raising not only of a Halifax, but a Provincial subscription, *that a Monument may be erected on the Grand Parade to the Memory of Joseph Howe, the great Patriot and Political Benefactor.* Shall it be said that while Canadians in the upper Provinces erect monuments to their public men far less gifted than Howe, we as Nova Scotians will continue dilatory and lukewarm in paying tribute to the memory of her most illustrious son? And thus I would have this Monu-

ment assume the attitude of Howe reclining in his
seat as he appeared in the House of Commons according to the portrait which appears at the beginning of this Book. This figure would repose
upon a base of granite, or Nova Scotia quartz, and
be placed upon the Grand Parade. The cost of the
whole work would fall very far short of the abilities
of the inhabitants of Nova Scotia to provide. A
similar monument to the model here indicated
stands upon one of the public squares in Baltimore, to the memory of George Peabody, the
philanthropist. The figure is seated in a reclining posture, and is admired by every one. I name
the Grand Parade as the site (not the Public
Gardens,) in order that his fellow-citizens may
have their great townsman continually before
them, in crossing to and fro this historic and interesting thoroughfare.

LAST ILLNESS OF HON. MR. HOWE.

It was a most remarkable coincidence that the death of two Dominion Lieut. Governors should have occurred within one month, respectively, after being sworn into office—viz: Lieut. Governor Howe, of Nova Scotia, and Lieut. Governor Boyd, of New Brunswick, cases only paralleled by the death of General Harrison, President of the United States, which took place in 1842. after being President just one month.

[I might state here that since I have undertaken this work, I have received many letters and much valuable information. from kind friends, directing my attention to circumstances and articles in connection with Mr. Howe's career, which information I take advantage of exclusively in the Appendix. To Martin Griffin, Esq., Ottawa, I am chiefly indebted for what follows in reference to Mr. Howe's last illness and death, taken from the Journals of the day. which Mr. G. has preserved and placed at my disposal :]

DEATH OF LIEUT. GOVERNOR HOWE.

[Halifax Morning Chronicle, June 2, 1873.]

" To-day man puts forth
The tender leaves of hope ; to-morrow blossoms,
And bears his blushing honors thick upon him :
The third day comes a frost—a killing frost,
And nips his root, and then he falls."

The death of the greatest Nova Scotian, Lieutenant Governor Howe, has painfully affected all classes of the community. For many years he had been the foremost figure in our history, the champion of the rights of colonists, and the triumphant enemy of veteran abuses in colonial government. His vigorous pen had made Great Britain acquainted with the wrongs which the system of irresponsible Government had inflicted upon us. His almost matchless oratory had awakened the people to a sense of their own dignity. There is scarcely one beneficial act in the code of laws affecting the American Colonies with which Joseph Howe's efforts are not in some way associated. Many of his rivals and friends were men of brilliant talents, and solid education, yet Joseph Howe contrived to lead them all, through the sheer force of genius. No British North American approached him in breadth of statesmanlike views—not one was his literary equal—not one could compare with him in favorably impressing a popular assembly. When more careful composition than that of extempore stump speeches was required of him he was not found wanting. His oration at the tercentenary of Shakespeare was absolutely

the best delivered on the occasion, although Great
Britain and America had selected their ablest men
to pronounce eulogiums on the poet, who still
holds the world enthralled. The address at Detroit, advocating the renewal of the Reciprocity
Treaty, is still remembered in the United States,
and as it were puts the capping stone to Mr.
Howe's fame.   *   *   *

To trace the life of the dead statesman accur-
ately would be to write the history of the Province for the half century just elapsed.   From 1827
until the day of his untimely death "Joe Howe"
has been the head and front of all great political
changes in Nova Scotia.

*   *   *   *   *   *   *

During his latter years the failure of his vigorous constitution, and, we say it tenderly now, the
decadence of his noble mind, had compelled him to
play a second part to those far beneath him in
virtue, in talent, and in reputation, is a melancholy
fact, and many have grown sad with the thought
that the foremost man of British America was not
its first minister.   The Tuppers and the Macdon-
alds forced themselves to the front—the old man
lagged behind—because his new associates lacked
generosity, and the weight of years had paralyzed
his strength.

*   *   *   Strongly as we regretted and resented
Mr. Howe's desertion of a party, whose principles
we believed just, we now would look with favor
upon any movement made by the Dominion Gov-

ernment to mark its appreciation of his services to
British North America. If Cartier dead is to be
honored, Howe dead should not be forgotten.

MR. HOWE'S ILLNESS AND DEATH.

The community was startled yesterday morning
by the announcement of the sudden death of the
Lieutenant Governor, Honorable Joseph Howe.
The news spread rapidly; flags were displayed
at half-mast on Government House, the various
Provincial and City buildings, some private houses,
the citadel, Her Majesty's ship, " Royal Alfred,"
and most of the merchant vessels of all nations in
port. The electric telegraph carried the news in
all directions, and soon the whole continent knew
that the foremost man in Nova Scotia—foremost
not only from the office he held, but from the
part that he had taken in the public affairs of the
Province for nearly half a century—was dead.

Mr. Howe, as is well known, had been in poor
health for several years. Nevertheless his death
was most sudden and unexpected. His disease—
if he had any disease other than a general breaking down of the constitution—is believed to have
been an affection of the liver. On his way from
Ottawa to Halifax to enter upon his duties as
Lieutenant Governor he stopped at Boston to con-
sult a physician. The one whose attendance he
desired was absent, but another eminent medical
man prescribed for him, and encouraged him to
believe that with rest and care he would recover

his health and strength. Since his arrival in Halifax, a little over three weeks ago, Mr. Howe, though by no means a well man, seemed to be improving. He continued to act under the advice of the Boston physician, and did not think it necessary so have any medical attendant here. During the recent fine weather he took frequent carriage drives with his relatives and appeared to be benefitted by them. He was last out on Thursday, when he extended his drive farther than usual, going as far as Deer's well known inn at Preston, ten miles from Dartmouth. When he returned he was a little fatigued, but otherwise was well.

On Friday he suffered all day—as he had often suffered before—from pain in the chest, which distressed him much and prevented him taking any rest. On Saturday the pain continued to trouble him. His wife and his son William (his Private Secretary) were continuously with him, and he would not allow them to leave him for a moment. Although he suffered much from the pain his condition was not such as to excite any alarm in the household. Unable to lay down to sleep or rest, he spent the night in his study, sometimes walking the room and sometimes sitting in his chair. About half-past four o'clock his wife and son urged him to go to his room and try to sleep. He said he would do so, and left the study. He entered his bedroom, but before he reached the bedside he staggered and fell. His son, who

was beside him, caught him and gently laid him
down. He retained consciousness and conversed
with his wife and son, telling them, in reply to
their questions, that he suffered much but they
could do nothing for him. Towards the last his
words seemed to indicate that he felt that his end
was at hand. In less than ten minutes from the
time he left his study, in the stillness of the Sabbath
morning, just as the sun was commencing to
throw its flood of light over the peaceful city, *his*
light went out and he entered upon his rest.
Joseph Howe, in his 69th year, was dead. So suddenly
did he pass away that there was no time to
summon physicians or friends, and only his wife and
son stood by his bedside.

His death, illustrating so forcibly the uncertainty
of life, was referred to in most of the churches
yesterday. In some instances the people received
the first news of the sad event from the preachers
at the morning service.

DEATH OF MR. HOWE.

[Halifax Evening Express, June 2, 1873.]

It did not occur to us that within two weeks
[after referring to the death of Sir George
Cartier] we should have the melancholy task
forced on us of writing for our readers the
obituary notice of Mr. Howe. Old, broken-down,
dying, as he seemed, he was yet so familiar to us,

his name was so incorporated with the politics of
the day and the history of the Province that his
death seemed a remote contingency ; it seemed as
if he must never die, but must always be Joseph
Howe, the man who in every household in the
country was familiarly known, and in every public matter had a hand, in every dispute a part, and
in every contest a species of candidature.

But the end has come for him. On Sunday
morning he yielded up his spirit. The grey head
that all men knew, that was carried erect to the
last, is low enough now. The busy, tireless hand
that performed so much labor as printer, journalist, politician, statesman, minister, is powerless.
The eloquent tongue is still. The eyes that spark-
led with so much of the light of humor and the
fire of genius are lustreless. And the ears that
for forty years or more had been so often filled
with the plaudits of thousands will soon be filled
with dust. Ere this is published the wires will
have carried to all the continent the news of his
death ; and all who are familiar with the events of
the past twenty-five years in the British Provinces,
will know that an able if not a great man is dead.
But it is in Nova Scotia that the sense of loss will
be most manifest and the grief greatest. The
news of his death will be known in the country
towns and will spread to the scattered villages ;
and everywhere there will be regretful and kindly
words spoken, mayhap manly tears shed, in
memory of Joseph Howe.

Those who followed him, perhaps against their
better judgments and for his own sake alone, will
find themselves justified now ; and those who opposed him while loving him will feel perhaps a
pang of regret that even with a patriotic purpose
they gave pain to the latter years of that once
popularly worshipped man. The farmers driving
along the country roads will stop to talk over his
life and tell anecdotes of his conflicts. The tiller
of the soil driving afield will have his mind full of
the strangeness that comes over one on hearing of
the death of a great familiar man. Those whose
threshold he has crossed and by whose fireside he
has made himself at home, will recall his humor,
his kindness, his sympathy, his winning ways, his
many stories that he told them as the night deep-
ened and the logs in the chimney grew dim towards the hour of retiring. We need hardly speak
of the regrets of those who during so many years
have been aided by him who never aided his own
very much, who have lived in positions in which
he placed them, and had a quietude in the public
service which he never had, till it came to him at
last, a premonition of the quietude of the grave.

The dates of Mr. Howe's official positions are
given in the statistical and biographical volumes
of the time. He was a member of the Assembly
from 1836. In 1840-41 he was Speaker. He
was Indian Commissioner from 1841-2. He was
Collector of Customs in 1842-3. He was Provincial Secretary from 1848 to 1854, when he assumed

the Chairmanship of the Railway Board. In 1855 he was defeated in Cumberland by Dr. Tupper, and remained out of Parliament till 1856, and in that year, having been elected for Hants on the elevation of Mr. Lewis M. Wilkins to the Bench, again took his seat in Parliament, under the leadership of Chief Justice Young. In 1857 the Hon. J. W. Johnston defeated the Liberal Administration, and Mr. Howe resigned the Chairmanship of the Railway Board. In 1860 Mr. Johnston's Administration was defeated, and Mr. Howe again accepted the Provincial Secretaryship, which office he held till 1863. In the election of 1863 Mr. Howe ran for Lunenburg, was defeated, and again thrown out of public life. On the death of Moses Perley, in the same year, he was appointed Fishery Commissioner by the Imperial Government, which position he filled up to the period of the abrogation of the Reciprocity Treaty. The political contests during the six years preceding Mr. Howe's defeat in Lunenburg, were very violent and hard ones.

* * * * * * *

It was at one of the earliest public meetings in Nova Scotia that he first declared himself by implication the leader of the anti-Union agitation. Dr. Tupper was speaking and, if we remember rightly now after six years nearly, was comparing the opposition to the Reciprocity treaty to the opposition to the Union, when Mr. Howe rose and amid a hush of breathless excitement contradicted

Dr. Tupper, and in a stern voice said that he had not opposed the treaty on its merits but because it had been negotiated by the British Ambassador "without a Nova Scotian at his side to give counsel or advice." [This is evidently in reference to the manner in which the Quebec (Confederation) scheme was conducted.]

JOSEPH HOWE—DEAD!

[Halifax British Colonist, June 3, 1873.]

No announcement more solemnly sad or startling could head this column. Joseph Howe, who for the past forty years filled so large a space in the eye of Nova Scotia, and who four weeks ago came among us to occupy the highest position which his country could bestow, has passed away forever!—It would be difficult to exaggerate the grief, the regret, the full-flooded sympathy, with which the sad tidings were heard on Sunday morning, as word passed with electric speed from lip to lip throughout all the city.—What shadows we are, and what shadows we pursue! Only a month ago Mr. Howe entered upon the well earned position of Governor of his native Province. He had reached the goal of his ambition, above the turmoil and the strife of party politics, surrounded by hosts of admiring and sympathising friends, with promise of leisure and repose, after a life of conflict, and toil, and many vicissitudes. And now he is suddenly called away ; he has fought his last battle, and he sleeps his last sleep.

Mr. Howe had reached the verge of the promised three score years and ten. His death, therefore, can hardly be called untimely. The years left their mark upon his countenance a quarter of a century ago. Well built, strong, sturdy, he was not a man to husband his health or strength. His stock was at one time so great that he considered it practically inexhaustible. He retained all his mental and physical vigor till about three years ago, when he was prostrated by a terribly severe and protracted illness, from which he never fully recovered. The contest in Hants in the spring of 1869 was what killed him. But the people of that noble county made all the compensation in their power by returning him to his place in Parliament last year without the trouble of a contest, or of one hour's personal canvass.

It was well understood by himself and his friends that his malady was such that his death might have occurred any day or hour within the past two years. Only an originally powerful constitution enabled him to fight off the great enemy so long. It is no secret that he was himself perfectly aware of the exceptionally frail tenure by which he held his life. Still he bore up manfully under the impending stroke ; and when death came it found him still in harness, doing his work like the brave, true man that he was. He was very ill when he left Ottawa towards the end of April.

When he reached Halifax his wan countenance told of his sufferings; and he was visibly weaker than we had ever seen him before. Still his eye had not lost the old lustre.—The grasp of his hand was as cordial and firm as ever, and his face still brightened into the old sweet smile. It was hoped that the bracing air of the seaside would renew his strength, and that he would at least have weathered our summer months. Last Thursday he drove some twenty miles over a rather rough road. He seemed to enjoy it well, but it was too much for his failing strength. On Saturday he was ill, but not much worse than usual. On Saturday night he was restless and ill, but still kept up a cheerful heart. About four o'clock on Sunday morning he became much worse, and complained of loss of sight. At Mrs. Howe's request he moved from the library to his bedroom. While walking these few steps his strength gave way, and after a short struggle with pain, he passed away to his rest. He died in the arms of his son and his wife, there having been no time to summon any other friends. He was in full possession of his faculties till the last, and was able to give a most graphic and deeply affecting account of the pain he was enduring.

The bright morning sun rose on the city on the first Sabbath of June to find signs of mourning and sorrow everywhere, from Government House to the humblest home that the news reached. Flags drooped at half-staff on the Citadel and all the public buildings, and half-mast on the shipping. Earnest prayers were offered up in the Churches for the bereaved widow and family, and touching allusions were made to the departed Governor.

THE DEATH OF MR. HOWE.

[From the Halifax Citizen, June 3, 1873.]

The community was shocked on Sunday morning by the intelligence of the death at an early hour, of the Lieutenant Governor, Hon. Joseph Howe. So sudden was the event, and so unlooked for, that many persons could not believe it, but the melancholy fact was only too true.

Mr. Howe had been in ill health for some time, but nothing to justify the belief that he might not live for some years, though it was well known that his once vigorous constitution was shattered. He had been daily in the habit, since his arrival here, about three weeks ago, of driving out in company with Mrs. Howe, and seemed to derive benefit from the exercise. On Thursday last he drove as far as Preston, and appeared none the worse, though a little fatigued. On Friday, however, a pain in his chest, from which he had suffered for a long time, again attacked him, and became so violent that he could not rest. The principal portion of Friday, Friday night and Saturday was spent in his study, sometimes reclining on a sofa, sitting in his chair, or walking about the room.—About half-past four on Sunday morning, at the solicitation of Mrs. Howe, he left his study to go to his bedroom and endeavor to gain a little rest, but ere he reached the bedside, the exhausted powers of nature would no longer sustain him, and he staggered and would have fallen had not his son William caught and gently laid him down. He still retained consciousness, but in less than ten minutes from the time of leaving his study, the soul of JOSEPH HOWE had passed away. He was in his 69th year. The sad event was so sudden and unexpected that there was no time to summon friends or physicians, and his wife and son were his sole companions.

When the sad news became known, a universal feeling of regret and sorrow prevailed. Flags were hoisted at half-mast all over the city, and on most of the shipping in the harbor.

> " Ashes to ashes, dust to dust.
> He is gone who seemed so great,
> Gone, but nothing can bereave him
> Of the force he made his own
> Being here, and we believe him
> Something far advanced in State,
> And that he wears a truer crown
> Than any wreath that man can weave him.
> Speak no more of his renown
> Lay your earthly fancies down.
> In the vast Cathedral leave him
> God accept him, Christ receive him."

HON. MR. HOWE'S FUNERAL.

[Chronicle June 5, 1873.]

"The remains of the late Hon. Joseph Howe, Lieut. Governor of Nova Scotia, were interred in the Camp Hill Cemetery, yesterday afternoon.

"The citizens generally acted on the request of the City Council in closing their places of business during the funeral hours. In fact, there was scarcely any business done during the afternoon. Public and private buildings were closed and flags hoisted at half-mast throughout the City and on the vessels in port. From all parts of the City, men, women and children gathered at Government House and along the route of the procession to witness the obsequies. For two days there had been a constant stream of visitors at Government House to see the body of the dead Governor; and now, as the time approached when the coffin must be closed, and all that remained of "Joe Howe" must be committed to the ground, the stream increased, hundreds pouring in to take a last look at the features of the dead statesman. The corpse lay in the large room in the north wing of the building. It was enclosed in a coffin of polished mahogany, richly mounted with silver. The plate on the cover bore the simple inscription :

JOSEPH HOWE,

Died June 1st, 1873.

Aged 68 years.

" Among the visitors were some who had not seen Mr. Howe for years, and these could not help re-marking how unlike the Howe they knew and loved in his prime were the emaciated form and careworn features of the dead ; but to such as had seen him in his last days, and observed the effects produced on him by age and anxieties, the features appeared natural and had an air of calm repose. The hands of loving friends had strewn the corpse with choicest flowers. To one bouquet was attached a card bearing the initials of the donor and a passage from Mr. Howe's well-known poem "Our Fathers :"

> Not here ? Oh, yes, our hearts their presence feel,
> Viewless, not voiceless ; from the deepest shells
> On memory's shore, harmonious echoes steal ;
> And names, which, in the days gone by, were spells,
> And blest with their soft music * * * *

* * * If fitly you'd aspire,
Honor the dead, and let the sounding lyre
Recount their virtues in their vestal hours;
Gather their ashes, higher still and higher,
Nourish the patriot flame that history dow'rs,
And o'er the old men's graves go strew your choicest flowers.

"Relatives, whose tearful faces showed the sorrow they felt for one who was near and dear to them, moved softly about the room. Old men and women, youths and maidens, and young children passed through silently, and dropped tears as they gazed for the last time on the face of Howe. Outside the building, on the grounds of the Pleasant street front, was a scene in which gaiety and solemnity were combined. The solemn-looking hearse stood at the door waiting for its burden. Around it gathered the officers of Her Majesty's army, whose uniforms of scarlet and decorations and trimmings of white and gold flashing in the sunlight, had additional brilliancy from the contrast with the sombre black of the civilians standing by; the officers of the navy in uniforms of dark blue with gold trimmings; officers of the local militia forces in brilliant dress; members of the masonic fraternity wearing the beautiful aprons, badges and jewels of their mystic order, and some of them surpassing in richness of appearance the brilliant costumes of the military; members of the national societies with badges covered with crape; and private citizens in plain funereal garb of black, the whole forming an imposing scene seldom witnessed at the funeral of an untitled civilian.

" Meanwhile the men of the army and navy (for whose presence the community are entitled to the kindness of General Haly and Admiral Fanshawe) and the local volunteer forces, had been drawn up in open line along the route of the procession. First, at Government House and stretching southward, were the blue-jackets from Her Majesty's ships of war, then the 87th Royal Irish Fusiliers, the 60th Rifles, the Royal Engineers, the Royal Artillery, the Halifax Field Battery, the Halifax Garrison Artillery, the 66th Halifax Volunteer Battalion of Infantry, the 63rd Halifax Volunteer Battalion of Rifles—the whole lining both streets along the route, which was from Government House, through Pleasant, Morris and South Park streets, Spring Garden street to Camp Hill Cemetery.

" A few minutes before 4 o'clock a short service was conducted in an upper room of Government House by the officiating minister, Rev. J. K. Smith, pastor of the Fort Massey Presbyterian church. At this only the relatives and immediate personal friends of the deceased were present. This over, the relatives and friends took a last look at the remains, the coffin was closed and removed to the hearse, the minute guns began to peal from the saluting battery at the citadel, and Colonel Laurie and Mr. Stairs commenced the arrangements of the funeral procession. The various bodies and the citizens were formed in fours (abreast) and took up their stations in the following order :

Division of City Police under a Sergeant.
Officiating Ministers.

PALL BEARERS.		PALL BEARERS,
Sir W. Young,	THE BODY.	Colonel Luard,
Sir Edward Kenny,	Drawn in a hearse.	Captain Courtenay,
Dr. Almon, M. P.,		Col. Bremner.

Members of Family.
Relatives.
Invited Mourners.
Members Executive Government of Nova Scotia.
Admiral and Staff.
General and Staff.
Senators.
Judges of the Supreme Court.
Members of the House of Commons.
Legislative Councillors.
Members of the House of Assembly.
Mayor and Recorder.
Aldermen of the City.
Civic Officials.
Custos and County Stipendiary Magistrate.
Justices of the Peace.
Warden and Councillors of Dartmouth.
Officers of H. M. Navy.
Officers of H. M. Army.
Officers of Militia.
Private Friends of Deceased.
North British Society.
Charitable Irish Society.
St. George's Society.
Germania Society.
Citizens.
Officers and Members of the Grand Lodge of Freemasons
Carriages.

" All being in readiness the signal to start was given and the procession moved off. " Not a drum was heard, not a funeral note." Bands of

GRAVE OF HON. JOSEPH HOWE IN CAMP HILL CEMETERY.

music were there, but their instruments were en-
cased in crape, the directors of the arrangements
having decided to have no music. The streets
through which the procession passed and the
houses along the route were crowded with spectators. The people with one accord turned out to
attend the funeral or to see it, and the solemn
mein of all made the demonstration a most impressive one. A little before 5 o'clock the cortege
reached the cemetery. Only a small portion entered, as the services at the grave, conducted by
Rev. Mr. Smith, were very brief and had ended
while yet the larger part of the procession was
approaching the cemetery. All that was mortal
of Joseph Howe was laid in the earth, and the
thousands who had assembled to perform the last
sad duty turned from the solemn city of the dead
to the mourning city of the living.

"The funeral was, without doubt, the largest that
was ever witnessed in the city of Halifax. The
only one that at all approached it was that of
Lieutenant Governor Sir John Harvey, twenty
years ago, which was largely a military affair."
The cut here presented is a true representation of
Mr. Howe's last resting place.

APPENDIX.

THE WELSFORD AND PARKER MONUMENT.

(British Colonist, July 19th, 1860.)

On Tuesday last the people of Halifax and its visitors were witnesses of a scene which, we think, will live long in their memory. It was not so much that upon that day a certain ceremony was performed—for deep is the interest of Nova Scotians in the fate and history of their fellow-countrymen, the mere fact of funeral honors being paid to their dead would not evoke any extraordinary interest. But the peculiar charm of the proceedings of Tuesday last consisted in the fact that this is the first time that Nova Scotia has shown herself really alive to the characters of her children. Hitherto she has been content to see the skill or valor of her sons mingled with and most probably forgotten in the glories of the Empire. Old England has won this battle or achieved that significant triumph in scientific research—and among the warriors or philosophers there may have been a Nova Scotian whose name, if mentioned at all, has been either not noticed or soon forgotten. It was not till the Crimean War broke out, and the news was brought us that among the heroes who distinguished themselves, our countrymen were first among the first in the wearisome labor of the trenches or the fiery onslaught of the breach, that the idea was suggested by some of our citizens that it was time that Nova Scotia should assume her proper place and do honor to herself by claiming as her own the renown of her children. Two well known Nova Scotians were stated to have fallen in the assault on the Redan. One whose name was as a household word amongst us—well known and well beloved, of easy manners, sociable habits and lively humor, who is there in Halifax who does not remember WELSFORD? Of Captain Parker we knew personally less—but falling as he did by the side of WELSFORD at the Redan in that ill-judged, ill-fated but heroic charge, we couple them together as twin Nova Scotians, gallant, unfortunate, but not to be forgotten.

The idea once started was speedily caught up, and a handsome subscription list was soon filled. To this list, the Legislature, under different administrations. has most nobly voted handsome sums in aid. A committee was appointed who did their best to obtain designs and to carry some or one of them into execution, but month after month—we may say year after year, passed on, and still the monument was—nowhere. It would be useless here to go into an account of the failures

THE WELSFORD AND PARKER MONUMENT.

of the committee to obtain a plan for the monument, or a piece of ground on which to erect it. Other countries, greater and wealthier than ours, have been baffled in their plans for similar works. Let the past be now forgotten. We shall have enough to do to deal with the present and the future. We have great pleasure in stating that, as far as we can gather from the voices of all around us, whatever regret there may have been as to the delay in this matter, all is now forgotten, and there is a general feeling of satisfaction as to the monument and the proceedings at its dedication.

The day appointed for the solemn inauguration was Tuesday, July 17th, 1860. A few hours before the time arranged for the ceremony, the sad but hardly unexpected news spread through the community that our beloved and venerated Chief Justice, Sir Brenton Halliburton, had breathed his last. The death of this patriarch seemed to give additional solemnity to the occasion. One more Nova Scotian had been taken from us. Just as we were met together to do honor to our fellow countryman who had fallen at the cannon's mouth, we were warned that the cannon was not the only instrument of death, and that old age was as sure, if less speedy, than the sword.

Tuesday came in with clouds and showers, and it was feared that the dedication must be postponed. Up to ten o'clock the weather was uncertain, but at about that time the sun burst out and the wind veered round, blowing gently to the west, as if to bear to the dead in the Crimea the tale of the honors that were being paid them "at home." The day thenceforth was lovely, the sun shone cheerily and the breeze blew softly. At half-past one o'clock the gallant volunteers began to muster strongly on the parade. Then marched in the societies, and last of all, in great force, the Masons, all forming a square round the parade. At two o'clock they moved off in order, marched along Barrington street, entering the south gate of Government House, where the Masons formed a double line, through which, under the rich banners of the lodges, the executive committee, typed with mourning badges, escorted His Excellency Earl Mulgrave and Her Ladyship, the Admiral and Lady Milne, the General and his Lady, with their respective suites, together with the other gentlemen, clerical and lay, military and naval, who were to take their places on the platform, and we hope we do not give offence, as we mean none, in naming here and not before, the Executive Council, the Speaker and several members of the Assembly and the corporation.

All these honorable bodies found themselves upon a spacious platform upon the western face of the monument, and in front of them a noble series of semi-circles, row behind row, of the matrons and maids of Halifax. These were hedged in by a band of soldiery—one side of which was composed of our gallant militia who looked well and acted well,—long may it be before we have to write that they fought well and died well—and behind these bristling live hedges were crowds of citizens, male and female, who, as usual, were orderly and peaceable beyond belief.

His Excellency opened the proceedings by calling upon the Rev. Mr. Scott (Presbyterian) to invoke the blessing of the Almighty by a prayer. The Rev. gentleman accordingly, in a strain of fervent piety, implored God's blessing upon the proceedings of the day.

His Excellency then addressed the vast assemblage. He spoke of the great satisfaction which he felt in being present upon so interesting an occasion. He alluded briefly but feelingly to many Nova Scotians who have distinguished themselves, among the rest to Sir Edward Belcher, Sir Fenwick Williams and General Inglis. He spoke with interest of the volunteers, and concluded an eloquent address with an evidently heartfelt allusion to the loss which the Province had just sustained in the death of the Venerable Chief Justice, a loss upon which, we may be permitted to say by the way, no one seems to be able to touch without becoming eloquent and pathetic.

Then followed *the* address of the day—the funeral oration — the panegyric — the mingled hymn, half mourning, half triumph for the dead, delivered by Rev. G. W. Hill, Rector of St. Paul's Church. Due honor was paid to George Long, the architect, who stood near the Reverend Orator,

in his uniform as one of the Chebucto Grays.
Then, at one paragraph near the close, the lion
upon the summit of the monument was unveiled,
and the cheers of the assemblage greeted this, the
solemn publication of honor paid to our dead.

Some complimentary remarks of the Reverend
Orator, Mr. Hill, called up Major-General Trollope,
who, in an energetic and humorous speech, praised
the volunteers for their attention and proficiency,
and stated his earnest desire that the whole population of the Province should become soldiers, and
prepare to defend their country in these trying
times, when no man could say what great events
an hour might bring forth.

Then followed thirteen minute guns—the last
tribute to the memory of the brave deceased ; and
then three hearty cheers for the Lieutenant
Governor, and three more for the Admiral, and
then three for Lady Mulgrave and the fair
daughters of Acadia, which were developed into
three times three—and then three—but we must
stop. God Save the Queen was sung, and " God
save her," say we heartily—and then the band
played, and the troops and militia formed and
passed off, and then the ladies, some on foot, others
in their carriages, moved away, and with them and
among them the motley crowd wended their way
homeward, or to pleasure, or to business, and then
amid a few lingering spectators, and workmen
busy at the cemetery wall, rose in lonely state the
WELSFORD and PARKER monument.

DEPARTURE OF THE DUKE OF KENT.*

"This summer (1800) His Royal Highness, the
Duke of Kent, took his final departure from Halifax. The usual addresses were presented by the
House of Assembly, His Majesty's Council and the
people of the Town. He embarked in H. M. Ship
Assistance on the 3rd August, and sailed on the
4th. His embarkation was attended with full military ceremony, the troops lining the streets. His
Royal Highness, accompanied by the Governor and
Council and the principal Navy and Military
Officers, proceeded on foot through the avenue
formed by the troops to the King's Wharf, whence
he reached the ship under salutes from the bat-
teries, the artillery corps and the ships of war.
Several of the old inhabitants not many years since
recollected the scene, and could describe the feelings evinced by the townspeople on the occasion.
His tall commanding figure in full military

---

*I am indebted to the Halifax Historical Society (a most use-
ful and popular institution) for the following and several other
interesting articles, published in one of the recent volumes.

H. R. H. THE DUKE OF KENT,
Father of Queen Victoria.

uniform, his hat surmounted by the lofty white plume, then worn by the fusiliers, could be seen above the heads of the surrounding crowd as he walked down the line with a smile of recognition for his friends, on passing them, amidst the plaudits of the crowd.*   Though the Duke exhibited on all occasions the most kind temper in civil life, and his manner and conversation with those he liked almost amounted to familiarity, yet his sternness in military affairs never forsook him.   Eleven soldiers had been sentenced to death for mutiny and desertion, and had been left by the Duke for execution, which was carried into effect under his orders a few days after he left our shores.   On the 7th August, those unfortunates were brought out on the Common, dressed in white, with their coffins, accompanied by the Revd. George Wright, the Garrison Chaplain, and Doctor Burke, the Roman Catholic clergyman, in the presence of the whole garrison.   Eight of them were reprieved under the gallows, and the three who belonged to the Newfoundland Regiment were hanged.   Public feeling was against the Duke in this affair.   It was thought that on the eve of his departure he should have granted a remission of the death sentence, which, as General Commanding, he had power to do, until the King's pleasure should be known.

*Note.—After the Prince's departure Governor Wentworth occupied the Lodge on the Basin, which had been built on his land. He resided there for some time after retiring from the Government.

Three executions only a day or two after his departure, produced a disagreeable impression of His Royal Highness in the minds of the people of Halifax, who had just taken leave of him with so much kind feeling."

SUNDAY ON THE COMMON.

The Common was the usual resort of a large portion of the inhabitants on a Sunday afternoon during the summer months. It has been the custom for many years, and had continued to be so until discontinued by Governor Maitland, for the whole garrison, which usually consisted of service companies of three regiments, a park of artillery, and a company of sappers and miners, to parade on the Common every Sunday afternoon at three o'clock during the summer season. The Governor and his staff attended and the whole brigade, with their regimental colors, and the artillery, with their field pieces, formed a line and were inspected by the Governor or Commander-in-chief, after which they marched around the drill ground, passing before him at slow time, saluting him in open column of companies. No booths, however, were allowed on the Common for the sale of refreshments except on the King's and Queen's birthdays, when grand reviews came off.

Sunday presented a gay scene at Halifax in those days. There being then no garrison chapel

for the troops, the regiments in garrison, preceded
by their brass bands playing, marched in full dress
to St. Paul's and St. George's churches amid the
ringing of bells and the sound of martial music.
The carriage of the Governor (who was then always a general officer) in full military costume,
with his aides-de-camp, drove up to the south door
of St. Paul's, the whole staff having first assembled
under the portico which then ran along the
southern end of the church. His Excellency, followed by a brilliant display of gold lace and
feathers, the clank of sabres and spurs, and the
shaking of plumed hats of so many officers, many
of whom were accompanied by their ladies, on
entering the church, presented a most brilliant
spectacle. All this was followed by the old Chief
Justice Blowers in his coach and livery, the carriage of the Admiral, and those of several members
of Council. All being seated and the body of the
church full of fashion and dress, the peal of the
organ began to be heard and the clergy in surplice
and hood (he who was about to preach, however,
always in the black gown) proceeded from the
vestry up the east side aisle to the pulpit, preceded
by a beadle in drab and gold lace, carrying a large
silver headed mace, who, after the clergy had
taken their seats, deliberately walked down the
aisle again to the vestry with his mace over his
shoulder. The Rector, Dr. John Inglis, usually
preached in the morning, and the Curate, Mr. J.
T. Twining, performed the service. They were

frequently accompanied by other church clergymen on a visit to town, and in Lord Dalhousie's
time, his Chaplain, the Rev. Isaac Temple, always
took part in the service, frequently preaching in
the afternoon at 3 o'clock. On the sermon in the
morning being concluded, the troops marched
back to barracks and the general and staff returned to Government House, where they partook of
luncheon, and were again in requisition by 3
o'clock for the grand review of the troops on the
Common. There were no evening services in the
churches and meeting houses in those days, except
with the Methodists, who were quietly doing their
work in the old Argyle Street meeting house,
under the Rev. Wm. Black.

＊　　＊　　＊　　＊　　＊　　＊　　＊

St. Paul's Church is now, perhaps, the oldest
building remaining in Halifax. It was erected at
the expense of government in the year 1749, and
was esteemed one of the best constructed wooden
buildings in America. The oak frame and
materials were brought from Boston, and the
building was ready for divine service by the
autumn of 1750. It received an addition to the
north end with a new steeple somewhat similiar to
the old one in the year 1812. The first sermon
was preached in this building by the Rev. Mr.
Tutty on 2nd September, 1750. It remained in
nearly all respects as at its first erection until certain late alterations have changed its appearance,
particularly an addition to the south end from

which the fine old altar window, with its Doric
pillars and small panes, has been removed to make
way for a large Gothic window full of painted
glass, altogether incompatible with the architec-
ture of the building itself. The old escutcheons
in the galleries have been permitted to remain.
The walls below are covered with monuments and
tablets recording the deaths of governors, military
commanders, who fell during the old American
and French wars, and not a few of our leading
citizens. The most conspicuous are those of Governors Sir John Wentworth, Wilmot, Lawrence,
and Sir John Harvey, Capt. Evans of the ship
Charleston, who was killed off the coast of Cape
Breton in defence of a convoy against a superior
French force, Lord Charles Montague, late Governor of Georgia, who died of fatigue after a
journey in winter from Quebec to Halifax by land,
the Right Rev. Charles Inglis, first Bishop of
Nova Scotia, and his son Dr. John Inglis, third
Bishop of the Diocese, Baron De Seitz, who commanded the Hessian troops in the old war, General McLean, Hon. Richard Bulkeley, Attorney
General Uniacke, with a number of others of lesser
note. The first organ was purchased, partly by
private subscription, during the incumbency of Dr.
Breynton, about 1765. It was replaced by a new
one about 1829, but the old case of Spanish walnut
was preserved.

BANCROFT'S EULOGY OF LINCOLN.*

CRITICISM BY HON. JOSEPH HOWE.

From an unpublished manuscript in the possession of Sydenham Howe, Esq.

On the 12th of February, 1866, Hon. George Bancroft, the historian, delivered in the House of Representatives at Washington his " Memorial Address on the Life and Character of Abraham Lincoln."

Among his audience was Hon. Joseph Howe, who, hastening with chivalrous impetuosity to repel the slurs cast upon the policy and the statesmen of Great Britain, immediately penned an open letter to Mr. Bancroft, which he signed " Sydney" and purposed publishing in a Washington newspaper. Mr. Howe was, however, dissuaded from printing his criticism by an eminent diplomat, who feared that Howe's vigorous strictures might intensify the existing strain between the British and American governments.

---

*Printed by the permission and courtesy of W. R. Dunn, the owner of the copyright of this article which first appeared in a holiday edition of the *Halifax Chronicle.*

It was characteristic of Mr. Howe that, while often exchanging hard blows with military governors and secretaries of state in defence of Nova Scotia's rights and interests, he never became soured against the mother country. Even in the midst of his unsuccessful struggle against Confederation, he did not waver in his proud appreciation of the record, the constitution, and the worthies of our great empire. This trait is nowhere more signally illustrated than in the following letter, which is now printed for the first time.

Washington, February 13, 1866.

Sir,—When Abraham Lincoln died the whole British people mourned in sadness and sincerity. The Queen upon the throne, and Lords Palmerston and Russell, as leaders of the Lords and Commons, threw into official forms of graceful condolence the universal sentiment of a great people sympathizing with the widow and the fatherless in their distress, and with their kindred across the sea smitten by a national calamity. Nor was the sentiment of sorrow or its outward expression confined to the British Islands. In every colony and province of the Empire, wherever the flag of England floated or her drumbeat was heard, the press gave utterance to a common feeling of respect for the dead, and abhorrence of the crime by which the United States had been suddenly deprived of its chief magistrate.

Sharing in the feelings so universally expressed,

it was natural that, being in Washington yesterday, I should desire to pay respect to the memory
of the man whose loss you were selected, in presence of the Government and Legislature, to de-
plore, and whose virtues it was fair to assume that,
in some appropriate form of classic eulogy, you
would commemorate. I had seen in October the
burial of Lord Palmerston, who, without offence
to foreign nations, or insult to old opponents,
foreign or domestic, was laid to sleep in that venerable pile where rest the men who have made
our language undying and the history of our race
illustrious. It was natural, therefore, that, as I
had not seen Lincoln buried, I should desire to
see a whole nation bending over his grave and
hallowing his birthday by lamentation for his loss.
I did not suspect that handfuls of fresh mould
were to be snatched up and flung in the face of
any portion of the audience; I did not suppose
that in the presence of the representatives of
foreign powers, invited to participate in the sorrowful ceremonial, questions of foreign policy were
to be treated with offensive partizanship, and least
of all should I have imagined that the graves of
our illustrious dead were to be rifled of the
wreaths which, in all sincerity, we hung there, to
decorate the tomb of the man over whom our
dead and living statesmen had sincerely mourned.
Some trinkets were flung into the grave of Lord
Palmerston by a relative who, in his hour of intense sorrow, felt that diamonds were but dust;

and I would as soon have believed that an American gentleman could have been found to break the cerements and purloin those jewels as that another would attempt to dim the lustre of a great name, on an occasion where comparisons were odious and out of place, and would abuse the privilege of his position in a hall where all criticism and defence were denied, that he might disparage the living and the dead.

I confess that I was disappointed, every way disappointed. I had heard the graceful elocution of Everett, the vigorous and classic declamation of Phillips, the rich tones and blended piety and humor of Beecher. I remember the oratory of Clay and the massive arguments of Webster, and was certainly not much edified when Mr. George Bancroft read for three mortal hours, from a printed paper, an essay which the newsboys had been selling through the streets all the afternoon.

*   *   *   *   *   *   *

But, passing over the mere composition and the manner of delivery, I wish to enter my protest against the bad taste and utter want of candor and manliness of Mr. Bancroft. The occasion was one on which public discussion could not intrude. The hall, dedicated to legislation and to national ceremonials, were closed against every gentleman there, however deeply his nationality or personal feelings had been wounded. In an open public meeting any stranger might have risen, and, claiming fair play from the audience, have, on the spot, brought the speaker to book. Mr. Bancroft knew he was safe from any such intrusion. The men he assailed were not there, the classes he disparaged could not be brought into personal comparison with him ; and if there were Englishmen present who knew the difference, or Frenchmen who could distinguish the covert menace from the fulsome flattery, they were restrained by the genius of the place and by respect for the worthy man whose obsequies were being disturbed by this literary resurrectionist. We held our tongues. It was enough for us to observe that the reader at the desk read for more than an hour in his dreamy manner before there was the slightest applause; that though the political passages and personal attacks were applauded by a portion of the audience, at least three fourths of those present did not participate in those manifestations, and were evidently offended at a want of tact and taste which they had never anticipated, and yet had no power to control.

There is "a time for everything," saith the preacher—a time to embody national complaints in official despatches—to reason, to illustrate, to reclaim. All this had been done for the American people with great industry and ability, by diplomatists enjoying their confidence ; and behind all this there is the final arbitrament of the sword, whenever the President and Congress choose to draw it, and every man and woman in the audience knew that, when drawn, every gallant officer in either service who sat before them would spring to his feet to defend his country's interests and honor. But everybody felt that the last place where grievances should be hunted up, or where unkind words should be spoken, was on Abraham Lincoln's birthday or beside Abraham Lincoln's grave. It is very satisfactory to know that thousands in this city should share and express that feeling, notwithstanding the artful manner in which, towards the close, the speaker sought to dodge and avoid the frank expression of his opinions on the questions of the hour.

I will not follow your bad example, and, while doing justice to the statesmen I respect, seek to disparage the worthy man with whom they have been most unfairly compared. If Abraham Lincoln had his faults and weaknesses, like other people, let them be forgotten in presence of his great services and of his great loss.

You tried to make your audience believe that the English aristocracy despised him because he was a working man. Did you know no better? Did you not know that a large portion of the aristocracy of England are sprung from working men—that Peel's father was a cotton spinner, that Gladstone's father was a merchant, that Brougham commenced his public life in a Scotch attic—that George Stephenson and Shaw, the life guardsman, had hands and feet as large as Lincoln, and yet were not despised in aristocratic England? Burns was a peasant's son, yet his truest friend and patron was Lord Glencairn. There is not a year that the House of Commons is not recruited, or the peerage adorned, by new men, springing by force of talent and energy to the highest grades of public life from the humbler classes of society. The difference between your system and ours is that, when a man has risen in England, he may found a family and leave them for generations above the ordinary casualties of life. This privilege is open to the whole body of the people. Lord Clyde, the hero of Alma, the pacificator of India, sprang from as humble an origin (with all respect to your truly modest and great soldier, be it said) as General Grant. The Queen gave Clyde a peerage and a pension, and every poor lad in Scotland knows that his sword may win for him the same honorable distinction and permanent provision. I hope your distinguished leader may fare as well, but, if he does, he will fare better than all the soldiers who achieved your independence, for whom no permanent provision was made, and whose descendants collectively hardly own as much visible property as a single successful trader in New York.

Lord Lyndhurst died recently, full of years and of forensic and parliamentary renown. He was the son of a poor American artist. He leaves behind him his peerage, and an estate which may be transmitted for generations. A century hence an American traveller may find all that can illustrate his life—the trees he planted, the books he read, the manuscript he valued, treasured with religious

care on the property he bequeathed ; and find, side
by side with the works of art painted by his father,
the portraits of his sons, eminent in arms or in
statesmanship, hanging upon the walls, graceful
memorials of the past, open to the people on holi-
days, and calculated to inspire in all classes a generous emulation. A few years ago Daniel
Webster stood at the head of the Boston bar and
in the very first rank of American public life. As
a great lawyer, a great orator and administrator,
he had few equals, and perhaps no superior. I
remember him well——the space he occupied in the
public eye, the part he acted in public affairs.
Daniel Webster, in England, would have risen as
Copley rose ; he would have entered the charmed
circle by sheer force of talent, farmer's boy though
he was ; he would have embellished the Peerage
with his name and left a permanent provision for
his family. He died, and I leave to those who
know the facts to say how sad a contrast may be
drawn between what is and what might have been.

You have your system and we have ours. We
prefer our own. We delight to see England stud-
ded with the palatial edifices which embellish
every county, and in which all that is curious and
venerable in the bygone life of our country is care-
fully preserved and blended with all that is fresh
and new in our modern civilization ; and we know
that almost every one of these is a centre of intellectual life and of social refinement. The youth
reared in these " stately homes" go into our public

schools and colleges and wrestle for their distinc-
tions with the sons of commoners and citizens.
They go into the army and navy, where a severe
discipline equalizes all ranks. They go upon the
hustings, where any poor man's son may beat
them ; or, if successful, they study in the noblest
school of eloquence and laborious public life in
Europe, to fit themselves for the high duties of
senators when called up to the House of Lords.

Of this class were the two statesmen that you
have thought fit to scold and to disparage. Both
were born to rank and affluence. They might,
had they chosen like thousands of the youth of
this country, have given themselves up to coarse
pleasures, to idleness and dissipation. It is true
that neither of them ever split rails, drank hard
cider or lived in a log hut, privileges which seem
to be highly valued by a certain class of orators
in this country. But they were bred to all the
manly exercises of England, and a month before
he died I would have backed Lord Palmerston to
beat Mr. George Bancroft in a canter round the
park. From his youth upwards Lord Russell was
a student of literature and politics, associating
with all who were eminent for freedom of thought
and advanced public exertion. At a very early
age he gave us a valuable contribution to history ;
and at a later period a charming biography of
Moore, who was his personal friend For nearly
half a century, that he had been in public life, he
has been the friend and fellow worker of Grey

and Brougham and Landsdowne, of Molesworth
and Buller and Sydenham, of Cobden and Huskisson and Bright ; and it is safe to say that to every
great measure of practical reform, in church or
state, in law, politics, or finance, Lord Russell has
given, not to " his order," but to the people of
England, his able and manly support. You affect
to desire an extension of the franchise, and, if sincere, why did you not tell your audience that to
Lord Russell and his friends the people owe the
Reform Bill of 1832, and that his administration
would announce on the meeting of Parliament another wide extension of the franchise ? But I
would shut out of view everything that Lord Russell has done for the improvement of the British
Islands and take the single measure by which he
gave self-government to the outlying Provinces of
the Empire, and I am free to state that, in con-
ferring upon all our great colonies a more perfect
system of administration, and a more thorough
control over their own affairs than any state in
this Union enjoys, he did a greater service to the
world at large than Mr. George Bancroft could
confer if he lived for 500 years. And yet this is
the man to whom you would deny the free expression of his opinion on a question of doubtful
policy, and whom you would lecture upon the
manner in which he should perform his duty to
the great country that, for half a century, he has
served with all fidelity and honor.

To compare Lord Palmerston with Mr. Lincoln

is to compare people totally unlike in training and culture, in mind and manners, in pursuits and qualifications.   You might as well have compared a dray horse and a hunter, a smart frigate and a monitor.   *   *   Lord Palmerston never split rails or floated down a river on a raft, but he was a man, every inch of him, and had he been born to poverty and privation would have met the hardships of life with his characteristic cheerfulness and resolution.   But he was born a gentleman, an " aristocrat," if you will, and received from the society and public schools of his country the personal and mental culture they are so well calculated to impart.   He had no turn for writing dull books, but he had a turn for making history, for parliamentary discussion, and the administration of affairs.   1 have no desire to write his life or to record his services.   They are to be found in the parliamentary and diplomatic history of his country for the last fifty years.   Called to the highest place in the councils of his sovereign, Palmerston displayed a vast amount of practical talent, of varied information, of ready eloquence, combined with a plastic power to conciliate and bind men together, without which all statesmanship is often unavailing.   I have heard this great man often—in parliament, where the most appreciative audience in Europe listened with intense interest to his wisdom or enjoyed the classic flavor of his wit,—

> " While his eloquence played round each topic in turn
> Shedding lustre and life where it fell."

But I have heard him elsewhere—at great gatherings of the working classes—of fellows with as big feet and as horny hands as any that are to be found on this continent; and I have seen them time and again clustered round the orator in whose statesmanship and true human sympathy they had boundless confidence.

Recalling some of those scenes yesterday, "Oh! for an hour of old Mondego," rose involuntarily to my lips, and I wished from my soul that "Pam," in the flesh, could have descended beside the orator of the day, and, hostile and prejudiced as a portion of the audience might have been, ten minutes would have sufficed to mark in everybody's mind the difference between the statesman who could defend his foreign policy in a speech of seven hours, spoken without a note, and the person who had tasked his perverted ingenuity to defame him.

But you thought proper to discuss in a most disingenuous spirit the Alabama claims and the slavery question. With reference to the first, permit me to say that it had already been elaborately and ably treated by the Secretary of State and by your Minister to England, and let me add that your ill-natured reference to this question, like all your other references to foreign affairs, was inappropriate and ill-timed. An Englishman is ever ready in all courtesy to pay his debts or to give a reason why he declines, but he does not like to be asked for money in a church or at a funeral. Nobody more sincerely regrets than I do the irritation which has grown out of these maritime depredations, and perhaps few persons more ardently desire that some means may be hit upon, by the very able men charged with the adjustment of this vexed question, to save the honor of two great nations and preserve the peace between them. Wise men, hoping for an adjustment, should desire to calm, and not increase, the irritation. I have been in England seven times, and have often, for months together, mingled with all classes of its population, from the highest in rank to the lowest orders of its varied industries, and I deny that there exists in that country any desire to treat this (country) unfairly, to prey upon its commerce or to dismember its organization. Had there been any such disposition, England and France would have been combined, the blockade would have been broken, the Southern rivers cleared, and the Confederate States at this moment would be an independent nation. This was not done, because Lords Palmerston and Russell, and those who governed England, exercised a forbearance, under strong temptation, worthy of all praise. Englishmen preferred to mind their own business. They paid, during the war, fifty times the amount of the Alabama claims, in the enhanced price of cotton, rather than go and take it ; they maintained the inhabitants of their great manufacturing principality by subscriptions, rather than do wrong ; and they gave up the trade of the Southern States, to which they were entitled under the Reciprocity Treaty ; because they knew that the blockade was forced upon the Government of this country by the exigencies growing out of the Civil War. Having done all this, without going into the question of the Alabama claims, I can quite understand why those claims have been rejected.

But the English Government should have sympathized with this country, because the slavery question was one of the issues to be tried out by the war. Why? Did the people of the United States ever sympathize with us in dealing with that most difficult question, or show the slightest desire or design to follow our example? Lord Mansfield decided in 1772 that a slave touching the soil of England should, from that moment, be emancipated and disenthralled. Did your Free States follow our example? No ; they accepted Fugitive Slave Laws, and not many years ago colored men were arrested, even in Boston, and dragged back to the plantation. In 1833 Parliament voted £20,000,000 sterling to purchase and emancipate our slaves in the West Indies. Did you follow our example? No ; but for over thirty years thereafter you continued to import, to breed, to sell, and to whip your slaves, and while you grew rich upon their labors, rarely failed to point to the declining trade of our tropical colonies and laugh at the misplaced humanity of John Bull. In England respectable colored persons may be seen in society. I never met one at any gentleman's table in the United States, although I have been tolerably familiar with its society for the last five-and-thirty years ; and I could not but remark that, in an audience of several thousands, admitted by ticket or by invitation, there were not five black faces to be seen.

During the war 1812-15 some hundreds of negro families were carried off by our naval commander-in-chief from the southern plantations and were flung into the Maritime Provinces. For three years they were maintained out of the military chest and then settled on crown lands. We afterwards paid to your Government a heavy indemnity for the offence of making these people free. In 1837 they were enfranchised. A few years afterwards they were allowed to sit on juries. Their testimony was never rejected by any court in British America. We have, in fact practically solved long since, within the Queen's dominions, all the questions about which this country is convulsed day by day, and yet you undertake to lecture our public men for a want of sympathy with the negro !

" But slavery was planted by the English." Why, all North America was planted by the English, but surely the present generation, who have had nothing to do with slavery for thirty-three years, are not to blame for what people did before they were born ! A king ninety-four years ago might have upheld the slave trade and no living

Englishman be to blame. Witches were burned by your ancestors, I presume, about the same time; but it would be very unfair for me to upbraid you or the New Englanders of the present day with the fanaticism and inhumanity of a bygone age.

Trusting that you will pardon the freedom with which I have repelled a most unfair attack on the policy. institutions, and public men of my country, I remain,

Your obedient servant,

SYDNEY.

The Honorable George Bancroft.

MR. HOWE'S GREAT DETROIT SPEECH.*

[I have referred to this great speech in the body
of the work, and as its contents are suitable to the
present day, as they were thirty years ago, I have
no doubt the reader will be interested in its re-
publication and perusal here. The occasion was
the "Great International Commercial Convention"
called to meet at the City of Detroit on the 14th
July, 1865. There were present upwards of five
thousand of the Merchants and chief business men
and politicians of the United States and the British
Provinces, and Mr. Howe was called upon by the
delegates of the latter to address the meeting as
their spokesman. This speech has long been out
of print. I am indebted, however, to Dr. George
Stewart, of Quebec, for a copy of the speech preserved in pamphlet form, revised and corrected
by Mr. Howe himself at the time, after it had
passed through the hands of the reporter.]

Hon. Joseph Howe, of Nova Scotia, took the
floor and made a long and eloquent speech. He
said : I never prayed for the gift of eloquence till
now. Although I have passed through a long

---

*To publish the whole of this great speech would occupy as
much more space as we now give; but all the material points
are preserved, and will well repay perusal.

public life, I never was called upon to discuss a question so important in the presence of a body of representative men so large. I see before me merchants who think in millions, and whose daily transactions would sweep the harvest of a Greek Island or of a Russian Principality. I see before me the men who whiten the ocean and the great lakes with the sails of commerce—who own the railroads, canals and telegraphs, which spread life and civilization through this great country, making the waste plains fertile and the wilderness to blossom as the rose. I see before me the men whose capital and financial skill form the bulwark and sustain the Government in every crisis of affairs. (Cheers.) On either hand I see the gentlemen who control and animate the press, whose laborious vigils mould public sentiment—whose honorable ambition I can estimate from my early connection with the profession. On those benches, Sir, or I mistake the intelligence to be read in their faces, sit those who will yet be Governors and Ministers of State. I may well feel awed in presence of an audience such as this ; but the great question which brings us together is worthy of the audience and challenges their grave consideration.

What is that question ? Sir, we are here to determine how best we can draw together, in the bonds of peace, friendship and commercial prosperity, the three great branches of the British family. (Cheers.) In the presence of this great

theme all petty interests should stand rebuked—
we are not dealing with the concerns of a City, a
Province or a State, but with the future of our
race in all time to come. Some reference has been
made to " Elevators " in your discussions. What
we want is an elevator to lift our souls to the
height of this great argument. Why should not
these three great branches of the family flourish,
under different systems of government, it may be,
but forming one grand whole, proud of a common
origin and of their advanced civilization ? We
are taught to reverence the mystery of the
Trinity, and our salvation depends on our belief.
The clover lifts its trefoil to the evening dew,
yet they draw their nourishment from a single
stem. Thus distinct, and yet united, let us live
and flourish. Why should we not ? For nearly
two thousand years we were one family. Our
fathers fought side by side at Hastings, and heard
the curfew toll. They fought in the same ranks
for the sepulchre of our Saviour—in the earlier
and later civil wars. We can wear our white and
red roses without a blush, and glory in the principles those conflicts established. Our common
ancestors won the great Charter and the Bill of
Rights—established free Parliaments, the Habeas
Corpus, and Trial by Jury. Our Jurisprudence
comes down from Coke and Mansfield to Marshall
and Story, rich in knowledge and experience,
which no man can divide. From Chaucer to
Shakespeare our literature is a common inherit-

ance. Tennyson and Longfellow write in one language, which is enriched by the genius developed on either side of the Atlantic. In the great navigators from Cottereal to Hudson, and in all their "moving accidents by flood and field" we have a common interest. On this side of the sea we have been largely reinforced by the Germans and French, but there is strength in both elements. The Germans gave to us the sovereigns who established our freedom, and they give to you industry, intelligence and thrift ; and the French, who have distinguished themselves in arts and arms for centuries, now strengthen the Provinces which the fortune of war decided they could not control. But it may be said we have been divided by two wars. What then ? The noble St. Lawrence is split in two places—by Goat Island and by Anticosti—but it comes down to us from the same springs in the same mountain sides ; its waters sweep together past the Pictured Rocks of Lake Superior, and encircle in their loving embrace the shores of Huron and Michigan. They are divided at Niagara Falls as we were at the revolutionary war, but they come together again on the peaceful bosom of Ontario. Again they are divided on their passage to the sea ; but who thinks of divisions when they lift the keels of commerce, or when, drawn up to heaven, they form the rainbow or the cloud ? It is true that in eighty-five years we have had two wars—but what then ? Since the last we have had fifty

years of peace, and there have been more people
killed in a single campaign in the late civil war,
than there were in the two national wars between
this country and Great Britain. The people of
the United States hope to draw together the two
conflicting elements and make them one people.
And in that task I wish them God speed!
(Cheers.) And in the same way I feel that we
ought to rule out everything disagreeable in the
recollection of our old wars, and unite together as
one people for all time to come. (Cheers) I see
around the door the flags of the two countries.
United as they are there, I would ever have them
draped together, fold within fold—and let " their
varying tints unite, and form in heaven's light,
one arch of peace." (Applause.) He thanked
the Board of Trade, and the people of the city for
the hospitality extended to the Provincial Delegates, and proceeded as follows to the general ex-
position of his subject :—The most important
question to be considered at this great meeting of
the commercial men of North America, involves
the relations which are to subsist between the inhabitants of the British Empire and the citizens of
the United States. Before we can deliver a
rational judgment upon this question it becomes
us to consider what those relations are now. The
British Government controls the destinies, and re-
gulates the trade of 250,000,000 of people, dis-
tributed over the four quarters of the globe, and
in the British Islands alone the machinery in con-

stant running order does the work of 800,000,000 more. Now, in what spirit has the British Government, controlling this great empire, dealt in commercial matters with the United States? It has extended to them all the privileges of the most favored nation, and has opened up to them, on the most easy terms, the consumption for everything that they can produce, of all these people. Millions of emigrants, and hundreds of millions of money have flowed in here without any attempt, by unwise laws, to dam up the streams of industry and capital. Leaving those of her Provinces that have Legislatures free to regulate their own tariffs, Great Britain restrains them from discriminating, as against the productions of this country, even in favor of her own. Though burdened with an enormous debt, and always compelled to confront the military monarchies of Europe with a powerful force by land and sea, the people of England prefer to pay direct taxes to burthening commerce with heavy import duties. Year by year the highest financial skill of the nation has been employed to discover how its tariff could be simplified—port charges reduced—obsolete regulations removed; and year by year, as trade extends and revenue increases, taxes are reduced or abolished upon articles of prime necessity, consumed by the great body of the people. I notice that some writers in the west complain that wheat is sent into this country from Canada, duty free; but it should be remembered that the surplus of all the cereals, ground or unground, is not only admitted to the British Islands duty free from the United States, but to almost, if not to all, the ports in our widely extended Empire. It is sometimes said that because this country admits breadstuffs from Canada, manufactures free of duty should be taken in return. But Great Britain and the Provinces take annually an enormous quantity of breadstuffs and meat from this country, but do not ask from you the privilege that some persons would claim from us.

In three departments of economic science Great Britain has made advances far outstripping in liberality the policy of this or of any foreign country. France and the United States continue to foster and extend their fisheries by high bounties, but she leaves her people, without any special encouragement to meet on the sea, and in foreign markets, the unfair competition to which they are subjected by this system. Great Britain throws open to the people of this country the coasting trade of the entire Empire. * * * I assert that Great Britain, with a liberality which would do honor to any Government, has thrown open this whole trade without any restriction. She says to us, if not in so many words, " You are all children of mine, and are dear to me. You are all on the other side of the Atlantic, possessing a common heritage ; make the best of it." (Hear, hear.) Your vessels are permitted to run to Halifax, from Halifax to St. John, from St. John to British Columbia, and from

British Columbia to England, Scotland, or Ireland.
They are allowed to go coasting around the British Empire until they rot. But you do not give
us the privilege of coasting anywhere from one end
of your Atlantic coast to the other. And now I
hope that our friend from Maine will acknowledge
that in granting this privilege, with nothing in
return, Great Britain gave you a pretty large slice.
(Cheers and laughter.)

       *   *   *   *

When the civil war broke out, one-half the sea-
board of the United States was blockaded, and all
the advantages of the Reciprocity Treaty, so far as
the consumption of the ten millions of people in
the Southern States was a benefit to the Provinces,
were withdrawn. Assuming that the treaty runs
over ten years, it will be seen that for the whole of
that period the people of this country have enjoyed all the benefits for which they stipulated,
while the British Americans, for one year of the
ten, have derived no benefits at all, and for four
entire years have lost the consumption of one-
third of the people with whom, by the treaty, they
were entitled to trade. Recognizing the political
necessities of the period, British subjects have
made no complaints of this exclusion, but it ought
to be borne in mind, now that the whole subject is
about to be revised.

       *   *   *   *

Mr. Chairman, let me now turn your attention to
some of the topics touched upon by other gentle-

men in the course of this three day's debate. Some
gentlemen seem to be apprehensive that if this
Treaty is renewed it will lead to illicit trade along
the frontier. For a long time your duties were
lower than ours. Mr. Sabine said he was once a
smuggler. At that time he could not carry on
trade or business at Eastport and be anything else.
The traders on the whole coast of Maine were engaged in the same business, and so was Massachusetts ; and small blame to them. The smuggler is
a check upon the extravagance of governments, or
the increase of taxation. (Cheers.) Any country
that raises its tariff too high, or increases its taxation too far. will be kept in check by smugglers.
The boot was formerly on your leg ; it is now perhaps on the other. You have been driven into a
war which has created a large expenditure and
increased your taxation. It would perhaps pay at
this moment to smuggle some articles from the
Provinces into this country. You are entitled to
defend yourself against it. But at the same time
bear this in mind, that one of the main objections
in the Maritime Provinces to this treaty was, that
it gave to your people the power of smuggling.
And that power you possess, and may use to any
extent you please. (Laughter.) Over thousands
of miles of coast we can not afford to keep revenue
officers. Down come cutters from Maine, with
flour, pork, salt, &c. ; but who can tell what they
have in the salt ? (Great laughter.) Why, sir, we
sometimes laugh at Yankee notions ; one of those

is what is called white-eye in the Provinces—a life-destroying spirit which these coasters bring and deluge our coasts with ; and it comes in the salt. (Laughter.) So in like manner with the tea, tobacco and manufactures. Why a fisherman can land on any part of our 5,000 miles of coast, and when challenged by our custom house officers, he can answer that he has a right to land there. The custom house officer withdraws, and the white-eye is landed. And I tell you what we do to adapt ourselves to the circumstances. We are free traders, and we maintain our Government, have an overflowing treasury and carry on our public works, with a tariff of ten per cent. (Hear, hear.) The only way we can keep out smuggling is to keep our tariff so low as to make it not worth while for any one to smuggle. Let me now draw your attention for a moment, to the value of these North American Fisheries. You have behind and around you here, boundless prairies, which an all-bountiful creator annually covers with rich harvests of wheat and corn. The ocean is our prairie, and it stretches away before and around us, and Almighty God, for the sustenance of man, annually replenishes it with fish in myriads that can't be counted, having a commercial value that no man can estimate. The fecundity of the ocean may be estimated by the fact that the roes of thirty codfish annually replace all the fish that are taken by the British, French and American fishermen on the Banks of Newfoundland. In like manner the

schools of mackerel, herring and of all other fish
that swim in the Bays and trim around the shores
are replaced year by year. These great store-
houses of food can never be exhausted. But it
may be said, does not the free competition which
now exists, lower the prices ? No. Codfish have
never been higher in the markets of the world
than they were last summer. Herrings are now
selling in Baltimore for $13 a barrel. Thirty
years ago I used to buy No. 1 mackerel in Halifax
for $4 a barrel. They now cost $18, and I have
seen them selling since the Reciprocity Treaty was
signed for $22. The reason of this is, that relative
to all other employments, fishing is a perilous and
poor business, and that, with the progress of settlement and growth of population in all these great
States and Provinces, to say nothing of the increased consumption in Spain, the Mediterranean,
the Brazils and the West Indies,—all that your
fishermen and ours can catch will scarcely supply
the demand. I placed before the committee a
paper, signed by two American merchants carrying on trade in Prince Edward Island, which
proves that under the Treaty, your mackerel fishery has flourished and expanded to an extent unexampled in its former history. Taking two years
prior to the existence of the treaty and contrasting
them with the last two years, they show that
your mackerel fishery has grown from 250 vessels
measuring 18,150 tons, valued at $750,000 and
manned by 2,750 men and securing a catch worth

$850,000, to 600 vessels measuring 54,000 tons, employing 9,000 men and securing 315,000 barrels, worth $4,567,500. So with the herring fishery, it is equally prosperous. I have seen two American seine boats take 500 barrels of herrings, at Baltimore prices worth $6,500, on the coast of Labrador in a summer afternoon. The net fishing is also profitable. The Bank earns and the Mill grinds while the banker and the miller sleep. The fisherman sets his nets at night, and finds in the morning that a kind Providence, without a miracle, except the " wealth of seas"— that standing miracle—has loaded them with a liberal hand. These fisheries, sir, are sufficient for us all. The French, who are anxious to build up a powerful navy, maintain 10,000 men by their bounties in these North American waters, and it is most creditable to our fishermen, that in the face of these bounties and of yours, they have been able, by strict economy and hardy endurance, to wrestle for a share of these ocean treasures, to maintain their families and increase their numbers.

Mr. Howe also dealt with the coal and lumber interests in the same argumentative manner.

In closing the speaker said, I must now touch upon a subject of some delicacy and importance. It has been urged by Mr. Morrill in Congress, and by the people of the United States that the treaty ought not to be renewed, because it had bred no friendship toward them across the lakes—that in their struggle the sympathies of the Provinces were against them. Well, if that were true in its fullest extent, which it was not—if they had not had one sympathizer among the native people and British residents of the Provinces, it could fairly be plead in response that when Great Britain was at war with Russia the sympathies of the American people were very generally with the latter country. I was in the United States at the time, and was perfectly astonished at the feeling. Russia was at that time a country full of slaves, for the serfs had not been emancipated, and England was at war with her to prevent her aggressions upon and making slaves of the weak neighbouring countries. How the American people could sympathise with Russia was a perfect puzzle at first sight, and could only be explained in the same manner that much of the sympathy for the South on the part of the British subjects could be explained. And when the Canadians once had a rebellion within their borders, where were the sympathies of the American people then ? Were they with the Canadian Government or were they with the rebels ? Why, they (the Americans) not only sympathized with them, but I am sorry to have to say it, they gave them aid along the frontier in many ways, and to a very large extent. I am happy to have it to say, that during the whole four years of the late rebellion in the United States there has not been developed a particle of evidence to show that a single citizen of any British North American Province had put a

hostile foot upon your soil. (Loud applause.)
Everything of which complaint could be made
has been the act of your own rebellious people, in
violation of the hospitality and right of asylum
everywhere extended to them on the soil of Great
Britain and her dependencies. I make these remarks in no spirit of anger or of excitement, but
to show how unfair it is to hold any Government
or people responsible for the actions of a few evil-
disposed individuals, as well as how natural it was
for the sympathy to be aroused in the minds of
people on one side or another. In our rebellion,
when its attention was called to their acts, the
United States Government exerted itself to keep
its own citizens within bounds, and all that could
have been asked of the Provincial authorities
has been freely done to prevent any cause of
complaint against them. It is something to be
able to say, that during the four long disastrous
years of the war just ended, not a single act of
which complaint could be made has been
committed by a Canadian. Notwithstanding
the false reports that were circulated, I do not believe there was a single intelligent citizen of my
Province, at least, who did not believe that the
capture of the "Chesapeake" off the coast of
Maine, by rebellious citizens of the United States,
was nothing less or more than an act of piracy.
And so of the St. Albans raid. The Government
of Canada acted most promptly and nobly in connection with that affair ; and has repaid the money

which rebellious citizens of the United States had carried into their territory from the States banks. (Hear, hear.) As to their harboring the rebels and extending to them the right of asylum, is there a single American here who would have his Government surrender that right? There was not an Englishman, nor an Irishman, nor a Scotchman, nor an American who would not fight three wars rather than give up that sacred right. (Applause.) How many excellent citizens of the United States were there among them at this moment, and how many were there who had helped them to fight their battles, who dare not go back to their own native lands across the ocean on account of political offences? The American people would not give these people up to their respective Governments and thus surrender their right of asylum ; they would every man of them fight first. (Applause.) It is very proper that criminals should be given up, and a treaty for that purpose has been made between England and the United States. They could sympathize with political offenders, but need not sympathize with criminals. When Abraham Lincoln fell by the hand of the assassin the act was reprobated throughout the Provinces as well as throughout the British Empire. (Hear.) But admitting that a large number of people in the Provinces sympathized with the rebels, what of that? Did not a very large number in the Northern States sympathize with them? Nobody ever saw two dogs fighting in the street, or two cocks fighting in a back yard, without having his sympathies aroused, he scarcely knew why, in favor of one or the other of the combatants, and generally the weakest. (Laughter.) Suppose a good deal of feeling was excited in some portions of the British Provinces, was that any good reason for refusing to allow us to trade with our brethren south of the Lakes? The sympathy expressed for the South ought to be well balanced by the young men whom they had drawn from the Colonies into their conflict. (Hear, hear.) For one ton of goods sent to the Southerners, and for one young man sent to aid their cause, we have sent fifty tons and fifty able-bodied soldiers to the North. The people of the Provinces might lay the charge against you of having seduced their young men away from their homes and left their bodies bleaching on Southern plains or rotting in Southern prisons. Only a short time ago I met no less than thirty British Americans going home on a single vessel, after having served three years in the war, and having left scores of their companions behind to enrich the soil. At Washington I met with a brave son of one of my colleagues in the legislature of Nova Scotia, who held the rank of lieutenant in a Massachusetts regiment, with only one leg to take back to his home instead of two. (Loud cheers.) I met another veteran from my Province who had fought in twenty battles and was on his way home. In my own family and person I have suffered not a little by this unhappy rebellion. I have five boys, and one of them took it into his head to enter your army. He has now been for nearly two years in the 23rd Ohio regiment, and has fought in all the battles in which that regiment has been engaged during that period. He was in both the great battles under Sheridan, in which Early's forces were scattered and the Shenandoah valley cleared. (Loud and long continued applause.) All the personal benefit that I have derived from the Reciprocity Treaty or hope to derive from its renewal, will never compensate me or that boy's mother for the anxiety we have had with regard to him; but when he produced the certificates of his commanding officers showing that he had conducted himself like a gentleman, and had been faithful and brave, it was some consolation for all our anguish to know that he had performed his duty. (Enthusiastic applause, during which the speaker's feelings nearly overcame him; as this subsided, a gentleman proposed "three cheers for the boy," which were given with great vivacity.) I know that it has been asserted by some, and I have heard it uttered since I came to the Convention, that if the Reciprocity Treaty is annulled the British Provinces will be so cramped that they will be compelled to seek annexation to the United States. I beg to be allowed to say on that point that I know the feeling in the Lower Provinces pretty thoroughly, and believe I am well enough acquainted with the Canadians to speak for them also, and I speak for them all, with such exceptions as must be made when speaking for any entire population, when I make the assertion that no consideration of finance, no question of balance for or against them, upon interchange of commodities, can have any influence upon the loyalty of the inhabitants of the British Provinces, or tend in the slightest degree to alienate the affections of the people from their country, their institutions, their Government and their QUEEN. There is not a loyal man in the British American Provinces, not a man worthy of the name, who, whatever may happen to the Treaty, will become any the less loyal, any the less true to his country, on that account. There is not a man who dare, on the abrogation of the Treaty, if such should be its fate, take the hustings and appeal to any constituency on annexation principles throughout the entire domain. The man who avows such a sentiment will be scouted from society by his best friends. What other treatment would a man deserve who should turn traitor to his Sovereign and his Government, and violate all obligations to the country which gave him birth! You know what you call Copperheads, and a nice life they have of it. (Laughter.) Just such a life will the man have who talks treason on the other side of the lines. (Applause.) The very boy to whom I have alluded, as having fought manfully for the "Stars and Stripes,"

would rather blow his own father's brains out
than haul down the honored flag under which he
has been born, the flag of his nation and of his
fatherland. (Cheers.)   I do not believe there is a
young Canadian in the American army who does
not honor his own flag as you honor yours, and
they would be worthy of being despised if they
did not.   If any member of the Convention har-
bors the idea that by refusing Reciprocity to
British America, they will undermine the loyal
feelings of the people of those Colonies, he is
laboring under a delusion, and fostering an impu-
tation upon the character and integrity of a great
and honorable people of the most dastardly kind
that can by any possibility receive a lodgment in
his breast. (Loud and continued applause.) Some
gentlemen from Maine asked me if we were not
building fortifications in the Provinces. Well, after
so many threats from Northern newspapers, that
so soon as the rebellion had been put down and
Mexico attended to, the face of the army would
be turned towards Canada, it was not to be won-
dered at that the mother country should become
a little anxious about her children so far from
home, and send out an experienced officer to report upon the situation. The officer did not report
any armed force in sight, but reported that, if
they did come, Canada was in a very poor condition to receive them ; and it was resolved to build
some further fortifications at Quebec, and there
has been some talk about places further westward,

but no action has been taken. But what do we see on the other hand? I passed down the Penobscot river a few weeks ago, and what did I see there?—a great frowning fort, of the most approved pattern, looking as new and pretty as if it had just come from the mint. (Laughter.) At Portland, also, I observed some extensive fortifications in progress, and have been informed that you are at work in the same line at other points, so that nothing need be said if Canada did invest some money in costly fortifications. But I have no faith in fortifications. I do not rely on military defences:

> We need no bulwarks,
> No towers along the steep;
> Our march is o'er the mountain wave,

and our homes are in the mart, on the mountain and the prairie, wherever there is good work to be done, and God's gifts to be appropriated. I have faith in our common brotherhood—in such meetings as this—in such social gatherings as that magnificent demonstration which we all enjoyed so much last night. I sincerely hope that all thought of forcing annexation upon the people of Canada will be abandoned, and that if not, you will seek a more pleasant sort of annexation for your children and children's children. It was a novel mode of attaching them that the people of Detroit adopted in lashing a fleet of their steamers together, and getting up such a grand entertainment, and there was no question that it had a strong tendency to promote one kind of annexation, especially among the young people. (Laughter.) As a measure of self-protection, I put myself under the care of a pretty little New Brunswick woman, and charged her to take good care of me until we got safe ashore. (Laughter and applause, twice repeated.) I fear I am detaining you too long. (Cries of "go on" from all parts of the house.) In conclusion, let me say, that in dealing with this subject, I have spoken in an open, plain manner, and kept back nothing that ought to be said upon it, considering the limited time at my disposal. My friend Mr. Hamlin wished us to "show our hands"; we have done so and shown our hearts also in all sincerity. The subject is of vast importance to us all. Though living away down East, I take a deep interest in the great West, and I trust God will spare my life long enough to permit me to explore its vastness more thoroughly than I have yet been able to do, that I may the better discuss the great interests created by its commerce. British America has a great West, as yet almost entirely undeveloped, out of which four or five States or Provinces may yet be formed, to pour their wealth down the great Lake Huron into Canada, and through the Straits, past the city of Detroit, to the ocean, while the manufactures of the United States, of England and of the Provinces go back to supply the wants. The moment Providence gives me opportunity, I will return to the West and examine its resources, and understand its position, in order that I may lay before my own people, and the people of the Provinces generally, and the capitalists of the mother country, an adequate idea of its importance, with a view of promoting a more active settlement and development of the territory on both sides of the boundary line, for the trade would be as valuable to the world on one side as on the other.

MR. CHAMBERLAIN ON THE FEDERATION OF THE EMPIRE.*

Mr. Chamberlain then reviewed the growth of the feeling for Imperial Federation, and he said : " Although experience has shown that the final realization of our hopes of Federation is a matter of such vast magnitude and great complication that it cannot be undertaken at the present time, it does not follow on that account that we should give up our aspirations. It is only a proof that we must approach the goal differently and not try to do everything at once, but seek the line of least resistance. The boldest might shrink appalled before an attempt to create a new government for the British Empire, with large powers of taxation, and legislation over countries separated by thousands of miles of seas. We may, however, approach this desirable consummation by a process of gradual development. We may endeavor to es-

---

*Extracts from a speech delivered by the Colonial Secretary at a festival in London given by the " Canada Club" in March, 1896.

tablish some common interests and common obligations, to deal with which it is natural that some
sort of representative authority should grow up.
The greatest obligation is the Imperial defence.
The greatest interest is the Imperial trade. The
former must be reached through the latter, as was
the case in the creation of the German empire.
At first the Reichstag was convened to deal with
the commercial interests of the German States.
Gradually it embraced national and political objects and became the bond of unity and the basis
of the empire."

Remarking that it was natural that Canada
should take the initiative, Mr. Chamberlain cited
the resolution of the Ottawa conference in favor
of a customs arrangement between Great Britain
and the Colonies, and also Mr. McNeill's resolution
in the legislature on Tuesday in favor of an ad
valorem duty on foreign imports. Although he
foresaw a very serious dislocation of trade with
England if such a proposal became effective, Mr.
Chamberlain asserted that the proposal merited
respectful consideration.

"This proposal," Mr. Chamberlain proceeded,
"would involve at least a small duty on food and
raw material and would thus increase the cost of
living and the pressure on the working classes.
It would also tend to increase the cost of production and would therefore prejudice us in competing
with foreign countries in neutral markets. *It is
useless for us to shut our eyes to these facts.*

" In return we should get a very small consideration in the shape of a preference, maybe two per cent., and perhaps even five per cent, in competing with foreign manufacturers in the Colonial markets.

" This is a very startling proposal for a free trade country and seems in its platform impossible to be adopted. I am a pronounced free trader, but at the same time I am not so pedantic that, if sufficient advantage were offered, I would not consider a deviation from the strict dogma. But so far no sufficient quid pro quo has been offered to induce England to take certain loss and possible risk involved in reviewing altogether her present commercial policy. The preference would be much smaller in the case of British goods imported into the Colonies than in that of Colonial goods imported into Great Britain. It is still more important that our foreign trade is so gigantic in proportion to the foreign trade of the Colonies that the burden of taxation would fall with much greater weight upon the United Kingdom than upon the Colonies."

Mr. Chamberlain then proceeded to invite the Colonies to continue their efforts and he expressed the opinion that if the Marquis of Ripon's despatch to the Governors of the Colonies on this subject in 1895 had not closed the doors to more favorable proposals which might be advanced in the future, and he called particular attention to Lord Ripon's statement that an arrangement creating a customs union comprising the whole empire, by which the aggregate customs revenue might be equitably proportioned among the principal communities, would in principle be free from objection. Mr. Chamberlain regarded a possible alternative. "Its advantages to the Colonies would be so enormous," he continued, "that it appears to me that the Colonies themselves will be bound to give such a suggestion their careful consideration."

Going into details he said: "In such a general free trade arrangement it is quite clear that exceptions must be made in the case of articles such as tobacco and spirits, which are chiefly taxed for revenue purposes. If we are to make even the slightest progress in such a direction, protection must disappear *and the only duties must be revenue duties, not protective duties in the sense of protecting industries of one portion of the empire against the industries of another.* I cannot help thinking that if a council of representatives of the whole empire should be called to consider such an arrangement, although the subject would present many enormous difficulties, still with the existing good will and the ultimate goal in view, something like a working agreement would be reached, and free traders, even if they had to abandon their principles, to some extent, must remember the enormous gain that would compensate for the loss of our dealings with foreign countries. For the states forming the empire are after all more likely to develop an increase in prosperity, population, wealth, power, commerce and enterprise than any foreign states."

———

Since the foregoing was put in type the Chancellor of the Exchequer delivered his Budget Speech in the House of Commons on the 15th of April ; and I make the following extract in reference to it from one of the Associated Press newspapers. Why should England attempt to change her free trade policy with regard to the rest of the world, on account of her Colonies, while she is undergoing such great prosperity?

" During the afternoon the Chancellor of the Exchequer, Sir Michael Hicks-Beach, made the budget statement. He said that the surplus of 1895-96 was £4,210,000 and he estimated the expenditures for the current year at £100,047,000. The Chancellor said this had been a wonderful year and one of unexampled revenue, in spite of the fact that the expenditures had been the largest since the great war. The surplus was the largest ever known and a larger sum was devoted to the reduction of the national debt than ever before. The condition of the working classes, he continued, judging from the consumption of tea, tobacco and sugar, had materially improved."

NEW BRUNSWICK STATESMEN.

If the people of Nova Scotia were indebted to Mr. Howe and several of his great Responsible Government assistants for the freedom they enjoy this day, the people of New Brunswick owe no less a debt of gratitude to the memory of the two gentlemen whose pictures and sketches appear on the following pages; for although the introduction of real party Constitutional Government lagged behind Nova Scotia about ten years, still our heroes fought hard against " the old compact" and the changes came about in good time.   It seems to me that the Legislature of New Brunswick should not hesitate to erect a Monument to these gentlemen on Parliament Square in front of the Province Building.

HON. L. A. WILMOT.

This gentleman was one of the leading champions of Responsible Government in New Brunswick, and the greatest orator that this Province has ever produced. In his prime (in the forties) he was the peer of any of the great rhetoricians of Europe or America—far ahead of most of his contemporaries in the two hemispheres, and scarcely behind the ablest of them. The writer, in his fifty years' peregrinations, has listened to many of the great orators of England and America, political and clerical ; and for holding an audience spell-bound and breathless, as it were, moving them at will to tears or to mirth, Wilmot was matchless. Compared with Howe he was more showy, but less solid. He had a fine resonant voice, commanding figure, and piercing eyes, which were prominent among his natural gifts, while his " action" was all that a Demosthenes could have claimed for it. He was equal to any demand made upon him, whether as a political debater, a platform lecturer, or a Sunday school speaker—in all these capacities he shone brightly and effectively, delighting all and infusing himself, so to say, in the whole corporeal essence of his listeners. He was a man of strong impulses, emotional, fiery, nervous—not at all times, even in critical moments, reliable in judg-ment—if at times violent in speech, it was like smoke from the fire, it soon passed off into thin air, for his heart was in its place, and his kindli-ness of disposition always the same. He was the son of Mr. Wm. Wilmot, at one time a member of the House of Assembly ; and it is said that this gentleman was expelled from the house, on motion of one of the members, on the charge of being a Preacher, which meant that as Mr. Wilmot did occasionally hold forth as a local preacher in one of the Churches, he therefore came under the pro-

EX-LIEUT. GOVERNOR, HON. L. A. WILMOT.

hibited ban, which provided that ministers of the gospel were ineligible to a seat in the Legislature ; and it was positively inconsistent and shocking for a "dissenter" and "lay preacher" to represent the people on the floors of the House in violation of the laws of the land and against the peace of the King's most excellent Majesty, his crown and dignity ! ! !   But the absurdity of the whole proceeding is contained in the fact that there was no law whatever justifying the expulsion—for the law was, as it is now applicable to regularly ordained Ministers of the Gospel, and not to laymen, no matter how often they may preach God's word to erring mortals.   The resolution of course was carried, and on leaving the House the hon. gentleman, pointing to his little boy standing in the lobby, (the subject of this sketch, then about 12 years of age) said to the Speaker : " Sir, the time will come when that lad (pointing to him) will see that justice is done to my memory, by vindicating on the floors of this House the rights that belong to all classes in this Province, and when all churches shall be placed on one footing." Here was prophecy fully fulfilled, equal to old Testament times. L. A. Wilmot lived long enough to turn the tables altogether upon the supporters of the old one-sided system, and give effect to the denunciation and hopes of his father.

HON. CHARLES FISHER.

If Wilmot was a great orator, Fisher was a great Constitutional Lawyer. Each was essential to the other, as companions in arms on the side of the Responsible Government army. It used to be said that Fisher made the balls and Wilmot fired them, meaning thereby that while the former drew up the resolutions, the latter spoke to them with telling effect—not that Fisher was incapable of doing full justice to his own views and wishes, for he was a debater of no mean order and fully understood the subject he took in hand, which is not always the case with Parliamentarians of pretentions. He was a man of dignified, stately presence, and never failed to impress the House by the force of his

HON. CHARLES FISHER.

utterances. Privately he was not always to be understood—there was a non-committalism about him, even in important matters, which many of his friends could not account for, as though he always felt that his best counsellor was himself, and the less he divulged to others it would be all the safer for his side. It was the want of this frankness which caused the most political capital to be made against him at election times. On the floors of the House, however, he was outspoken and manly —his language lucid and fluent, and his appear-

ance in debate commanding and statesmanlike.
To Wilmot and Fisher are the people of New
Brunswick mostly indebted for the free govern-
ment of which they are in possession this day.

R. L. HAZEN.

This gentleman is here referred to as the
great political antagonist of Wilmot—the two
having been pitted against each other—for
and against Responsible Government—in the
earlier stages of the agitation. Though not the
equal of Wilmot as an eloquent speaker, he was a
foeman not unworthy of the steel of the former.
It was said of Hazen that he never took very
great interest in work, but somehow or other these
lazy men manage to hold their own and hit hard,
and exhibit the fruits of much study, when the
time comes for action. At all events, Hazen always exhibited great strength of mind and will
whether at the Bar or on the floors of the House;
and was perhaps the most formidable opponent
with whom Wilmot had to contend. Hazen was
backed up by all the old Tory influence of the
day, especially the old office holders of Fredericton and their adjuncts; and yet he was not so
much opposed to the principles of Responsible
Government, as he was to the danger he thought
of carrying those principles too far—although the
old folks generally said they believed in Respon-

sible Government, but it was in the abstract—
the details of the system were the disturbing elements in their opposition—in fact it was everything—for the details meant the surrender of
office on the forfeiture of the confidence of the
House—they meant that the Heads of Departments should be in the House. They meant, in
short, too much against them to be regarded with
complacency, and so the advocates of the old
system fought hard, but the fates were against
them. R. L. Hazen is remembered as a fine, stal-
wart, gentlemanly man, in manners as well as
looks. Although to the manor born, he was always approachable by the humble—as a lawyer
he was high-minded, and far above the petty
tricks of the special pleader. On the floors of the
House the same dignity was manifest, and for
which no member was more highly respected—if
what was considered by his opponents to be of
him on the wrong side of politics he was known to
be honest in his convictions.

SIR LEONARD TILLEY.

This gentleman came into politics among the
new school of Liberals, just about the time that
Responsible Government was won by the old
Liberal party and recognized by all parties in
New Brunswick, in 1855. Mr. Tilley, perhaps,
was the most successful and lucky politician that

this Province has yet produced—if success can be measured by his lengthened tenure of office, for with the exception of a couple of years perhaps, he continued to occupy an official position, of one kind and another, almost from the day he was first elected for St. John, until his final retirement from the Dominion Government, extending over a period of probably thirty years. It must have been luck or abilities to account for this favourable showing, but no doubt it was both conjoined with a suave and kindly bearing. Mr. Tilley became the first Provincial Secretary in the first Responsible Party Government of New Brunswick, on its formation in 1855—an office which was looked upon at the time so difficult to fill on account of its financial duties, that nobody thought Mr. Tilley—then quite a young man—was capable ; but his first budget speech settled that doubt, for he succeeded in its delivery and the marshalling of his figures far beyond expectation, and was pronounced from that moment to be " a very clever man"—according to a colloquial expression. He was among the young reformers who gave to this Province all the great changes the people enjoy this day—such measures as vote by ballot, enlarging the franchise, quadrennial Parliaments, reduced expenditures in all the departments, &c., &c. As a Liberal he was ever consistent and firm, and strictly honest as a politician. Such a thing as " boodling" and jobbing with contractors and other such acts of spoliation, no Liberal of that

SIR LEONARD TILLEY.
Ex-Governor of New Brunswick.

day would countenance for a moment. It remained to a later period for this Upas Tree to be planted by designing hands and take root in our soil to the destruction of every interest, life and property perhaps included.

When "confederation" was proposed in 1865, Mr. Tilley threw himself into the struggle, as an ardent supporter, and when the measure was finally carried he became a member of the Dominion Government. From that moment old party lines throughout the new Dominion became obliterated—it was then a fusion of parties—old Tories and even old Liberals as well as young, clasped hands like brothers, and performed what might be called a pilgrimage to Mecca (Quebec) to worship at the new shrine set up by our (Upper Canadian) modern Mahomets—and so they went, a strange mixture as I thought at the time, for in my opinion it is as natural for a man to be born a Tory or a Liberal as it is to be born a Poet—the blood and the spirit go together. whence the inspiration comes.   But then it must be allowed that in order to carry out the new project the best men of the Provinces were required, and they had to ignore their old differences and throw themselves into the new work ; besides there could be no dividing issues—it was like the building of a new house—the partitions had not yet been set up —no tenants had yet got in to wrangle with one another and call names and make a great noise generally.   So that the fusion of parties in 1866 was quite natural and right, in the construction of this new Dominion. We are told that the chameleon takes its colour from the bark of the tree upon which it feeds. We have been in business as a Dominion, nearly thirty years, but the party complexion of the Government, with a short interregnum, has continued Tory to the present day. The big rod has swallowed up the little rod —the laws of gravitation have not failed to draw the smaller bodies to the larger; while the former Liberals in their own Provinces have long since become so absorbed that they are all alike pronounced to be Tory, — and on the other hand, what is now called the Liberal Party, embraces some of the old Provincial Tories — so that the goose and the gander plied with the same sauce cannot at this time of day say one to the other —" you're another," for both parties have been scratched alike and overcome by the genius of the times.

The following in reference to Sir Leonard Tilley's political career, given in detail, I copy from Morgan's Parliamentary Companion :

Tilley, Hon. Sir Samuel Leonard, K. C. M. G., C. B., P. C., son of Thomas M. Tilley, Esq., of Queens County, N. B., and great grandson of Samuel Tilley, Esq , formerly of Brooklyn, N. Y., a N. E. Loyalist, who came to New Brunswick at the termination of the American Revolution, and became a grantee of the city of St. John (see Sabine's American Loyalists), born at Gagetown, Queens

County, N. B., 8th May, 1818 ; educated at the County Grammar School ; married first to Julia Annie, daughter of Jas. T. Hanford, of St. John, (dead) 2nd November, 1867 ; married Alice, eldest daughter of G. Chipman, Esq., of St. Stephen, N. B. ; was a member of the Executive Council of New Brunswick from November, 1854, to May, 1856, from July, 1857, to March, 1865 ; and again from April, 1866, until the Union, during which several periods he held the office of Provincial Secretary of that Province, and from March, 1861, to March, 1865, was leader of the Government. Has been a delegate to England on several occasions to confer with the Imperial Government on important public business. Notably, regarding the Union of the B. A. Colonies, and the construction of our Intercolonial Railway, has also repeatedly served on like missions to the sister Provinces, was a delegate to the Charlottetown Union Conference 1864 ; to that in Quebec same year, and to the London Colonial Conference, to complete terms of Union 1866–7. Holds a patent of rank and precedence from Her Majesty as an Ex-Councillor N. B. Created C. B. (civil) by Her Majesty, 1867, and K. C. M. G., May, 1879. Sworn of the Privy Council and appointed Minister of Customs for the Dominion, 1st July, 1867. Resigned Nov. 1873 on appointment as Dominion Governor of New Brunswick. Sworn as Minister of Finance, October, 1878. Sat for the City of St. John in Legislative Assembly of N. B., in the spring of

1851, after which he resigned, and from June, 1854 to June, 1856, when defeated on the Prohibitory Law question and the Government resigned, from June, 1857, to March, 1865, when defeated on the Union Policy of his Government, and again from 1866 until the union, when he resigned to accept a seat in the Commons and represent New Brunswick in the Dominion Cabinet.

The Prohibitory Liquor Law of N. B. was introduced by Mr. Tilley as a private member. Amongst other measures of importance introduced and carried by the Government of which he was a member may be mentioned the following: Vote by ballot and extension of the franchise; an Act authorizing the construction of the European and North American Railway as a Government Work, agreeing to pay three and a half twelfths of the cost; an Act granting facility for the construction of certain Railways. Was Lieut. Governor of New Brunswick, from 15th Nov., 1873, until 11th July, 1878; returned to the House of Commons at the General Election, 1878; appointed Finance Minister in October; occupied that office until 1885, and was re-appointed Lieutenant Governor of New Brunswick, November of that year, which position he occupied until September, 1893.

SIR EDWARD BELCHER.

I failed to recall in the body of this book, among "distinguished Nova Scotians," the name of Admiral Sir Edward Belcher, and so I give his record here :

Sir Edward Belcher was born in Halifax in 1799. He was a son of the Hon. Andrew Belcher, a member of "the old compact" Executive Council, and a grandson of a former Chief Justice of Nova Scotia and a descendant of Governor Belcher of Massachusetts. Who does not remember "Belcher's Wharf," nearly at the foot of "Jacob's Hill," both so called in my boyish days over sixty years ago, and no doubt changed in name by this time. This was the property of the father of our sketch who carried on business as a merchant in the West India trade.

Young Belcher entered the Royal Navy in Halifax in 1812, and became Commander in 1829, passing in the meantime through the various grades—and for his excellent services as a Nautical Surveyor in command of H. M. Ships Ætna and Sulphur. he was made Post Captain in 1841, and a C. B., and in 1843 he was knighted. Between the years 1836 and 1842, he made a voyage round the world in H. M. Ship Sulphur (all sailing ships at that time) and wrote a very able narrative of his travels in connection therewith, which attracted great attention at the time. On the 15th of April, 1852. Sir Edward Belcher set out on an Arctic expedition in search of Captain McClure and Sir John Franklin, the searching fleet consisting of several men-of-war.

And now we come to a period in our hero's life when all the fame that had covered his name and works were to be tarnished ; and yet the circumstances which brought this about, will no doubt in time receive a more honourable explanation than what up to the present has been vouchsafed—for Sir Edward did not live long enough to vindicate or justify his conduct on that occasion. Finding his search to be vain and the danger imminent by which he was surrounded, he abandoned his ships in the Polar Regions, considering it impossible to bring them out of the ice, and thus he decided, rather than hazard his own life and that of his men. And so he returned home heartless and disappointed. The Admiralty was unforgiving. He was accordingly court-marshalled, and if not actually condemned, was never more employed in Her Majesty's service. Here was a life then rudely eclipsed and the former fame and glory of Sir Edward Belcher became as dead letters among his former admirers. But notwithstanding this cloud that passed over him the name of Sir Edward Belcher will ever stand out among his fellow countrymen as one who has reflected lustre upon his native Province. Sir Edward Belcher died on March 18, 1877, having risen to the rank of Admiral by seniority, (which could not be withheld) in 1872.

G. E. FENETY, AUTHOR OF THIS BOOK.

Founder and highly successful Publisher in St. John of the first Morning Newspaper printed in British America upon the present cheap plan. Until 1839, to obtain a newspaper ten cents had to be paid—now two cents—Thus "five blades of grass are made to grow where one grew before." Rowland Hill in England was the originator of

the penny postage.   Mr. Fenety was the originator of the penny newspaper in British North
America.

Appointed Justice of the Peace in 1855.

Director of the St. John Mechanics' Institute in
1847.

Appointed by the Government in 1857 a Commissioner to investigate the management and condition of sundry Government Institutions, such
as the Provincial Penitentiary, the Lunatic Asylum, the Light Houses along the coast, the
Marine Hospital and to report thereon, which
report was written out by the Secretary, Mr.
Henry Fisher.   Hon. Senator Wark is the only
surviving co-commissioner.

Appointed Queen's Printer in 1863, which office
he resigned in 1895.

Was Mayor of Fredericton five years—ran three
times without opposition.   Retired in 1887 of
his own accord, and was succeeded by J. D.
Hazen, Esq., now M. P. for St. John.

Director of the Joggins Coal Mines Association, St.
John.

President of the Auxiliary Bible Society, Fredericton.

Trustee of Fredericton Schools.

Director of Fredericton Central Fire Insurance
Company.

President of the Fredericton Gas Company.

President of the Forest Hill Cemetery Company.

President of the Historical Society—(now dissolved.)

Chairman of the Fredericton Board of Health.

Vice-President of the Church of England Temperance Society.

Delegate (in Bishop Medley's time) from Christ's Church Cathedral to the Diocesan Synod.

Delegate from the same to the Church Society.

Director of the Fredericton Leather Company.

President of the Fredericton Trotting Park Association.

Delegate from the City of Fredericton to Ottawa to confer with the members of the Dominion Government, in the interests of the Great Eastern Railway—since built.

President of the Fredericton Society for the Prevention of Cruelty to Animals.

Chairman of the " Wilmot Park" Board of Directors.

Of the above offices held from time to time—more honorary than remunerative, requiring considerable time to properly discharge the duties—Mr. F. continues to hold four of them.

During his Mayoralty the subject of this sketch

had the pleasure of introducing to Fredericton audiences the following distinguished persons :

Joseph Cook, the celebrated Thinker and Lecturer.

Rev. Henry Ward Beecher.

The Marquis of Lansdowne (Governor General.)

Rev. Dr. Talmage.

Justin McCarthy, the ex-leader of the Irish Party in the House of Commons.

Sir Frederick Middleton, Commander of the Canadian Military forces.

Sir John A. Macdonald.

MARITIME WIT. ANECDOTE AND HUMOR.

[Most of the anecdotes given below have been floating about
for many years, from mouth to mouth, but not in print. I
thought they might be of interest to the younger readers of this
book by collecting them together, as far as I knew, and publishing them here.]

What Impudence Can Do.

Her Majesty's Dock Yard, some years since, if
not now, was like the Citadel, a sealed book to all
visitors. A stranger from abroad was very anxious to gain admission, and my friend in Halifax,
a fine portly looking gentleman, who would pass
for a General any day, undertook to chaperon him
and see what *he* could do. Now, over the Dock
Yard gate were the words "no admittance," and to
make the injunction more convincing. a Sentinel is
always pacing just inside the gate with a drawn
bayonet. Our portly Haligonian told the stranger
to follow close behind him, and marching forward
and into the gate-way, he commanded the Sentinel
thus "let this gentleman pass in," and away he
went with a most dignified air, the stranger following. The Sentinel, of course, took our friend for
some one high in authority, belonging either to

the army or navy.   But so it was done.   So much
for good looks and impudence.

Supreme Court Judges.

The Court had been sitting several hours beyond
the usual dinner time, as the lawyers were anxious
to take their departure by the "next train" and
wished to "get through," and therefore no recess
for fortifying the inner man was thought to be
necessary ; but not so with one of the Judges of
the lean kind, who suddenly rose from his seat
and declared, that although he was a judge he
was also a man, and no man could weigh evidence
upon an empty stomach, and for his part he intended to go out and get a strengthening plaster.
" Why," said a brother judge of the full-blooded
order sitting beside him, " look at me—why I
have had nothing to eat for the last 24 hours,—
nor to drink either for that matter; and 1 could
sit here all day if necessary—*Crier, adjourn the
Court !*" followed immediately at the end of this
avowal.

A General in Disguise.

When General Coffin resided at Westfield in the
neighborhood of the Nerepis, N. B., (say 70 years
ago) Sir Howard Douglas, the Lieut. Governor,
paid him a very unexpected visit.   Now the General was an amateur farmer, and he worked with
his men from early till late among burnt stumps
and clearing up.   When the Governor arrived on

the ground he came suddenly upon the General,— who was begrimed with smut and resembled a laborer of the dismal type,—and thus addressed him, " my man, is General Coffin at home, or about here?" The General without looking up replied :—" I think he is, Sir, in the house there, and you might walk in, and if he is not there just take a seat and I will go and find him." The Governor went in the front door and the General in the back door and up stairs as fast as his legs could carry him, and at it he went washing and doffing his laborer's clothes and donning his military garb, sword and even spurs, all of which did not take him many minutes, and then he marched down stairs and into His Excellency's presence with the air and dignity of one who had never done an ignoble day's work in all his life. This may be called military strategy worthy of a Buonaparte.

The Proof of the Pudding.

Four of us on one fine summer morning started from St. John for an excursion to Hampton, N. B., in a large open carriage and " pair "—there were no railroads, and the village was the only Hampton then known, and contained only one tavern, whither we made for. On the way up different topics were discussed. One of the company raised the question as to whether a man weighed heavier before dinner, or after, which had been an old unsettled problem. The company was divided in opinion—those on the side of the weight being no more after dinner, argued on the principle that a person was more buoyant after eating, and therefore more elastic and light, and it was propounded that a fish, no matter how heavy, when placed in a tub of water did not add anything to the weight of the tub and water, so long as the fish did not touch the sides or bottom of the tub. However, it was a knotty question only to be decided by ocular demonstration. When we reached Hampton, all pretty hungry (not thirsty) we went into a store in order to weigh, each one for himself, *before* dinner, upon a Fairbanks scale; and then to weigh again *after* dinner. This could be the only test in favour or against the argument. So far so well. After dinner—we did not spare ourselves—we again proceeded to the same store and went through the same process of weighing, when—lo and behold, each man had added to his weight an average of three pounds. Nobody said a word after that.

The Intoxicated Member.

The hon. gentleman had the floor, but was in such an intoxicated state, that he was obliged to clutch the back of a chair in order to maintain his perpendicular. Members felt that they were in for a long (anti-Scott Act) speech, and there was no way of compelling silence. At length an hon. member cried out " I move that the Speaker take the chair." The Bacchanalian member, thinking it was meant that the chair that he depended upon was to be taken from him, he at once attempted to resume his seat, but in doing so he came with a crash to the floor—whereupon L. O'Connor Doyle remarked "the hon. gentleman has lost his seat, but he still has the floor."

Kill-Kenny.

It is related that Sir Edward Kenny had a dinner party in his house at Halifax, at which Doyle was present. In taking a glass of wine the host swallowed a piece of cork, which happened to be in the glass, and it came very near choking him, whereupon after the danger was all over one of the guests remarked "you came very near going to Cork that time, Kenny." "I think," said Doyle, "it came nearer to Kill-Kenny." [This was in print before.]

A Swearing Parson and Washington.

When "Bill Williams" was driving the Stage between Fredericton and Woodstock, he had on one occasion a high church dignitary as a passenger among others. They stopped on the road to dinner—after dinner Bill was in a hurry to get off, the Clergyman had finished and was up to time, but the others lingered at the table and thus delayed matters—Williams losing all patience rushed into the room, and cried out, gentlemen, it is time we were off, there is that little Clergyman outside swearing like thunder. This reminds me of the story in "Harper." General Hamilton showed bad generalship at the battle of Long Island, he retreated when he should have advanced. Washington coming up was in a great rage and swore terribly at Hamilton for his blundering. Now Washington was always reported to be a highly religious man—"he would never tell a lie." A person at the time hearing of the great man's oaths would not believe it possible—accordingly to set the matter at rest he sought out the chaplain, and asked him if it was true that the General sometimes swore ? Well—very seldom ; but when he does it is beautiful to hear him, he swears in such a polished way, like a real gentleman ! Now, probably one of the above stories is about as true as the other—both wanting " the essential element."

" *Bob Ray.*"

Everybody in St. John forty years ago knew Bob, one of the kindest and most humane and charitable men who ever lived there—but he was a great practical joker. The Lake Lomond darkies had cause to remember him. He would get half a dozen of them couped up in a certain shop and strike them over the shins and heads without mercy, and they would sing out " O Massa Ray—don't, don't." After thus belaboring them until he got tired, he would give each of them " something to drink " and new articles of clothing, such as socks, caps, brogans, &c.   But the darkies always knew what was coming when Bob had them under surveillance, which made them " grin and bear it."   On one occasion in company with some friends he was staging it from Annapolis to Halifax.   When they stopped for dinner at a certain public house, he made up to the landlady about dinner, and he put his hand behind his ear (common with deaf people) pretending not to hear and caused the lady to sing out at the top of her voice.   When at the dinner table, some half a dozen travellers being seated around, Ray at the head of the table, the lady of the house happened in the room, when he asked her some question, whereupon the lady screeched out an answer so stentoriously that it set the whole table in a roar —but they all suspected that this was another of Bob's practical jokes.   The lady cut stick out of the room very fast.

A Great Astonishment.

One of the Dominion Ministers a few years ago was on an official visit to Fredericton with his Private Secretary.   Now the latter was well acquainted in that city, and he introduced the Minister to a well paid official of that place.   In the course of conversation the official, by way of a joke, asked the Secretary if he could not manage to obtain for him through the influence of the Minister an office under the Dominion Government —the Minister not perceiving the joke, looked at his Secretary and the Secretary looked at the Minister, when the latter queried "how would the vacant tide-waiter-ship in Chatham answer?" of course meaning what he said. The Secretary was so tickled that he burst out into roars of laughter, to the great astonishment of all present, inasmuch as said Secretary, up to that moment had never been known even to *smile*, no matter what fun was going on.

He Wished to be Kept Alive for a Couple of Days Longer.

One of our well known politicians who was about dying and very anxious about the result of the Dominion elections, begged of the doctor to do all that was possible to keep him alive two days longer, by which time the result would be known, when he thought he would die happy.

Two Witty Parsons.

The Reverends Messrs. Waddell and Dripps were once in a row boat crossing a sheet of water, near Truro, the day being somewhat cloudy, and rain threatened. The former remarked "if we don't hurry along we shall get Dripping wet," whereupon the latter replied, "Well, I suppose we shall be able to Waddell through it."

The Halifax Robbing Room.

Over the Barristers' door, when the Court was held in the Province Building, the words "Robing

Room," were inscribed upon a sign board. Some wag added another letter B, so that it was made to read *robbing* room, which annoyed the Lawyers very much. When Doyle came along he remarked: No wonder at the annoyance, for the sting is in the *Bee*.

The Rat Terrier.

Another of Doyle's jokes was made on one occasion when the House was in session. An honorable member was declaiming bitterly against a fellow member who had promised him his support in a certain measure but had backed out. At this moment a terrier dog had found his way into the room and barked frantically, to the great disgust of the Speaker and Sergeant-at-Arms. "Put him out, put him out," was the universal shout—whereupon Doyle rose and said "Mr. Speaker, the dog means no harm—he only smells a rat!"

"Going Through the Mill."

Mr. S. G. W. Archibald, Master of the Rolls, was a very active and mischievous lad and up to all sorts of tricks. On one occasion when playing about a Water Mill, in his native town of Truro, he slipped and was carried by the water through the sluice and was taken out on the other side more dead than alive. On one occasion in the House of Assembly a petition was before the House for aid to a family in the country who had been burnt out and lost everything. The member in his pleadings said that the family had gone through everything in their sufferings and were fully entitled to the sympathies of the House. Archibald remarked : "Why, Mr. Speaker, I have gone through the mill myself, and although I nearly lost my life on the occasion, the only sympathy I got was the whole town laughed at me, and it is doubtful if the people have got over it yet."

An Odd Lawyer.

There was a certain legal gentleman in St. John, one of the ablest in the profession, but at times eccentric—sometimes on going out of his office he would forget to turn the key in his door. One day a young lawyer, whose office was on the same floor, called upon Mr. Blank to obtain certain points, and finding the head out he saw a book lying upon the table which contained the desired information, and as Mr. Blank had always been very friendly to him, he thought he might borrow the book for a short time, for he felt that if the owner was in he would loan it to him without hesitation. Accordingly he walked out with the book under his arm. In a couple of days afterwards he returned, and finding Mr. Blank in his office, the young lawyer apologized for what he had done. "Oh, my dear fellow, no apology is necessary—I am always happy to be of use to young beginners ; but, d—— you, if you ever take such liberties with my property again, I'll kick you as far as I can send you." The young man thought it was time to—put.

Calves Did it.

A well known lady was on her trial in St. John before Chief Justice Ritchie, on a charge of having purloined goods from her employers. She was a very pretty woman and on taking and leaving her seat in the prisoner's box morning and night, she was not very punctilious in taking off and putting on her rubbers, but showed a little higher than modesty warranted, and all in full view of the jurymen. The trial lasted several days—the Judge in his charge bore down heavily upon the prisoner, so much so that all present thought she would be brought in guilty. But, no,—she was declared innocent. A wag in the Court Room said that *calves* did it. It remains, however, up to this day a problem whether the wag meant the calves in the jury box or in the prisoner's box.

The Gridiron and the Mason.

When the Masonic Hall in Halifax was kept by Mr. Sutherland, say seventy years ago, there used to be a *great* deal of cooking done in the kitchen, and a great deal of feasting among the Masons up stairs. On one occasion a young man was a candidate for the honours of Masonry and a knowledge of their secrets; but as the hour for the initiatory steps to be taken had not yet arrived, the aspirant thought he would in the meantime explore the lower regions to see what things looked like— going into the kitchen he espied a large gridiron over the red hot coals, preparatory no doubt to the cooking of a beef steak. His curiosity and suspicion were quickly aroused, and so he asked the person in charge, what that big gridiron was for ? The answer was "I understand a new Mason is to be made to-night. and it must be got red hot." It did not take the young man long after that to find his hat and coat.

The Pretenders.

A member on the floors of the Nova Scotia House of Assembly was complaining that another member (Mr. Stewart) had made promises to him in regard to a certain measure and afterwards had changed his mind—whereupon Doyle interposed : "What more can you expect, the Stewarts were always Pretenders."

What !—All Dead ?

The story of a rather remarkable occurrence is told of a gentleman who arrived recently in Fredericton from a few weeks tour. On reaching the depot he instructed the coachman to drive him to the residence of a gentleman with whom he had been staying before his departure—but he was startled with the answer : "Why, he's dead." Then take me to Mr. so-and-so's, and again the coachman's answer came : " And he's dead, too." The gentleman then concluded he had better hesitate before proposing another place, so he told the driver to take him to some one who was alive —and he took him to one of the hotels, where everybody was eating, which convinced him there was some live people in Fredericton after all.

- - -

A Slippery Customer.

In my travels through Nova Scotia collecting subscriptions for the " *Novascotian*," I had on my list a subscriber living at Granville, opposite Annapolis, who was in arrears four years ($16)—a pretty heavy newspaper bill; but then in those days (60 years ago) publishers were not as they are at the present day, exacting in their demands, as they should be. However bad the credit system is in 1896, it was a great deal worse in 1830. On inquiring in Annapolis where our debtor lived on the other side, I was informed, and told at the same time that I might save myself the trouble of crossing the ferry for he (naming the person) never paid any body, and yet was a well-to-do farmer. I replied, " Well, I will try." On arriving in Granville my man was pointed out to me, chopping a log on his farm a long distance from the house. On accosting him and pulling out my book and reminding him of his indebtedness, he replied very blandly—" Certainly, the amount had run up too much—it should have been paid long ago, and I will go and fetch the amount, you just wait here," and away he went at full speed for the house a long distance off but in full view, to " fetch the amount." He politely asked me to take a seat (upon the log) until his return. The last I saw of that man was his back, and from that day to this he has remained in shadow, for he forgot to return and " fetch me the amount." I saw him enter his house *to get the money,* but he never came back to my knowledge. On taking my seat upon the log I ruminated in the man's favour, and against the one who told me " he would never pay," for how could such a slow man run so fast to " fetch me the amount ?" Feeling safe in the fellow's integrity, I remained seated upon the log fully three-quarters of an hour, expecting every moment to see him coming over the hills with the money, but he came not. It then for the first time dawned upon me (I was young then) that the fellow was only fooling, and so I turned my face once more towards Annapolis, wondering how many more such men there were in the world. It is very likely, however, that the man has long since paid that debt ($16) in the great debt of nature, (for no doubt he has gone to his reward long ere this) when he was called upon to render an account of all his doings in this world, and where lies and evasions avail not, and where to " cheat the printer" is set down as one of the greatest sins a man can be guilty of.

He Was a St. John Man.

A story upon St. John is told by a St. John man. It appears that when the deputation from

St. John went to Ottawa some time ago to urge the importance of granting subsidies for a Trans-Atlantic Steamship line, Mr. P——— was one of the deputation. Each member of the deputation had spoken and each delegate appeared to say two words for himself and one for St. John. Finally it came to Mr. P.'s turn, and in his stately manner and measured tone he said :

"I am here, Sir Mackenzie Bowell, to endeavor to get a steamer subsidy for St. John. I want you to particularly notice that I am not here looking for anything for myself."

The Premier replied : "Mr. P———, I would like to have your photograph."

"You shall have it, Sir Mackenzie, if you promise to put it up in your office."

"I shall do that, Mr. P.———," said Sir Mackenzie, "and every time I look at it I shall say to myself there is the portrait of one man from St. John, N. B., who did not want something for himself."

Only an Item.

The clever member for Northumberland, N. B., (J. W. Johnston) afterwards of the House of Commons, was one day trying to catch the chairman's eye (Hon. John H. Gray,) the House being in Committee, in order to direct attention to certain items in the bill before the House to which he (Johnston) objected, and feeling that the chairman was trying to avoid him, he became louder

than ever in calling upon the chair—so at length
the chairman managed to *see* Johnston upon his
feet determined to be heard, when the former said,
" Mr. Johnston, to what item have you reference ?"   " The *item* before me !" said Johnston
and sat down.

ERRATA.

The typographical errors will explain themselves.

At page 226, 2nd paragraph, read 1865, instead of 1855.

Page 228 read " conservatism" instead of " conversation."

Page 229 read " reputed to be a Justice" instead of " deputed."

Page 226—For " statute of Apollo," read " statue," &c., &c.

than ever in calling upon the chair—so at length
the chairman managed to *see* Johnston upon his
feet determined to be heard, when the former said,
"Mr. Johnston, to what item have you reference?" "The *item* before me!" said Johnston
and sat down.